THE BRIDE OF ALMOND TREE

Robert Hillman has written a number of books including his 2004 memoir *The Boy in the Green Suit*, which won the Australian National Biography Award, and *The Bookshop of the Broken Hearted*, published by Faber in 2019. He lives in Melbourne.

The Bride of Almond Tree

ROBERT HILLMAN

faber

First published in the UK in 2021
by Faber & Faber Ltd, Bloomsbury House
74–77 Great Russell Street
London WC1B 3DA

First published in Australia in 2021
by The Text Publishing Company, Swann House,
22 William Street, Melbourne Victoria 3000, Australia

Printed in the UK by CPI Group (UK) Ltd, Croydon, CR0 4YY

© Robert Hillman, 2021

The right of Robert Hillman to be identified as author of this work
has been asserted in accordance with Section 77 of the Copyright,
Designs and Patents Act 1988

*All characters, names, places and events in this book are fictitious and any
resemblance to persons, living or dead, places or events is entirely coincidental*

A CIP record for this book
is available from the British Library

ISBN 978-0-5713-36642-2

MIX
Paper from
responsible sources
FSC® C020471

2 4 6 8 10 9 7 5 3 1

Chapter 1

HE SAW HER for the first time since returning from the war out on Cartwright's Track. He'd hitched a lift home with Nat Fish. She was walking. He didn't get Trout to stop for her because she was almost home but he waved, and she waved back. She was two years older since he'd last seen her, and her fair hair was longer, and in her green summer dress she seemed more a full-grown woman. They were friends, he and Beth, if friendship were applied in a broad way. He had always chatted with her down at the Almond Tree shops, where she'd run a stall each week selling donated odds and ends—jams, teddy bears, potted plants—to help support the strugglers of the town. The commitment to charity must have come down to her from her mum, Lillian, who knitted jumpers for pensioners. It didn't show up in her other daughters. Gus and Maud, both older than Beth, were more devoted to marathon arguments with their husbands and Franny, the second youngest, to marathon flirtation.

Wes had admired Beth for her kindness. As one of the small Almond Tree community of Quakers, he saw in her far less self-absorption than among his brethren in the faith. She considered herself a Marxist—she'd told him before he went away to war.

'Are you, then?'

'Well, not officially. You don't get a placard or anything. But Di Porter's been coaching me.'

'Di from the high school?'

'She used to be. Now she writes to me from the city.'

She said this in an embarrassed way, as if it might seem a type of boast for a young woman from a country town to claim membership of a cadre in a massive world-wide movement. All the same, as shy as she was about it, she didn't make a secret of her Marxism: that would be a betrayal of convictions. She was ridiculed, as she knew she would be. But not by Wes.

Now, when Beth waved to him she smiled, and the smile roused something in him he'd never experienced before: attraction to a woman. It was as if, by bits and pieces, certain vital components had been patiently accumulating in his heart, waiting their opportunity to be connected.

The smile; its welcoming quality: a bolt.

What next? A shower and shave; clean shirt and trousers; give your boots a bit of a birthday. Go and see the young woman in question, show that you like her. Hope that she also likes you. All going well, maybe the pictures. Or bonfire night, which was tomorrow. Beth might enjoy coming to the bonfire night with him.

He called in the next day at the Hardy farm off Cartwright Track with a bunch of beach daisies and tinsel lilies. Hardy ran a dairy herd of three hundred with a contract down the rail line that gave him the money he needed to extend his shack north, south, east and west for his four daughters. Gus and Maud, being older, had been given boys' work and roared about the farm on old Nortons from the age of ten and eleven, doing tasks they kept up after they married, shouting at the Ayrshires and whistling up the dogs. Hardy ran sheep as well, a thousand, and bred angora rabbits galore, the special province of Franny, second youngest to Beth.

Wes was directed down to the paddock of granite outcrops where Hardy was looking for a headstone. The grave he intended to mark was not for a human but for a horse called Kildare which had given up the ghost after a legendary life that included two Almond Tree Cups and a swim of a mile across Scullin Reservoir. Other horses had died over the years; they were picked up by Denny Christian from the abattoir and on-sold to a pet food factory off the highway at

Maccleworth. Only Killy merited a burial.

Wes found Hardy at work with a set of cold chisels and a mason's hammer, attempting to knock a chunk off a boulder the size of an elephant. Wes, like most Quaker males, had been trained in masonry and carpentry and, although not yet a master like his father, knew what to do with a cold chisel. He handed Hardy the tinsel lilies and daisies and had a block free of the boulder in ten minutes.

Hardy gave the bouquet a shake. 'What am I supposed to do with these?'

'For Beth.'

'What's Beth supposed to do with them?'

Wes lifted his shoulders. 'Stick them in a vase.'

Hardy nodded. 'She'll be reading,' he said. 'The collected works of Red Joe Stalin. Can try the flowers if you like. This is courtship, is it? Romance?'

'That sort of thing.'

Hardy handed Wes the bouquet and picked up his tools. 'Stay for a cuppa? Then you can try your luck with the professor.'

Bob Hardy wished Wes all the luck in the world. Of all his daughters, he loved Beth the most, and while he admired her intellect, hated the idea of losing her to the university in the city. He wished she would see in Wes the makings of a decent sort of husband. The army was over for him, nothing to impede him settling down. As Bob knew from chatting with Wes's father Marcus at the shopping centre, he'd come back from the islands with bullet holes in his shoulder and left thigh, now healed, and a medical discharge issued by a surgeon who'd judged he'd never walk again. Twenty-one, tall and cheerful, he'd started to build a place of his own on a patch he'd purchased from Neddy Gosling above the high-water mark of the river. Strolling back to the house with Wes, Bob imagined Beth giving up university, marrying Wes, raising three or four kids.

But that was nonsense. She wouldn't be marrying anyone. Could he blame her? Maud and Gus lived with their husbands under the vastly extended Hardy roof and nothing in their domestic habits acted as an enticement to marriage. All the luck in the world, but he had to concede that he was going to lose his daughter to the university. And to politics, of course.

Fetched from a region of the indoors, Beth appeared in the kitchen doorway dressed in what would normally adorn a scarecrow of the fields—a faded brown twill shirt left unbuttoned at the cuffs, and a bunchy blue woollen skirt. Wes stood to show courtesy but Bob gestured for him to sit down.

'Wes! How lovely to see you.' And a smile full of warmth.

'What are the flowers for?'

'You.'

'Me? Why?'

'Friendly gesture.'

5

Beth chuckled, not quite at Wes's expense. 'Wes, were you going to ask me out? You were, weren't you?'

'Thought you might like to come to the bonfire tonight, Beth.'

'You and me?'

Beth's mum had just put down a pot of tea on the table, cups and saucers, sugar and a jug of milk. And some shortbread biscuits. She was humming the wedding march from *Parsifal*, satirically.

'Mum, could you put these flowers somewhere? In a vase.'

Beth waited until Wes had taken a few sips of tea before enclosing one of his hands in both of hers. 'Wes, you're a lovely man, but I'm going to university in the city. I'd barely see you. And in all honesty, I don't want a boyfriend. I have politics. The Eureka Youth League takes up all of my spare hours. Do you see? You'd be wasting your time.'

'This is going well,' said Lillian.

Bob Hardy, leaning against the wall, was looking at his feet, shaking his head.

'And in any case, Wes, I never go to bonfire night. It's to celebrate the torture of a human being with fire. It gives me the creeps.'

Bob Hardy allowed a snort of laughter to escape.

'Hadn't thought of it that way,' said Wes, rubbing the back of his head. His dark curls had returned after his army haircut.

'Well, you might. As a Quaker. Does that sound pompous? Sorry.'

Wes plunged in again. 'Your dad here says you've been reading.'

'Nothing escapes Dad's attention.'

'The Life and Times of Red Joe Stalin,' said Bob Hardy. 'That'd be right, professor? She says that Red Joe clobbered the Germans on behalf of the working man.'

'Dad, I said nothing of the sort. I simply said that if the Soviet Union hadn't defeated the Germans, the Allies would have lost the war. Just common knowledge.'

'Want to make your way with the professor, Wesley, better get yourself a big red flag.'

Beth said: 'Dad, give me a break. You don't have to find fault with everything I say.'

Franny called from outdoors: 'Casey, you mongrel! Let it go!' Lillian raced to the back door.

'Just be Casey with a rabbit,' said Bob Hardy. 'Get out of their hutch, the buggers. Want to persist with my lovely daughter, Wesley? No shame in backing off.'

Wes nodded and took a last sip of his tea. 'No, Bob. Beth has been clear.'

Beth said: 'I'm sorry I disappointed you, Wes. I truly am.'

As Wes stood, he glimpsed through the window above the kitchen sink Franny, long hair flowing, in pursuit of a dog with a huge white bundle of rabbit between its jaws. Behind Franny came Lillian.

Chapter 2

THE CUNNINGHAMS were one of three families of Quakers in the Almond Tree shire, all neighbours on the stretch of country that ran down from the hills to the river west of Chinese Town. They were known, the Quakers, more for painstaking carpentry and care of the land than for their peculiar doctrines. Their fences were split rail instead of barbed wire, each joint fitting perfectly, the posts fashioned into hexagons with an adze and sanded as smooth as a table surface. The three homesteads were clad in hand-cut lengths of ash weatherboard. The roofs had higher gables than any other dwellings in the shire, meant to accommodate an attic space, and were shingled in oblongs of red gum cut and sanded as if prizes were being awarded for regularity of shape. The Quakers were orchardists. Bing cherries and apple varieties. The rows of trees ran as straight as if drawn with a T-square from the pasture hills to the highway, screened by big, branchy cypresses. The fruit the Quakers produced was superior to any other harvest in the valley, and its abundance as great as a biblical prophecy. Other orchardists in the valley, some of them, had adopted a theory first proposed by Mick Coverdale who grew cider Gravensteins on the old flood plain past Rubicon.

'Quaker spells,' said Mick. 'From the Egyptians.'

The Quakers called themselves the Society of Friends but were happy to go by the more common label. They had come to Almond Tree in 1880 from Tasmania, where there were plenty of Friends, to establish a presence in central Victoria, where there were few. It was the 1880 contingent that had built the houses with shingled roofs and planted the apples and cherries. It was not the custom of the Almond Tree Quakers to go about converting Catholics and Anglicans and atheists to their austere faith, and the three families—Cunninghams, Trents and Farebrothers—had never become four, or more. They held their meetings in their homes, except for the London Annual Meeting, as it was known, held not in London but in Melbourne. They steered clear of local politics, did not run for shire office, but in 1916 George Fox Farebrother spoke at the Mechanics Hall during a debate on conscription. He said that the Society of Friends opposed violence as a means of settling disputes in all places, at all times. This whole non-violence business came as a surprise to most of those in the hall—a big crowd—and was taken as an insult to the many Australian volunteers who had died at Gallipoli and in France and Belgium. George Farebrother endured the shouts of 'Shame!' and 'Mongrel!' in stoic silence before finishing with, 'That's all I have to say.'

In the end, the Friends families were not especially doctrinaire. Four Almond Hill Quakers volunteered for non-combatant roles in the Great War without causing much of a fuss, and two of the Trent girls served as nurses in France. And the Cunninghams gave their blessing to Wes when he took on a non-combatant role in the 6th Division, bearing the wounded away from the battle at Wewak in New Guinea. It was a Japanese POW with an uncompromising sense of duty who had shot Wes in the hospital of a holding camp—a Webley pistol, wrested from an officer—as well as a nurse. The Quakers had prayed for the Japanese soldier on the day he was hanged—as they thought. The soldier had been executed by firing squad several weeks before prayers began.

Wes had returned to Almond Tree with a fixed plan to marry, raise children and avoid battlefields. If a man fell out of an apple tree and broke his neck, rotten luck. But a man's flesh ploughed open by a 58 mm Arisaka cartridge was a disaster. When he'd waved to Beth a few days back, he'd thought: 'Oh, that's Beth Hardy, all grown up.' He should see if he could meet up with her again. He had more to discuss with her after the war. There was Charlotte Brontë, many others. Recovering in hospital at Moresby, he'd been given the job of military censor, something he could handle on his back. A big canvas bag of books had been sent to the troops by a charity in Melbourne. Wes was to assess a share of the books for any possible pro-Japanese sentiment before they were made available to the patients; classic novels, Lone Star westerns. Wes's home schooling under Mrs Farebrother hadn't exposed him to the classics, but he read them with enthusiasm. When he took his bouquet to Beth Hardy, he thought that famous books might give the two of them something lively to talk about. Thought, perhaps twice, and fleetingly, of Beth Hardy's brow deeply engaged by something by a Brontë sister.

He was influenced by Beth's criticism of bonfire night and stayed home until seven in the evening. But in the end the habit of years prevailed and he dragged some old timbers and a farm gate that the termites had made a mess of to the site of the bonfire on Paddock Reserve.

Three weeks from summer and it was barely dusk at seven-fifteen. The bonfire wouldn't be lit until seven-thirty, but fireworks were already exploding over Paddock Reserve, the red tissue paper the tom thumbs came wrapped in lay scattered everywhere. Half of the families of Almond Tree had been attracted to the bonfire, some thousands, all those with kids, and more families arriving at the same time as Wes. Like Wes, they hauled fuel for the bonfire, items of ruined furniture, garden waste, piles of newspapers, an ancient single-bed horsehair mattress, a tall wooden wardrobe with its two mirrors intact reflecting the Southern Cross. At its base, the bonfire covered the space of a smallish dwelling, tapering as it reached up into the evening sky. Wes had arrived to add his timber to the heap just as Ern Masters from the fire brigade was scaling a ladder to attach the guy to the top. The guy was a stuffed figure representing General Hideki Tojo with a yellow face, a black moustache and round spectacles. The crowd pressed in as Ern tied the general to the tall stake around which the bonfire had been built. 'That's for Darwin, you evil bastard!'

A match was dropped into the kerosene-soaked base of the bonfire while Ern Masters was still at the top of the ladder.

'Better get a wriggle on, Ern!'

Ern could see the humour. He stayed where he was, waving a handkerchief as the flames scaled the sides of the construction. 'Mother, Mother, don't let me cook!' Then hurtled back down and heaved the ladder away from the flames.

The fire seemed to change its mood and for a few minutes, dwindled and sulked. Then it found fuel that pleased it and burst skywards striving for the figure of Tojo. The crowd kept as close to the heat as possible before being forced back. As the flames reached Tojo, the crowd in festive mood sang a raucous chorus of 'Waltzing Matilda'. The cloudless evening sky was illuminated in all the patterns of the Milky Way.

Wes was the only Quaker at the bonfire. His brothers and sisters in the faith sensed without being told that nothing good could come of watching a figure incinerated on a heap of debris, but they never rebuked Wes for dragging fuel to the bonfire each year. The abiding policy of the Quakers of Almond Tree was to permit Friends and non-Friends alike to come to their own conclusions about the burning of effigies, and everything else in human experience. This was not so much a belief of the broad Quaker movement as an expression of the benign temperament of George Fox Farebrother. Wes, since childhood the most cheerful of humans, enjoyed all spectacles of laughter and hijinks and never had a word to say against rituals of any sort. He was told by his army comrades that the natives of New Guinea ate each other and was fascinated.

But here at the bonfire, no, he was not his normal self. Beth Hardy had asked him if he thought, as a Quaker, he should attend a celebration of torment. Here in the hooting crowd, with Tojo burning like a torch, he was full of regret.

He next saw Beth a couple of days later down in the hardware store buying lubricating oil for, as she said, 'the printer'. She not only smiled at Wes, but gave him a light sisterly hug. 'I'm so glad I ran into you, Wes, because I think you might be able to help me with some printing.'

'Printing?'

'Posters I want to put up around the shire, the Eureka Youth League. Dad got me an old press that Dizzy Hall scavenged from the tip. You can only print one poster at a time. But I can't get the ink right. You're so clever about things like that. Could you come over and help me out?'

'Of course, Beth. When?'

'Do you think this afternoon? Say three?'

'I'll be there.'

He made his way to Beth's place by driving his father's ute along the firebreak then down to Cartwright's Track. He could hear from fifty yards off a shouting match underway, women's voices. Probably Gus and Maud, both famously noisy. On the back veranda the three Hardy dogs, still haunted by the fireworks, emerged from their kennels to implore a pat and a kind word.

It was Bob Hardy who answered Wes's second knock.

'Wes, handsome Wes. What, back for more?'

'Beth asked me to help out with her printing press.'

'Could say a glutton for punishment, could say as game as Ned Kelly. She's out in the barn printing a world history of Red Joe and his comrades. Come back for a beer when you're done Wesley. Or when she's done. Shouldn't be long.'

Wes eased the barn door open and called to Beth, who was at the bench, occupied with a roller and a tray of ink. Hardy's tractor and his red Dodge flatbed took up the space beside the bench. Half a dozen chickens had perched themselves on the tractor to study Beth while she worked. The less curious birds, fifty or more, preferred their coop at the back of the barn, keeping up a muted chorus of chicken contentment. Beth looked up from her task and smiled. The illumination of a bare overhead light bulb brought out all the features of impatience in her expression. She had bunched her long hair on the top of her head with a green ribbon.

'Wes, thanks so much. I know you're busy with your house. But this damned thing!'

'I wanted to tell you that you were right,' Wes said, inside the barn now. 'I went to the bonfire, but I shouldn't. It was in my head, what you told me.'

Beth looked baffled. The roller she held in her hand remained poised above the ink tray.

'What I told you? What did I tell you? I didn't tell you anything.'

'You said I oughtn't go. Quakers oughtn't go, you said.'

'Did I? Well, I should mind my own business. Sorry.'

'No, no. You were right. So how can I help?'

'This,' she said. With ink-stained fingers, she indicated a square of thick brown linoleum into which lettering and a picture had been carved. The lettering read: *Sheepskins for Russia* and the picture showed a smiling sheep. The smaller lettering under the sheep read: *Winter in Leningrad! Brrr! You can help our Comrades in the Soviet Union by sending a shilling postal order to the address below. Each shilling helps!*

'I'm printing posters,' said Beth. 'I'll put them up around town. It's important.'

Wes peered closer at the linocut. 'Your sheep's happy about giving up its skin?'

Beth, ignoring the comment, held up one of the printed posters on ten-by-twelve-inch cartridge. It was a mess, the lettering barely legible.

'The ink's too thick,' Wes said. 'Thin it with some turps.'

By trial and error the right consistency for the ink was found and a perfect poster printed. And another. Finally twenty, all the sheets of cartridge Beth had on hand. 'Wes, I'm so grateful.' Over the hour of cooperative engagement with the task, Wes asked about the Eureka Youth League, whether he should join up. Also, what was a 'communist' anyway? Beth stated by rote the aims of the Communist Party of Australia, but then added immediately that communism wouldn't suit him.

'Why not?'

'We're not Christians, Wes, not anything.'

'I can keep quiet about God.'

Beth said that wouldn't be fair to him, or to his family. 'Being a Quaker's in your blood, Wes. You can't

16

just forget it and replace it with communism. It has to be your life.'

Wes was fascinated by her commitment. Christianity notwithstanding, he had never had a solid commitment to any emphatic belief. In New Guinea, he had found it impossible to identify anything that gave the soldiers on his own side, the Australian side, a moral advantage over the Japanese. The Australians, with their mocking way of dealing with war and bloodletting, their satirical smiles, their shrugs, never seemed wholly serious about anything, while the Japanese appeared driven by stoicism and insanity. The Japanese prisoner who had shot him and the nurse had gravely surrendered the pistol, holding it flat in his two palms like an offering.

Better, of course, if the Australians won the war, but winning a war, should that make you proud? A stitcher attached to the 2/11th Battalion, a West Australian called Bluey Cook, superficial sutures, took pleasure in setting him moral dilemmas: 'What would you do if a Jap was about to bayonet your dad and you were sitting behind a Vickers? You'd give the Jap a burst, right?' Bluey Cook had only a muddled idea of what Quakers were on about, but he made up for ignorance with persistence. 'You don't want nothing to do with transfusions, but you give 'em to our blokes, you give 'em to the Japs. How does that go down with your archbishop?'

All that Wes could say he believed was that it was

wrong to murder, and war was murder. It had been instilled in him by his mother, Daisy, although it seemed so obvious to him that it may simply have been his temperament, regardless of instruction. At the same time, that Jap with the bayonet—yes, he would have pulled the trigger on the Vickers. And he had actually fired a Vickers. Thrilling.

He left Beth to her project, declined the beer with Bob Hardy. He was glad Beth had been so candid with him about the boyfriend stuff, which was nonsense. And relieved that he felt no impulse to pester her about it. She was going to university, a much more worthwhile ambition than hooking up with him. He would finish the house. One fine day, he'd find someone he could share it with.

But on the drive home, no more than ten minutes on the dirt track, he decided to give up on girlfriends altogether. He'd been to war, had shovelled the limbs and guts of hundreds of men, Australian and Japanese, into canvas bags and he'd given a fair try to observing Quaker love. Neither had taught him anything about life. He'd build the house, live there alone, grow cherries, honour God in whatever fashion, teach himself to cook. And that would do. Also read. Maybe Karl Marx. He recalled volunteering to go out in New Guinea and fetch back stray Japanese bodies. His real object was to detour past a particular green pool on the cove and gaze at it. Beth's eyes were the same green; you could lose yourself in their shimmer. The green was of a quality he'd seen only in that cove near Wewak, a small cove, clear to the white sand on the bottom. The creatures of the sea, bright fish, small squid, entered the cove through a narrow opening and dawdled in the warm waters. An enchantment to watch the sea creatures loitering in the green waters of the cove.

Later in his Almond Tree life, casting about for reading material that might mean something to him, he had taken up reading poetry and had come across one by D. H. Lawrence about a hot day in Sicily and a snake. A current developed between Wes and the poet. The man in the poem had thrown a piece of wood at a snake, forcing the creature to wriggle quickly and disappear down a hole in the ground. The man was disappointed in himself; he should have gazed at the beauty of the golden snake without interfering. 'I had missed my chance with one of the lords of Life,' he said. Wes had seen hundreds of snakes around Almond Tree, especially out by the billabongs on the flood plain, red-bellied black snakes a yard long and more, also tigers, browns, copperheads. He had stepped on them in unaware moments, bare feet, the fat girth of the creature moving against his sole. He had never thought of a snake as a lord of life. Then he did. That was poetry. Beth's eyes, their colour, the life that swam into them like bright creatures into the Wewak cove—that was poetry.

He barely glimpsed her again before she left for the city in February.

Chapter 3

BETH'S CURIOSITY about politics had been roused by Di Porter's classes on the industrial revolution, dwelling on the conditions of factory work in the English mills. Also, an incidental reference to remedies, such as the October Revolution in Russia. It all went over the heads of the second form pupils, except for Beth. At the age of fourteen, she had developed a sense of justice that coiled itself in her breast like a spring. She had concluded all by herself that the world could not go on in the way it had, the small number of haves and the masses of have-nots. But where her convictions came from was a mystery. Her family environment was more characterised by anarchy than anything else, four bickering girls with only eight years between them. Nevertheless, Beth came to Di Porter at the end of the second class on the mills with an enquiry: 'Mrs Porter, what is Red October?'

Di had a portrait of Vladimir Lenin displayed on the wall of her kitchen next to the Kelvinator, and a second portrait of Joseph Stalin beside the door that led into the living room. A guest of sometime past had written in a speech balloon that grew from Lenin's lips: 'Kiss me, I'm hard.' Stalin's speech balloon read: 'I'm yours for a rouble.' Di Porter hadn't thought it necessary to erase the irreverent messages, even when urged to do so by Beth, whose piety was more pronounced than Di's. 'Not so solemn, Beth. A little levity can't hurt.'

Di had come to Australia from Cambridge in 1931 to marry Beau Porter, a Melbourne boy, reading Economics at King's. The two had met in Cambridge while Di was at Girton reading History, both socialists who considered a long lecture at the Fabian Society followed by a meeting of the Constituency Working Group a grand night out. When they first set eyes on each other at a Labour Club picnic, she thought Beau the most handsome man on earth. More than that, his smile and gestures expressed a freedom that did not exist among Englishmen, even socialists, who were more class conscious in their way than the nobility.

On a plaid blanket on the banks of the Cam she plied him with questions about his homeland, surprised at her lack of interest in Australia up to this point considering she now found everything he said beguiling.

Beau loved Australia; that was what so engaged her. She did not know anyone who could speak of his love for his homeland, her homeland without a great deal of passionate ranting. Nobody loved England, particularly, except John of Gaunt. When she spoke about her own life, her political coming-of-age at eighteen during the General Strike of 1926, buttering bread for unionists on the picket lines, he listened as enthralled as if she were reciting battle scenes from the *Iliad*. Her father, a librarian at the London School of Economics, and her mother, a paediatrician, were both socialists, but not so you'd notice. They held their daughter, their only child, somewhat in awe. Their usual response to any decision of their daughter's was immediate acquiescence, and so it was when Di told her parents about Beau and said she would probably marry him after graduation. But Beau's father, who ran a printing works back in Australia, in Collingwood, was forced to call Beau home in the aftermath of the stockmarket crash. Beau's older brother, Horry, a barrister, took no interest in the business. While Beau left within a week, it was agreed that Di would stay on at Girton until the completion of her degree and join him in six months.

She married Beau six months later at Melbourne Town Hall on her twenty-third birthday and spent what would normally have been her honeymoon toiling in the printing works. She did everything from setting type to knocking on the doors of businesses up and down Smith

Street spruiking for contracts in her musical Wycombe Abbey accent. The stale winds of the Depression blighted all her efforts, and those of Beau. Her father-in-law, Lou, a union supporter all his life, was a dithering wreck after letting thirty workers go, and Beau, too, was ailing, a mystery complaint that caused dizziness, aching joints and sudden collapse. The medical consensus, not offered with much conviction, was that Beau would benefit from rest and clean country air. Di took him to Almond Tree, where his family kept a cottage on two acres, usually only visited at Christmas, and devotedly nursed him back to health. It was during the two years of her husband's convalescence that Di took on teaching at Almond Tree High and came to meet all the Hardy girls, Beth most memorably, intense but cheerful, too, enquiring, a curiosity.

Di raised twin girls in a terrace in Fitzroy, a short walk from the printing works. The business recovered, the printers who'd been let go returned over the space of six years, Beau's degree remained uncompleted. The works were left in Beau's hands in 1939 when his father succumbed to a heart condition that had niggled away for years. Embarrassingly for a socialist, Beau revealed a gift for profit based on economy of production and the Porter-Nolan Printing Works was written up as a model of efficiency. Lou's wife Joy retired to the Almond Tree cottage with a set of Everyman classics and a scheme to write letters to world leaders warning of the rise of fascism in Germany. Horry said she'd lost her marbles. Di spent a day each weekend at Almond Tree with the twins, correcting the diction of her mother-in-law's letters to Stalin, Roosevelt, King George VI, and tutoring Beth Hardy, at her insistence, in the political philosophy of Karl Marx.

Now Beth was off to university herself, and as Bob Hardy watched Beth packing in her room he was sobbing all down his stubbled cheeks. Beth heard the moist, gurgling sounds and looked up in alarm.

'What's the matter?'

'I'll miss you, honey.'

'Oh, that. Don't worry.'

'Yeah, well. You know.'

Beth reminded herself that tears like this were, after all, sincere, and set aside the packing to console her father. She put her arms around him and patted his back.

'I'll be all right, Dad.'

'Remember,' said Bob Hardy, 'you've got as much right to be there as anyone else. Being at the university.'

Beth had no need for reassurance.

Chapter 4

PATTY CUNNINGHAM was writing to Beth Hardy on a green pad of the sort nurses carried to record a doctor's directions. She used a fountain pen which may have been the fanciest in Japan—a gold-plated Mont Blanc won in a game of fifty-two-card draw from a surgeon in Bougainville. The ink she was forced to use was an inferior brand that clogged the nib and had to be watered down, so that the script on the paper varied in its register from stark black to the grey of a pigeon's plumage. She wrote with the pad on her knees and with the intense concentration of one who had to battle every second to remain awake.

Patty, at twenty-four the second oldest of the Cunningham girls, had gone straight from her non-combatant role as a nurse in Bougainville to volunteer nursing with the British Commonwealth Occupation Force in Hiroshima. On her third day in her Hiroshima quarters, she gave herself time to write to Beth, whom she loved, before falling asleep. Strictly speaking, she was still on duty but after forty hours on her feet in the wards, she'd been allowed a six-hour break. No such thing as a nurses' dormitory in Hiroshima. On her arrival two days earlier, Patty had been assigned a tent that housed four, not the worst accommodation she'd known, brand new canvas fitted with Perspex windows and small holland blinds that rolled down. Compared to Bougainville, it was Paris.

The three other nurses were all away at the hospital— they'd arrived a week earlier. Their humble personal odds and ends were left on upturned dried-apricot crates beside their camp beds: framed photographs, notebooks, a small cactus-like plant in a squat little vase. The Australian nurses in the Japanese hospital did not wear the traditional uniform of belted dress but rather army-issue khaki trousers and blouse and peaked cap. Preferred by every nurse.

'Off to the big smoke, baby girl!' she began, and then included a story of Beth as a five-year-old sitting on her haunches to study a tiger snake, and how this convinced Patty that the Hardy girl's curiosity was fearless.

And look you are fearless! All these big babies scared of the commies, but not you! Good on you, Bethy! And now after Queens you're staying with

Di Porter, Red Di. Isn't that good? She can keep building you up to become the first Aussie Stalin. Only darling, try not to murder a couple of million peasants, if you can possibly avoid it. I hear from Mum that my little brother Wes is gaga about you. You could do worse, once you graduate. Believe me, you could. I have the rank of lieutenant and for some reason this attracts every randy surgeon in the place, except for the Japs, who are extremely respectful. I get slobbered on every working day. The nursing here is bloody awful, Bethy, dear God, an atomic bomb doesn't leave much behind, including the Japanese people. Frightful injuries, but your big grown-up friend does her best.

Like the Japanese woman who had been harboured by her daughter for months and who was finally carried to the hospital with such awful burns that her entire chest was lifted off in one piece from her neck to her navel, her organs on display like an anatomy lesson. Others whose eyes had been melted in their face when they turned their gaze to the blast. Burns all over bodies like the bubbles in boiling porridge. Patty didn't mention these horrors. 'My stint ends in three months. I wasn't discharged at Bougainville, so I'm officially still in the corps as a volunteer. You know what a volunteer is, don't you? A dogsbody, and a mongrel one at that.'

Patty didn't explain why she'd volunteered for

Hiroshima. It wasn't clear even to her. Other than the faces of the Japanese POWs, which troubled her. It wasn't the shame of being a captive she saw there. Most had not the least vestige of shame. More a mask-like blankness, which may have been what was left of shame once it was exhausted. Those who were full of shame had died months ago by swallowing stones and metal fragments they picked up in the compound, stuffing them down their throats with a stick. The ones who were left couldn't be bothered. They wanted to go home to Japan. Defeat, wounds, the English voices all around them that made the sounds of crows cawing, all that they wanted was to see their homeland, as if it were the only conceivable destination for their trammelled souls, the only possible solace. When Patty treated the POWs in the Bougainville compound, they reached for her hand and implored in English: 'Japan. To go. Japan.' They did not know that the cities they longed for were rubble. One POW said: 'To go. Hiroshima. I please.' An orderly overheard and laughed. 'All gone, my yellow friend.'

Within weeks of the atomic blasts, the Yanks and Australians in Bougainville had surprisingly accurate details of the devastation, the casualties, and even the mechanics of a nuclear explosion. Two bombs, and the Pacific War was over. An Australian major, one of the more courteous, told Patty over a beer: 'Now we go and patch things up. A Commonwealth force is off to the land of the

Chrysanthemum Throne. And the Aussies are slated for Hiroshima. Are you coming, Patty, my love? Want to see what a mess an atom bomb can make? All you have to do is volunteer. More than a hundred thousand dead in one big heap. Some still struggling on.'

She went, not for the sake of the major, who had become her lover in a way so casual and comical as to be slapstick, but to see for herself the worst thing in the world. She was a woman who averted her gaze from nothing. But more than that, to experience this strange country that could produce expressions of both hopelessness and yearning on her patients' faces, a country of a thousand years of sublime culture and sublime madness.

In Kure harbour the wreckage of a hundred ships of the Japanese navy with blackened bows rose out of the sea, and the sea here was ugly enough as it was, chopped into an ill-tempered contest of small waves by the wind. But the sky was a motionless, cloudless blue. Further south, overland, the sky was the grey of gunmetal above what was left of Hiroshima, a no-man's land of rubble stretching for miles. Any possible rebuilding seemed a fantasy. But Japanese in shreds and tatters, mostly children, searched in the debris for God knew what, stooped over, eyes scanning. Patty saw a girl gnawing voraciously on a block of charred wood. Australian troops shouted at the scavengers, aimed their rifles. 'Fuck off, you little bastards!' They were ignored.

Just a God-awful mess, Bethy. The Japanese, so far as I can see, are completely baffled by defeat and don't know how to grasp it. The Aussie troops are arrogant and mocking. The hospital is a mess. What equipment and drugs we have is all from the Yanks. The Japanese doctors are demoralised, but competent, at least. Anyway, I'll be back at Almond Tree in about four months, maybe, and although you won't be there, let's arrange to meet at Di's place for a natter. I'll likely avoid the propaganda, if that's okay. I know you love the commies to bits, but to me they're nutcases.

Your loving and adoring friend, Patty

Not that she would be permitted to, but she wouldn't be sending any pics of Hiroshima. She had seen the site of the blast twice and it still defied any belief she could muster that a single bomb had caused such complete devastation. One odd thing: grass was growing among the rubble, weeds, some flowering. But not a tree anywhere, not a shrub. Standing back from the rubble, she thought if we can do this to people, we can do anything. If we can burn a hundred thousand to cinders, we can burn a billion. She knew that bigger bombs than the Hiroshima blast were ready to be dropped from bombers, she had been told by the major. 'This one was kid stuff. In a bit of time, they could wipe out Melbourne in a second.' And Almond Tree, every stand of Bing cherries, every house, the racecourse with the new stadium, the old shops with their timber verandas along Columbine Street, the old hospital by the river and the new one on Cardigan Square. Patty had said she would be home in four months, but she knew she wouldn't be home in less than a year. Maybe longer. Walking away from Hiroshima would be like pouring a canteen of water into the dust in front of a parched child. She knew that the major would endorse her request to stay. She had a life. Better expend what energy she had here. Almond Tree would live on without her.

Chapter 5

HORSE RACING and Quakerism were not natural cousins; nevertheless, Wes Cunningham had taken on the job of building the new stable area for the sixty-year-old course, regarded as the most beautiful racing track in the country. As a carpenter respected for his skill, he was given licence to incorporate features into the twenty-two stalls that would normally be found only at such sites as the stables of princes and millionaires. His designs called for the stalls to be built a third larger than normal to allow the horses the freedom to roll on the straw and sand floors without injury. The stalls were to be gated instead of left open at the front, to prevent punters offering a horse a lucky whack on the rear, an incitement to stumble forward for the confused beasts.

The gables of the roofs were high, so that no matter how wildly a horse reared it could not strike its head. The walls were dovetailed cedar planks, simply because it pleased Wes to treat cedar in this way. Gutters would edge the floors, to facilitate the cleaning out with a hose. The number of each stall would be inscribed in white on a black background. In copperplate. Really? Derek Morack the sign-writer could do it.

At Beth's initiative, he wrote to her once a month. at Di Porter's in Fitzroy where she was now living. He described the progress on the stables. He received letters in reply, lively and full of university and Communist Party gossip. Wes wrote: 'I've been dovetailing cedar. It looks beautiful, Beth. These stables, you could live in them if you had to. Can't tell you the happiness it gives me to make something proper. If you ever see the house I'm building above the river, you'll love every bit of it.'

Wes allowed his mother, Daisy, to read Beth's gossipy letters. She came to a point at which she felt she must say something. 'Wesley, you're not still holding a torch for Beth, are you?'

They were on the back veranda drinking tea, Daisy with the bible and Beth's latest letter on her lap. She never drank tea or ate anything without first reading verses from the New Testament.

Wes smiled. 'No, mother. The letters are Beth's idea. I asked her out once, five months ago and she said no. Very polite about it. We're friends, that's all.'

Daisy nodded. 'Because she doesn't want you, Wesley. She doesn't love you. Beth is a zealot. For her, romance is a folly. A waste of time when she's trying to convert the world to a utopia. And I know, Wesley, I know that we have something of the same mission. But not with guns.'

Wes's reply was a little less patient than was usual for him: 'She's not a zealot, Mother. You know as well as I do that she sold stuff down at the shopping centre to help out the poor in the shire before she took up politics. She probably gets it from her mother, who crochets those rugs for the poor. She has a good heart.'

'She doesn't love God.' The real issue.

'Mother, we're friends. Have been for years. You've read her letters, you can see there's no romance. We don't love each other and I have enough to keep me busy with the stables.'

Daisy nodded. 'I wish I believed you, Wesley.'

The construction of the stables would cost a fortune, considering the care Wes was taking. The track held only six meetings a year, and the Almond Hill Turf Club was unlikely to cover the expense through bookies' fees. No, the financing came entirely from one man, Sir Jim Morecombe, an enthusiast of the gallops whose fortune had been made miles away from Almond Tree in the city, where he ran a half dozen department stores. But before he left the town to become a millionaire, he'd developed a vision of the racecourse as a thing of beauty. Year after year, he poured thousands of pounds into its upkeep. The most stunning feature of the course was the giant oak in the middle of the mounting yard, ninety years old, with boughs that reached all the way to the fence of the yard. Roses of four shades were planted along the rear fence, just in the sunlight. The white grandstands, freshly painted each year, were thought to be masterpieces of late-colonial architecture.

It was Jim Morecombe's habit—he never insisted on the 'sir', discouraged it more than otherwise, but his wife was always 'Lady Mary'—to motor up to the turf club in his Bentley a couple of days a week if work was going on, and there was always work going on. He wore tweed on these visits, a green homburg and two-toned shoes of cream and brown. This outfit was his idea of 'looking the part' of a man of the turf. He always carried a hip flask of cognac which he would offer about to anyone craving a pick-me-up, even to the strappers. His generosity in every other way was equally legendary—lunch for the trainers with an appetite at the Chinese Town pub, the 'pigtail', which did not serve Chinese food but a wonderful roast lunch six days a week day-baked by Mandy Patterson and her two married daughters.

A hearty patron was a godsend, but Jim Morecombe had the annoying custom of hanging over Wes's shoulder while he was working. Wes at work exercised the concentration of a dog with a lamb shank to whatever task he'd set himself and had to exercise extraordinary patience when Jim wished to know exactly what his stable builder was doing at any given time. Bevelling the top of walls between the stalls. 'Don't want the neddies rubbing their heads against any surface that hasn't been smoothed.'

'You think of these things don't you, Wes?'

'I do, yes.'

'You Quakers make bloody good carpenters. Must go all the way back to Jesus. Ha!'

'Might do. Jim, don't put your clodhoppers on the cedar planks. You'll leave muddy marks and I'll have to sand 'em back.'

'Clodhoppers? Ha! These are from Italy, Wes, Italy, bloke in Milan makes then specially for me. No others made for anyone else, not the same. But yeah, I'll move my trotters if it pleases you.'

Wes wasn't simply bevelling the top beams of the fence stalls. He was fitting the beams into the corner posts without glue, since it had come to his notice that horses were oddly attracted to the taste of pearl glue and would gnaw at the timber to get at it.

Wes's true motive in building the stables was the welfare of the horses. From the age of fourteen, horses had been put into his care for their education on the back block of the Cunningham spread below the foothills with Chinese Town on the other side. He spoke to the colts and fillies in a conversational way, sure that they understood. 'It's a saddle. So that you can carry a rider.

Like a seat on your back. You do the leg work, the rider sits there smoking his pipe. That's the way it is. You get along on your four legs, the rider smokes his pipe. Never going to change. A couple of weeks, you'll like it.'

Treats did no harm. He brought the horse he was educating mashed apple and carrot in a big terracotta bowl from his mum's kitchen, let the animal drool for a few minutes while he stroked its face, then allowed it to drop its head and make itself ecstatic on the contents of the bowl. He saddled it while it was eating, and when it had finished the fodder, bridled it, then cantered it along the perimeter of the paddock.

Wes since a young age had been one of the best riders in the district, amateur or professional. He never rode against the jockeys who came to Almond Tree for the six meetings a year; he was too big and he had no registration. But he rode in the amateur race at each meeting, the Mad Mile, free to choose any horse he fancied, and often won. He would set aside a neddy with heart, one he'd given some stiffening. Horses have moods. Days come along when they have no interest other than going through the motions, as if the point of racing seemed fruitless. But any horse that Wes had lunged and taught to accept the bridle, the saddle, had developed an intimacy with, that horse would race for him, give it everything. And Wes loved winning the Mad Mile. It was the only time that victory became vivid to him.

He'd been asked to teach Beth to ride when she was thirteen. Bob Hardy had opened up his leg with a chainsaw and couldn't take on the job. Not that Beth was interested in riding a horse. Any creatures not equipped to make political distinctions seemed a waste of time to her. But Bob Hardy insisted that a farm girl should know how to get about on horseback, and asked Wes to take it on. It was futile. Beth rode like a robot, no feeling in her legs and the reins held so tight that the poor beast was left baffled as to her intention. Instruction irritated her. 'It knows what to do. Why does it need me to poke and prod it?' Yet even at fifteen, Wes two years older, there was an intensity in her that fascinated him. She said that preparing horses for racing was 'immoral' and after the second lesson, said that she didn't want any part of it. Too bad, for Wes delighted in watching her hair bouncing on her shoulders with the horse's motion.

Opposites don't attract, except for a short time; it's those with complementary tastes that attract, or else a broadly generous nature that can happily accommodate variance. What Wes identified in Beth was something that he admired without having a wisp of it himself. She wanted to alter the world. His own Quaker faith would never achieve such an outcome. He had no faith in anything that would be likely to alter the world.

But to believe in it. That was something.

Chapter 6

THE VARIOUS halls in which meetings of the Eureka Youth League were held all smelt of stale urine and sewers, as if the plumbing had been contracted, one hall after another, to the one slapdash tradesman. The number of halls available to the EYL was limited. Church halls were out of the question, not simply because committees of management were reluctant to facilitate a movement that was pretty much committed to the mass murder of the clergy, when it could be arranged. The RSL wanted nothing to do with communists, even when it was pointed out that some millions of Russians had given their lives to defeat the armies of the Third Reich. The choices were limited to Mechanics Institute halls out in the suburbs—those whose admin was in the hands of left-wing unions, by no means the majority—or oddly surviving shacks erected ages ago by such organisations as the World Brotherhood for Understanding between Nations and the Daughters of Non-Violent Dissent.

The stink meant nothing. The zeal of the Youth League brethren was such that they barely noticed it. If a portrait of the queen were displayed, it was turned to the wall for the duration of the meeting, but the tawdry furnishings, the dim fifteen-watt lighting, the oppressive heat in summer and the frigid cold of winter were endured not so much with stoicism, but with a sense of betrayal if the discomfort were so much as mentioned. The cause was the thing; a sore behind from sitting on an uncomfortable chair for three hours was insignificant.

Beth, deputy chair of the committee, was always seated at the front where the most uncomfortable chairs were located. Her back and behind bore the pain with pride. The committee of her branch comprised three EYL members, which left six of the rank and file in the audience: Valentine Tell and his French wife, Eloise, both twenty-one, and four students from Melbourne Uni: Christian and Helen from Law and Andy and Denise from Physics—unusual, since the physics people were politics averse and believed that solutions to social problems would mostly be solved by the behaviour of molecules and advances in technology in ways not yet revealed.

~

40

The issue of the moment was a visit to the USSR by one of the EYL kids, a kind invitation extended by the students of Moscow University. Take a first-hand look at what's being achieved by the Soviet people. Visit factories and newspaper offices, join in the joyous ongoing celebrations of the October Revolution that lasted into December. Also, performances at the Bolshoi. Ten days. All expenses paid. The candidate would leave on December 1st on the first flight between Australia and London, then fly to Vienna, then to Moscow.

The most obvious candidate was Beth herself. But her sheer competence excited a certain amount of envy. Beth ran the branch and one office holder after another surrendered to her in her suggestions. It had nothing to do with ego; it was simply that she was intellectually equipped to identify solutions that it was impossible to fault, so astute was she in managing dogma. Valentine proposed Beth, and his wife Eloise seconded. Made sense. Beth was the only Russian speaker in any branch of the EYL, three years of tutoring by Di Porter. Beth could also be counted on to provide a conscientious report on the Moscow expedition, including details of factories, most important, since it was the sacred view of the EYL members that the bitter conditions under which Australian working folk laboured were unknown to the workers of the Soviet Union, where the samovar was always kept warm and apples and pears were handed out liberally.

On the other hand, Beth's merit was—how can this best be expressed?—undemocratic. She certainly wasn't a show-off, but it put members off when official documents were always handed to her for interpretation—and the documents needed it. She grasped what was being asked of the members at a deeper level than the wording strictly suggested. When the Party Committee wrote to insist that charity was no more than a bourgeois strategy of placation, including a penny tossed to a beggar on the street, she paused to explain that a penny for a beggar endorsed a life of humiliating mendicancy that served merely to salve the conscience of those who benefitted from inequality. It would help the beggar more if we 'took ten minutes to enlighten him on the rotten system he was unwittingly perpetuating'. Nevertheless, when a vote was called for, all hands were raised. And Beth was chosen from the six candidates from other branches of the EYL.

She travelled in December at the end of her first year of university. Her mother thought the whole business 'interesting'; her father thought she would be shot against the wall of the Kremlin. For what? Being too pretty? Too clever? Too something. Beth's preparations for the visit were insanely comprehensive. She would be able to speak about the activities of the EYL down to the finest detail. Patty in Hiroshima wrote to say: 'Bring me back a bottle of the people's vodka.'

Exhausted by the three-stage flight to Moscow, and

overwrought as she was with the mission entrusted to her, she failed to notice at first that the delegation from Moscow University—six students—were reading entirely from scripts that they held out almost at arm's length as if uniformly long-sighted. It was all in English: 'The peoples of the USSR have outrageous good pleasure in making welcome brilliant socialist student of the famous University of Melbourne Elizabeth Hardy.' Beth replied in Russian: 'My pleasure!' One of the students came rushing up with her big black suitcase, retrieved from somewhere or other. 'Let me carry, please, Miss Elizabeth Hardy!'

The six excessively cheerful students were the only smiling people she came across on the freezing journey between the airport and the hotel. Muscovites stared at her pleated tartan skirt, her gorgeous blue jersey jacket and black overcoat of the highest-grade merino (from Di Porter) with what seemed a blend of curiosity succeeded by contempt, as if she had come from wherever to offer a special insult to the frumpy citizens of the Soviet Union. Beth had items from her own frumpy wardrobe in her suitcase and she resolved to wriggle into them as soon as she could. She was taken to a monster hotel by the rollicking students, who went so far in their comradeship as to accompany her to her bedroom, about the size of an aircraft hangar. On the centre of the bed, big enough to accommodate six people, sat a huge Persian cat in a state of supreme contentment.

'For you, dear Miss Elizabeth Hardy. For to keep you

happy. In the Australia, all the people have a cat for being a pet, yes? This is your pet, for happiness.' The Russian student in charge of cat introductions, Vasily, explained further that the cat belonged to the hotel, and that the cat's name was Duma. 'Someone will come to feed Duma two times a day, and take her to the toilet. You like to have this gesture of friendship, Miss Elizabeth Hardy?'

Beth liked cats well enough, but offering up Duma as a companion seemed very odd. She said: 'Oh yes, a lovely pussycat. Thank you!'

'Now we leave you to rest. Tomorrow in the afternoon you give your speech.'

'Should I keep it short? Do you think? My Russian is limited, as you see.'

'No, no, excellent Russian. One hour and a half an hour. In the People's Auditorium downstairs. One thousand students will attend.'

And so she was left with Duma, who implored attention and licked her hand with a tongue like an industrial rasp.

She noticed that the green block of soap in the bathroom would not lather, and the lights flickered constantly. The rug on the bedroom floor was actually two rugs, the one on top hiding a threadbare patch beneath. The portrait of Comrade Stalin on the wall was not defaced with comic captions like the portrait in Di Porter's house. It was as radiant as if printed only an hour before.

~

Ninety minutes? What on earth would she say? The shearers' strike, or even before that, socialism on the goldfields, the Eureka Stockade, Federation, the bicameral parliament, which she could represent as the hoodwinking of the people. She stretched out on a mattress that felt like it was stuffed with stones, but managed to sleep for two hours. When she woke, the image in her mind was that of Wes, his candid expression as he listened to her explaining the Marxist program. It made her smile, poor ning-nong that he was.

The window of her hotel room overlooked a broad street that ran off Red Square. Snow was falling lightly in a wispy breeze. She wondered what she was doing here. From Almond Tree? Her, Elizabeth Hardy. She sat at a desk set up in the corner and went to work on her speech. The Russians would know what a shearer was, would they? She thought of translating the lyrics of 'Click Go the Shears', for the sake of the humour Di urged on her, but in Russian it came out: 'Noisy Are the Workman's Tools'. The point she wished to make was that the right to organise as unions among the shearers was the beginning of socialism in Australia, the birth of the Labor Party, which would eventually evolve into communism.

As she wrote, she glanced through the window every so often at the falling snow. Plenty of foot traffic. Most seemed grim, shoulders forward. She wrote: 'The people who survived the Great Patriotic War are full of the pride of victory.' The cat on the bed purred deeply.

The speech she made the next day appeared incomprehensible to the audience of students, most of whom seemed to have come from an urban background and had no idea about shearing. Whenever the students cheered, it was in response to Beth's references to 'the Great Patriotic War' and the unparalleled suffering of the Russian people. Also to the warmongering of the Americans. She quoted Wes's sister on the devastation of Hiroshima, but made no mention of prospective Soviet nuclear weapons.

Her happiest memory of the visit was the day she stood in the centre of Red Square with the sponsoring students circled around her. The snow had gone for the day and the sky was bright blue. Here she was at the pulsing heart of the Soviet Union, where crowds gathered each year to celebrate universal justice. She felt exhilarated and turned in a circle with her arms held high. The students clapped and sang. Some soldiers passing joined in. They were singing the 'Internationale' and seemed delighted that Beth knew the Russian. 'A patriot!' they shouted as they clapped. 'In Australia, one day!' she called out. The Russians applauded. 'In Australia!' they replied.

Chapter 7

WHILE WES was away from the Quaker meetings in the army, the singing was ordinary. His was the voice, a rich tenor tutored by Penny Farebrother, that could carry any note without a hint of a waver, although those in the congregation who knew about singing might have noticed that Wes kept to sentimental ballads and folk songs that did not test his range.

The singing of hymns was largely ignored by Quakers—too many insincere lyrics voiced by Friends that meant nothing, or were at least dubious in their expression. But the George Fox Farebrother tradition was another matter. George in his day enjoyed singing, and the tradition had been preserved. 'The Ash Grove' and 'The Water Is Wide' were the favourites. When

Wes sang, there was no joining in, except in occasional phrases ('build me a boat that can carry two...'), such was the quality of his voice. George's surviving brother, Martin, who resembled his older brother right down to his pendulous earlobes, kept this idiosyncratic musical tradition. The singing enhanced Wes's allure to the Quaker maidens, seven between the ages of fifteen and twenty. Plenty of modest overtures were made, but with his heart set on avoiding courtship, he barely noticed even the prettiest of the Quaker girls. If Wes loved God, as he ought, he should think of marriage. But he didn't.

Wes loved God. God was a veil that covered the earth. But he had been raised to love God and it didn't require effort and made no difficult demands; just refraining from murder and exercising kindness. There was no broad program of redemption for the human race in his religion. But Beth, who had no god, had adopted a blueprint for the salvation of humanity that exceeded in its ambition anything he'd been able to imagine. It made the Quaker fraternity seem isolated and self-satisfied. On Martin Farebrother's radio—the only radio in the Quaker community—Wes heard the increasingly dire news of confrontation between the Soviet Union and the West. He also read, avidly, his sister Patty's letters from Hiroshima. You didn't need to be a genius to work out that it wouldn't be long before the Soviet Union developed the nuclear weapons that had made a wasteland of Hiroshima and the veil of God was ripped to shreds.

~

Beth asked him to visit her at University College just the once in her first year, before her trip to Moscow. They went for lunch at a small place in Parkville and were joined by an older man, a lecturer, also a communist. The conversation was almost entirely between Beth and her friend. He may have been fifty, with long, greying hair, handsome in an aging way. And everything he said to Beth was tinged with humour, and flattery. 'The comrades will adore you, Bethy. They'll have you in bed within days.' Beth said, 'Tush, tush!' Not with a smile. Wes blushed from his neck to his hairline. When Beth finally brought Wes into the conversation, it was to tell her friend—Louis—that Wes was building stables up at the Almond Tree racecourse. 'He's a very good carpenter.'

'Ah, a working man,' said Louis, and he reached across the table to pat Wes's shoulder. 'Me, I haven't done a day's work with my hands in my life, I'm ashamed to say.'

'Wes has begun to take an interest in politics. He asked me to tell him all about Marx. Didn't you, Wes?'

Wes didn't reply. He was disturbed by the way in which Louis kept touching Beth's hand. It wasn't jealousy, more a piercing disappointment. Beth certainly did not appear to be enjoying it. She didn't wince, but she stiffened.

'My great-grandfather, though, was a blacksmith. Up in Tocumwal. He married a woman who was 'above his station', as they used to say, and she insisted on her three sons getting out of trade and into college. Like D. H. Lawrence's mum. Sending old David Herbert to Nottingham Uni.'

'Lawrence was a famous writer, Wes,' Beth provided. 'His father was a collier.'

'Yes, I know.'

He wished Beth would tell Louis to stop. But it wasn't his business.

It was Beth who spoke up. 'Louis, stop that.'

'Pardon?'

'Stroking me.'

'I wasn't aware that I was doing so.'

'You're aware now, so please stop.'

Beth took her arm off the table.

'Am I annoying you?'

'A little. Yes.'

'Then I apologise.'

And he did stop. Instead he glared at Wes, in a sudden change of mood. Then stood and left without a word. Beth called after him but was ignored.

'He's like a little child,' she said. 'I didn't ask him to come. He invited himself.'

But he returned, pushed his way to the table and leaned over it. 'Be aware, mister carpenter. She's sapphic. I don't know why I was wasting my time.' He turned and left again.

'What does he mean?'

Beth didn't answer immediately, but sat with her elbows resting on the table, her arms folded.

'He means I'm a lesbian. You know what a lesbian is?'

'Beth, I'm not a fool. Yes.'

'I'm not, but it gives him pleasure to think I must be if I don't find him attractive, which I don't. I think you were a bit embarrassed?'

'Well, yes.'

'Sorry, Wes dear. If I wanted anyone to stroke me, it would be you, of course. But I don't. I can't think of boyfriends at the moment. You know the girl you should be asking out is my sister, Franny. She's crazy about you, Franny.'

Wes smiled. 'And Franny is what? Sixteen?'

'Twenty-one. We get married in my family at twenty-one. All she'll want to do is have sex and babies. But for me, Wes, there's justice. Do you see? I'm going to Moscow for a week soon.'

The waitress served the lunch, lamb cutlets and a salad. Wes picked at his. Beth wolfed hers down then started on Wes's left-behinds. He had ordered a glass of beer, for which he'd developed a taste in the army, strictly against the dictates of his faith. While she ate, Beth babbled about the obvious way in which we—we humans—had made the world, not any God, and that we'd also made injustice, which now had to be unmade.

Wes didn't interrupt. But when he'd paid the bill and was preparing to leave for the station, he said this one thing, heartfelt. 'I don't believe that God made the world, Beth. But I believe that without God, there can't be a world.'

He excused himself and wandered the city all the way to Spencer Street for his train back to Almond Tree. Every step on the way to the station jolted pain into his chest, as if his heart were treading on pebbles.

Two days later, Wes wrote to Patty in Hiroshima and received this reply in a fortnight:

I don't know what Beth means about her red comrades getting a bomb of their own to 'even things up'. If Beth could see what a single bomb can do, she wouldn't want to 'even things up'. She'd want to get rid of the bombs altogether. I just don't have any belief in the stupid propaganda of her mob, nor in anything the yanks have to say. Wes, this is the world. We're not going to get another one. I'm nursing patients at both the American hospital and the Japanese hospital who are sick as poisoned pups with radiation illness. Bloody awful. Oh, and about Beth's friend, Louis. I happen to know who you're talking about. I met him once at a teachers' college do; he came along with his girlfriend of the day, a kid of about fifteen. Not really, but young.

I didn't like him at all. One of those chaps who revel in being thought witty. Even then, he was a big show-off in the movement, so I gathered. Mind you, the chap who's paying attention to me is also a show-off, but in an attractive way. He's happy to be contradicted. But he thinks he's beautiful, which he ain't. I'd like to show him a picture of you, little brother, then he'd know what a handsome man looks like. Oh but Wes, it's so awful, Hiroshima. They have a mayor now and he wants to rebuild. The Americans say, Sure, go ahead. But what about the radiation? It's bad enough for me, what would it be like for people trying to live on the desolate waste?

His mother, Daisy, had made it her task as he was growing up to explain all the world's religions to him, those of which she had knowledge. She thought it important for him to understand that the God of the Friends was not the only god. She spoke once of a belief popular among the Roman legionnaires that the world was divided forever between good and evil, which were eternally in conflict. The legionnaires naturally thought of themselves as being on the side of good, murder and rape and torture notwithstanding.

Dropping an atomic bomb on the people of Hiroshima and another on the people of Nagasaki was an act of evil, but no more so than dropping bombs of any sort on human beings wherever they were. And yet Wes felt that his sister in Hiroshima was aware of something that transcended other examples of evil. She said in one letter, 'Something has changed, Wessy. My friend the major who was a physicist in civvy life, and will be going back to it soon, says that within a few years the Americans will have bombs that can kill a million people in a second.'

Beth sent him a postcard from Moscow, Lenin's tomb, guarded by two towering soldiers, impeccably outfitted with boots so highly polished that they looked as if an entire tin of Kiwi must have gone into each one. It amused him to imagine two less conscientious soldiers turning up for duty one day, caps askew, scruffy boots, unshaven, not even sure who Lenin was. Beth's message was corny. 'One of the world's great men. It made me weep to stand there in the queue. Best wishes.'

Beth must have said something to Franny, because she left the rabbits to come around and watch Wes while he built the stables. She was by far the prettiest of the Hardy girls. On her visits she wore lipstick, a deep pink without being red.

'Has Beth been talking to you?' Wes asked, pausing from his carpentry and looking Franny in the eye.

'Yep.' Franny was famous for her candour.

'And what did she say, if you don't mind me asking.'

'No, I don't mind. She says I should show myself off to you.'

'So that's what you're doing? Showing yourself off to me?'

'The lippy. Anything wrong with that? Beth's never going to marry you. She wants to be the Stalin of Australia. I'll marry you.'

'It's kind of you, Franny. And I'm not hoping to marry Beth.'

Franny could see he was reaching for a hammer, and since she was nearer, she handed it to him. 'See? I'm useful. Marry me.'

'Franny, this is nuts.'

'Is it?'

'Okay, I'll marry you in a week.'

Franny's face became as bright all over as her lippy. 'Really?'

'No, Franny, not really.'

'See, you're stupid! I'd make your life heaven, you idiot.'

She came every day, sometimes neglecting the rabbits. Always with lippy. She acted like an apprentice, asking the names of the tools and standing uncomfortably close to study Wes at work. She chattered ceaselessly about her rabbits and the arguments between Gus and her husband Pete, and Maud and her husband Algy. 'They don't know how to be married. They had babies just so they'd have more to argue about. The kids are happier with me than them. You know why? Because I love babies. Gus calls them halfwits, her two. Maud just ignores Jonathan, the poor thing. What you need, Wes, is someone who understands babies. You know why I understand them? Because I'm a woman. Gus and Maud, I don't know what they are. And Beth is goodness knows any sort of thing.'

He agreed, at least, to go riding with her down to Port Flats, a wide expanse of pasture that had been left to go to ruin once Nick Port had shot himself through the head with a shotgun when he tripped chasing a fox. No heirs. The shire said they had the right to claim the flats, but in the end couldn't be bothered. The rack and ruin of the pasture was perfect for riding, logs just right for jumping and a huge gallop from the bracken at the hilltop down to Port Creek. Franny was an excellent horsewoman, the best rider in the district, and had educated her gelding, Brown Snake, to do everything short of sitting for matriculation at the high school. Wes was not even the second-best local rider. That would be Byron Peters from over near Chinese Town, seventy years old, who now and then rode with Franny, and could outrace her if he chose, which he didn't.

Franny took the jumps at full gallop, whooping, and easily beat Wes to the creek, face flushed and her maple hair thrown everywhere. She worked Brown Snake to the flank of Wes's mare, Maggie, and put her arms around him, around Wes.

'See,' she said. 'I can do everything with you. A saddle cuddle. Isn't it nice? How long are you going to go without making love? Your whole life?'

'Maybe.'

'That's not human! Don't you see that you're not being human?'

Brown Snake nuzzled Wes's mare. Wes kissed Franny on the cheek. 'Better get back.'

'Peck on the cheek. Better than nothing. Not much.'

Franny turned Brown Snake's head for home and spurred him into a gallop. She called over her shoulder: 'You're mad!'

Chapter 8

BETH CAME home for five weeks in January and February. She had pictures of Moscow to show. Not really of Moscow, but of Russians, men and women, mostly unsmiling. Russians, so it appeared, were not used to being photographed in this way and appeared suspicious. The less happy the Russians looked, the more it pleased Beth.

'What do Americans do? Smile as soon as you point a camera at them. The Russians are real people.'

'Couldn't get a giggle out of any of them?' said Bob Hardy.

'I didn't try. That wasn't my mission.'

'Oh, you had a mission?'

'Of course. Do you think I was on holiday?'

'Jesus, on a holiday. Wouldn't want you to get caught up in a holiday.'

Franny took Beth aside, out on the back porch. 'You have to tell Wes something. You have to tell him that he'd never be happy with you.'

'I have told him that. We're just good friends, close friends. But I don't want a boyfriend.'

'Tell him he needs me.'

Beth spent most of the five weeks pasting up Sheepskins for Russia posters. She had chosen to go to the neighbouring towns in the shire—Victoria Bend, Wembley, Pullen—since most of the posters she'd put up last time had been torn down. How much impact the posters would have was debatable. The war was over, the Russians were now the enemies of the West, and people thought that the reds could find their own sheepskins.

To get from town to town, she needed a vehicle, also a licence—she couldn't drive. She asked Wes for help, and he was glad to give it. He drove Bob Hardy's old Ford truck, his spare, and spent most of his time shushing people who stopped to abuse Beth.

On the drive from town to town, Beth told Wes more than he needed to know about Moscow, the courage of the people recovering from the war, the patriotic parades, the rationing, which wasn't too bad, not as much food as in Australia, but then Australia hadn't had three million Germans plundering the countryside.

She also felt it necessary to give him details of German atrocities. He had to ask her to stop.

'Really, you Quakers have such an idealised way of looking at the world. Wes, the war has ended, but we can't just ignore what happened. Haven't you seen the pictures of the death camps?'

'Yes, I have, Beth. I wish I hadn't. "We Quakers" know very well the horrible things that happen in the world. But we focus on the good things. Like Gary Mullane. He gave a house to Lilly Copper when her husband died and left her with a mortgage on the shack they lived in. That gets into my heart. The world doesn't keep going because of death camps and war. It keeps going because of Gary.'

In Wembley, two boys stood watching Beth paste up a poster on the wall of the old Majestic Theatre, no longer in use, and as soon as she'd finished, urinated on it. Wes chased the boys, but they were too quick, and he laughed about it in the truck. Beth was infuriated.

'What do kids like that know about suffering? Spoilt little brats.'

'Oh come on Beth. They're kids, naughty boys.'

Beth fell silent.

Then: 'Okay, you're right. I don't really want a world with no naughty boys in it. Do you think I'm a bit humourless, Wes? Di says I am, sometimes. I don't like to think of myself as one of those communists who can't laugh.'

'You are, at times. A bit. Like my mum when it comes to God.'

'I'm getting better. Di says so, too. I'm getting better.'

'Good to hear, Beth.'

She fell silent again, but revived.

'I have a joke.'

'Do you, now?'

'It's a dirty joke. One of the women in the union office told me. Do you want to hear it?'

'Sure.'

'Well, it seems that Comrade Stalin had a new secretary to take dictation. Very pretty. And in the middle of dictating something—a letter, whatever it was—he was overcome by desire for the secretary and got her to bend over the desk while he enjoyed her from behind. In his exertions, he cried out, "I get the strength for this from the people!" And the secretary said, "Do I take that down, Comrade Stalin?"'

Wes smiled.

'See, I have a sense of humour.'

Back at the Hardy house, Franny was seething. 'Where have you been?'

'Putting up posters with Beth.'

'For why? Nobody reads them!'

Beth, out of sheer perversity, kissed Wes on the cheek. 'Thank you.'

'Don't let her kiss you! It's like being kissed by a witch.'

Beth kissed him again. Franny punched him on the arm, hard.

Lillian, who was making lunch, called: 'Hoi!' Then: 'Want to stay for lunch, Wessy?'

Wes declined. He knew Beth's kisses were satirical, but relished them.

Chapter 9

THE FIRE broke out in the scrub above Jefferson Road. By the time the brigade got there, it had taken hold on the hillside and was in the foliage of the ironbarks. It was running east along Jefferson Road toward Chinese Town, where all the houses were semi-decayed weatherboard and especially vulnerable. Fire trucks from the nearest town would join the fight, but they would need an hour to prepare and drive the distance.

The accepted practice for fighting bushfires was for anyone with a truck and manpower to get to the blaze and beat the flames back from the roadside until tankers arrived. But this was a day of February heat touching the century, with a mongrel of a wind shifting from north to north-east. One look would tell anyone that the fire would be up the hill to the spur and into Chinese Town in a half-hour.

Wes took Hardy's truck. Hardy himself, with a crook back from where a cow kicked him, couldn't join the fight. But out of the house dressed in a pair of her dad's overalls rolled up at the cuffs came Beth. Bob Hardy said: 'What the hell?' Wes said, 'Beth, you can't come.'

'I'm coming!'

'Beth, the men won't work with a girl. You can't come.'

Beth climbed into the passenger side, the overalls hanging around her small frame.

She said: 'In the Soviet Union, women fight fires.' She had no evidence of this.

'Yeah,' said Bob Hardy, 'and in Australia, girls stay home and make sandwiches for the volunteers. You're not going.'

She wouldn't budge, but sat there with her arms folded and an obdurate expression.

Wes couldn't wait any longer. 'I'll leave her in the truck,' he called to Hardy, and took off.

'I'm strong, Wes. You'll see I'm strong.'

Wes said, 'Shut up,' and drove to Jefferson Road like a madman.

The volunteers and the brigade vehicles, other than one truck, had left Jefferson Road for the Chinese Town spur. The fire was racing up the spur track, driven by the scorching north-easterly. The plan was to stop the fire crossing the spur track and force it up into the mountain ash on the hills. By the time Wes reached the others, flames were soaring on both sides of the track. The fire had engulfed two volunteer vehicles and killed five men. Wes drove through the flames, yelling at Beth to crouch on the floor. The only hope for the 150 residents of Chinese Town was for the volunteers to get ahead of the fire and turn it away before it reached the slope above the town. The heat in the truck was so intense that Wes feared Beth would die.

She kept muttering, 'I'm okay…I'm okay…' But glancing down, he could see her face dripping with sweat.

The trees were burning as if they'd been soaked in diesel. Whole canopies at the top of the ironbarks exploded into flame. The bare earth of the track was burning, and off to one side, where the Chinese Town pasture could be made out through the trees, the grass had become a carpet of fire. There was no way ahead. He and Beth were going to die on the spur track.

They had one chance. He knew from his boyhood that the old Victory mine on the spur might shelter them, if he could find it.

He pulled the truck off the track, opened the passenger door for Beth and urged her out. She struggled to her feet. 'Wes, we're going to die. I can hardly breathe.' And yes, the blue smoke was dense. The tree canopies above them rained down burning fragments. Before Wes could set off in search of the Victory mine, a brigade truck emerged from the smoke. Ernie Boyle was in charge.

'Can't get out, Wes. The fire's closed the spur track behind us. We're cooked, mate. Who the hell is this?'

'Beth Hardy.'

'Wes, what the fuck? What's she doing here?'

'Never mind that. You've got what? Four blokes with you? You all come with me. I'm looking for the Victory mine. Leave the truck.'

The fire was behind them as they climbed the hill, hunting them, and the heat was so fierce that the men cried out aloud and wept. Beth could only go three steps without tripping over the cuffs of her father's overalls. Wes picked her up and carried her, her legs wrapped around his waist and her arms wrapped around his neck. 'Sorry,' she whimpered, 'so sorry, Wes.'

He said, 'Shush.'

He knew he was heading the right way when he saw a massive granite boulder off to the side. And there it was, the opening of the Cornishmen's mine, perfectly hewn into the hillside. The Cornishmen, master miners, had found a vein of quartz at the top of the hill and had worked their way into the hillside, expecting to come upon the vein deeper down where the gold would be found.

Wes sent Tony Lodge in first, with a torch. The mine ran to one side and the other at intervals but Wes told Tony to head straight. These side tunnels were just speculative; it was only the one tunnel that penetrated deep enough to give the men safety.

'Here,' said Wes and the men flopped down on the damp floor of the Victory mine as the fire roared over them, thwarted. The sound it made was amplified by the mine, like a living thing seething with anger. The men put their faces against the wet wall of the mine, breathing in relief. Tony set the torch down and they all gave themselves to mutters of thanksgiving. None was louder than Beth. 'This is what the people of Stalingrad did during the siege, hid together in places where the fighting passed over them.' She was delighted. 'We're workers together.'

Tony said: 'I'm a bank manager.'

Behind where the men and Beth sat, creatures of one sort and another had stealthily sought the same refuge, a pair of bandicoots, a goanna, a half dozen copperheads coiled close to each other, two koalas, and a feral dog trying hard to look like it had undergone a radical conversion to peace and harmony. After some raised eyebrows, the visitors were accepted. The roar of the fire was as loud as ever. Tongues of flame leapt in through the mine opening, but without fuel, withdrew.

Beth filled the space that the men had no wish to disturb with memorised tracts from Marx. 'This is what he said about the causes of injustice, do you want to hear?'

'Yeah, go ahead.'

'He says we can't have a just society that is headed by a ruling class, because no ruling class has any interest in justice. But look at us here. We have come together for the very just cause of saving lives. You see, it's crisis that often creates justice. That's what we're doing. Making justice.'

Tony said: 'I'm just trying to stop a bushfire, lovey.'

Wes leaned close to Beth and whispered, 'Down in Chinese Town probably dozens of people are dead. Best give Marx a holiday.'

'Oh. Okay. Sorry. I was just excited. Sorry.'

Even so, she couldn't contain herself. She referred to the men as 'comrades' and pointed out that it was crisis that had brought animals that would normally avoid humans into the mine. 'We need a big crisis in the nation to bring people together, people who would usually avoid each other. Like a general strike. That would be good. Out of crisis, we get justice.'

Yuri Malkov from Wembley hadn't said a word. He sat with his head lowered, his fingers in his fair beard. Now he spoke. 'Do you know where I come from, miss? I am Ukrainian. The Russians murdered sixty people in my village. They drove tanks through the wheat. For why? We wouldn't join the collective is for why. I hate the Russians. I wish the Germans had crushed them. As well as the Jews. The Jews were on the side of the Russians. So, that is what I say.'

Wes intervened before Beth could respond: 'Cut it out, Yuri. A bit of decency.'

'I wouldn't carry the communist slut out of the fire. I would have let her burn.'

Wes reached out and seized Yuri's beard in both hands and pulled him forward. 'Now you listen to me. The Russians killed millions of your people. The Germans killed millions of Russians. Nobody wants to talk about murder as if it's a good thing. You treat this young woman with decency.'

Yuri said: 'She's a red slut. I don't apologise.'

Wes whacked him across the face, and again. Yuri's nose bled down into his moustache and beard.

'Lean your head back,' said Wes, 'and then shut up.'

Beth found a grubby handkerchief in the pocket of her father's overalls and offered it to Yuri, who accepted it after some hesitation.

Terry Hoskins said: 'You're a robust sort of fella for a Quaker, Wes.'

'Yeah, well.'

The goanna turned and stalked back up the tunnel for the entrance. Then the bandicoots. They must have known that the fire had passed over. The copperheads remained where they were. The feral dog padded away. The two koalas were unsure. Wes picked one up and carried it; Dale O'Conner carried the other. Out in the open, the fire had moved on. Everything was blackened. The two trucks were burnt out. Some way ahead, smoke could be seen rising from Chinese Town. Wes and Dale carried the koalas to a patch of eucalypts that the fire had leapt, and released them. They both scaled the same tree.

The men trekked along the spur road towards Chinese Town, not knowing what they might find nor what they might achieve. At Muckle Bridge that crossed Warward Creek, they stopped to drink. The smoke above Chinese Town was moving on, which probably meant that there was nothing left to burn.

One hundred and twenty people lived in Chinese Town, only thirty of them Chinese. In the late gold rush, in the mid-1870s, the Chinese had followed behind the European miners—mostly Welshmen and Germans—going through the tailings left on the creek banks and finding more in the left-behinds than the European gold-seekers had found after having first go. The Welshmen and Germans were infuriated, believing that what the industrious Chinese gold-seekers had found rightfully belonged to them. They were encouraged by the most outspoken to storm the Chinese camps with clubs and picks and rifles to smash the tents and wound or even kill the Chinese. Political pamphlets were in wide circulation in which trade unionist correspondents proclaimed that Australia always had and always would belong to the white man. Whole lists of offences were included in these pamphlets, the propensity of the Chinese for theft and rape, a secret plan of the Chinese to take over the entire continent of Australia and present it as a gift to the 'yellow Empress'.

The gold had petered out well after the Quakers arrived from Hobart and placed the Chinese under their protection, printing their own pamphlets reasoning that people were people whether from China or Cardiff or Munich. The Quakers didn't have to argue their point of view for long. The Welshman and the Germans departed, finding no reward for their toil. The Chinese stayed on, those who didn't return to Guandong, and built Chinese Town on the banks of Fish Creek. Many switched to market gardening and sold their spring onions, potatoes, string beans, tomatoes, carrots and cabbages as far afield as Castlemaine. The remaining Chinese attended the Quaker meetings, without counting themselves as Quakers—just Christian visitors. They might have chosen the Anglicans or Presbyterians in Almond Tree, but it had been the Quakers who'd stood up for them.

Now the town was gone. The fire had come down the spur road and destroyed one weatherboard shack after another. Many of the shacks had been the dwellings of the poorest of the region's whites. It was possible to buy one for a hundred pounds from Hoong Li, one of the remaining Chinese, who had come to own every house in Chinese Town when his fellow countrymen returned to Guangdong. He called himself the mayor of Chinese Town. Now he was dead. Wes found his body in a water trough for horses. God knew what he thought he was doing in the trough. Escaping the heat?

The whole of Chinese Town was a single main road

with four streets branching off. The fire had set upon the weatherboards as if they had been laid out like a gourmet feast. Some of the houses were still flickering with flame. The corrugated iron of the roofs lay twisted on the ground, bent and buckled as if in a rigor of agony. There were survivors, standing in a daze before their charred homes. Here and there a house had escaped the flames, although why was a mystery, when the homes on either side were blackened wrecks. Bodies felled by the radiant heat and smoke were strewn on the roadside, hoping to outrun the flames. The telephone lines were down so there was no chance of calling the Almond Tree ambulance. Instead, they hauled the bodies down to the small park Hoong Li had proudly set up ten years earlier. It was a ratbag of a park and didn't look much worse after the fire than before. They found twenty-two bodies. Many more would be found in the smouldering debris of the houses. Wes had to climb a charred gum tree to fetch down the body of a woman who must have believed she could find safety where she had no chance at all of avoiding being killed. She was hanging upside down, and it was difficult to free her. Wes knew many of the Chinese Town residents, but the woman was too badly burnt to recognise.

Three ambulances arrived and four brigade trucks from Targo and Barton. Two of the brigade trucks went on to Galilee, where the fire was heading. The ambulances took eight of the worst injured away to the Targo hospital. Beth and Wes went in the cabin of the ambulances and were dropped off at Almond Tree. Beth said: 'This is what we have instead of war. Bushfires.' She was exhausted. It was evening. She had the strength to put her arms around Wes and hug him. 'Wes, my gratitude. You saved me. My gratitude.'

It rained heavily that night and the fire barely touched Galilee. Funerals were held for the next four days. The smoke was still in the air. Wes made sure he attended as many as he could, and Beth came, too. The grief of violent death at the hands of nature is not the same as death by heart failure or cancer. Something has intervened, some malice in nature that can't be assuaged by the bowing of the head and a handkerchief applied to the eyes. The mourners stand puzzled that out of nowhere a catastrophic wall of flame scorched the life from a husband, a wife, a friend. In New Guinea, comrades shot by the Japanese earned the Japanese undying hatred. Here—what? Who should you hate, or what?

On the last Sunday of Beth's stay, Wes asked Beth to come to the Quaker meeting at the Farebrother house. She acceded, with reluctance. 'I won't be praying.'

It was a week after the Chinese Town bushfire. The Friends gathered on an assortment of Quaker-made chairs in the broad living room of the Farebrother house. Made-laine Cunningham, Wes's eldest sister, led the prayer, a brief few words. 'We have lost twelve of our visitors,' she said in a voice so soft it could barely be heard. 'We mourn each of them with our love.' The gathering fell silent.

Beth whispered to Wes: 'What are they doing?'

'Mourning. Sending love to the souls of those who died. They were all Chinese. Visitors. Christians, but not Friends.'

The silence went on for what seemed an age to Beth. Then Wes left her side and stood before the gathering, and began to sing. He sang three Quaker hymns. Beth was astonished at the beauty of his voice. She had no idea. Then he announced that he was now about to sing a special hymn for one of their visitors, Beth Hardy. He sang: 'The people's flag is deepest red, It shrouded oft our martyred dead...' Beth had roared out with great mobs of socialists the words of 'The Red Flag', but never had she heard the song given such poignancy. Tears came to her eyes.

In the afternoon, she agreed to take a walk with Wes. He showed her the stables, and the house he was building with the help of his fellow Quakers. She nodded. But she said: 'Wes, you know what's happening in the Soviet Union right now? Starvation, plague, typhoid. I have to dedicate myself to raising money for the people. And I'll be working part time next year for the United Metal-workers Union. As an organiser.'

~

Wes went with her to the station the next day with Bob and Lillian. Gus and Maud were in the middle of one of their epic arguments and didn't bother. Neither did Franny. When the train pulled out, Bob Hardy put his hand on Wes's shoulder. 'You've still got feelings for my Beth, haven't you?'

'Friendship, Bob.'

'Yeah, yeah, friendship.'

Wes went straight back to work at the stables, of course with Franny hovering around. She asked him if he ever thought about sex.

'No,' he said.

'You'd have as much fun with her as a sack of turnips.'

'I like turnips.'

'Take me to bed. You'll love it. I promise.'

'No, Franny. But you can pass me the spirit level.'

'I'll become a Quaker. Will that satisfy you?'

'Don't be crazy. You're not going to become a Quaker. Hand me the spirit level.'

Nothing daunted, Franny came each day. Sometimes she brought a rabbit and chatted about their various ways. She also told Wes something Beth hadn't mentioned to him. That Beth was going to London in the middle of the year for a few days. Why London?

Chapter 10

TO LONDON at first, then to Cambridge. She had a parcel to deliver to a certain Peter Corning, a reader in History at Jesus College. The parcel and instructions had been given to her by a friend of Bob Beaumont, the Deputy Secretary of the United Metalworkers Union, who was more red than Lenin. The friend did not give his name, and had the fugitive look of a man who would always keep his name to himself. Nor did he explain what was in the manila envelope nor why it was unaddressed. 'Comrade, the more important question is why you should wish to know?'

Beth would be staying in England for three days, and no more. She would be given a parcel to bring back. Bob Beaumont said she'd been chosen because of her 'exceptional reliability'. She couldn't help but ask if the mail wouldn't be just as reliable. Bob shook his head. 'No, no, I don't think so.' The ordeal of the flight would be a nightmare, and for a mere three days? She didn't say a word in complaint. It was an honour to have been chosen.

Carrying her humble little suitcase, she found her way in Cambridge to Peter Corning at Jesus. He swung open the door of his rooms for her with a flourish, kissed both of her cheeks and showed her to his desk. His rooms were packed with bookshelves, and a series of mediaeval prints, which he invited her to admire. He was a tall man, good-looking, no more than forty with dark hair worn long, dressed in this summer weather in a white linen suit, loosely worn and an incongruous black waistcoat. His right cheek was scarred from the corner of his eye to his cheekbone, a thin scar but immediately the feature that dominated Beth's interest. 'A duelling scar,' Peter explained touching the faint line with his fingertips. 'Cocktail glasses at close quarters. Didn't leave a mark on Reggie.'

Beth said, 'You might have lost an eye.'

'Might have, but didn't. One of the many things in life that didn't happen.'

He spoke with an upper-class accent and a rapid cadence.

'You have lovely rooms.'

'Do you think so? I can't stand them. Makes me feel like E. M. Forster, full of the wonder of literature. I hate literature, except for the Greeks. And old Leo, of course. I understand you speak Russian?'

'To a degree.'

'You're staying with us at Grantchester. You know, the church clock and all that. You must be exhausted. I'll take you there now in the Riley.'

'I have the parcel.'

'Oh, the parcel. That's for Benny Edwards. You'll see him tonight. We're giving you a little party after you have a sleep. You're very pretty for a commie, I must say. The women are usually dowdy. I'm not a communist myself. I just help out. But Benny is—do you say in Australia? "Fair dinkum"?'

The parcel remained in the suitcase. Beth's room in Peter Corning's Grantchester house was tiny. If the little bed hadn't been so narrow, it would have been impossible to move about. There was an upstairs and a downstairs and each of the rooms was as cramped as the bedroom. No children, apparently. One attractive feature was the view of the orchard that all the rooms provided. Beth was shown the bathroom in which there was no bath but a shower with three devices that regulated the flow of water, each of which (when she tried them before lying down) seemed to cancel out the other. She stuck to the cold water. While she showered, Peter stood outside the door and read Rupert Brooke's 'Grantchester' aloud in a singing tone.

'Do you like this, Miss Hardy, or if I may call you Beth, so I will. I happen to know that you are commonly called Beth. It's utter rubbish, isn't it? Silly old Rupert, forever taking his trousers down for the Cambridge ladies. Maybe I just envy him.'

'Yes! I like it!'

'There are clean towels in a pile in the corner. Fairly clean, at least. Shall I leave you alone now?'

Six people including Peter and his wife, Heather, were at the dinner gathering. Heather was dressed in loose, flowing garments without the least coordination, with a red scarf woven through her mass of blonde curls. Then two young men who appeared to be students, both looking awkward outside of a meeting hall. The most important guest was evidently Benny Edwards, judging by the deference shown him, but there was nothing commanding about his appearance. He was tall and stooped, skinny, with pouches of flesh hanging below his grey eyes, as if he'd lost weight and turned haggard over a short period. Before any food was served, Beth was asked to stand before a semi-circle of the seated guests and talk about the people's struggle in Australia. She said that the people of Australia were being misled about the mission of communism just as the Americans were. The so-called socialist Australian Labor Party harboured the worst anti-communists of any political party in the country among its Catholic MPs—men who would rather go to the stake than listen to the true Marxist program. The only hope for a communist Australia was to infiltrate the ALP and convert more and more MPs—not the Catholic die-hards—to the people's program. Which was what she, Beth, was attempting to achieve in her work for the United Metalworkers.

She was applauded heartily. Then Benny Edwards stood and shouted about the need to embrace violence in the workplace. 'If we see rivers of blood in the factories of Britain, we must accept that as the price of justice. Those who shrink from violence, from force, are shrinking from justice.' He unbuttoned his ragged brown cardigan, then his shirt and showed a chest of grey hair. 'This is what my heart says. Justice will require blood, here and in this young woman's Australia.' When he sat, he was applauded, more temperately than Beth.

Only the single dish for dinner—a vegetable stew, since the meat ration had been used up. No dessert, but some drop scones made without sugar. Folk songs around the piano, nothing in the singing to compare to Wes's gorgeous voice. Beth was allowed to head off to bed early, since she'd enjoyed only three hours sleep in the last thirty-six. The students said their farewells as Beth headed upstairs; only Benny Edwards was left behind, drunk and mumbling. She took the parcel down to him—this was the third time she'd offered it to him and had been told to hold on to it for the time being. She was again told to hold on to it. 'Tomorrow,' he said.

'Benny's sleeping on the sofa,' said Heather. 'Give it to him at breakfast.'

Beth slept deeply until awakened by a scratching at her door, and a voice.

'Benny?'

'Open the door, something to tell you.'

She did as she was told, still groggy with sleep, and found Benny, visible in the dim light at the top of the stairs. She stood baffled for a few moments, but when he tried to reach for her she pushed him away and called for Peter and Heather. She picked up one of her shoes and showed that she was prepared to use it as a weapon. Benny whined meantime, 'I meant no harm, no harm at all...'

Heather came from a doorway further down the corridor, then Peter. Benny stood trembling. Peter said, mildly, 'Really, Benny. Get downstairs.'

'Forgive him, Beth,' said Heather. 'It's not the first time. Too much to drink.'

'If he's staying in the house, I'm leaving.'

'No, no, no. Peter will drive him back to his digs. Go back to bed, Beth.'

She didn't close her eyes until she heard Peter's Riley drive off. Sleep came in fragments. After showering in the morning, she came down with the parcel.

'What am I to do with this?'

'Give it to Peter.'

Peter reached across the toast and tea, held the parcel for ten seconds, then handed it back.

'What now?'

'Now,' said Peter, 'you put it in your suitcase and take it back to Australia.'

'Take it back? The same parcel? I don't understand.'

Peter nodded, then sipped his tea. 'Beth, my dear, it was a trial. Were you under surveillance by your security people? It appears not. There's nothing in the parcel other than twenty pages of algebraic equations, and also a few poems, Jabberwocky, I think, and some Browning.'

Beth was left exasperated. 'Seventy-two hours of flying for a joke? Do you have any idea of the pain you get in your legs and back on one of those BOAC things? For nothing?'

'For something, Beth,' said Heather. 'We want you to come back next time with real intelligence. A pain in the legs is a very small price to pay for the mission.'

'You want me to become a spy?'

Peter said with an equivocal gesture of his spread hands, 'Beth, "spy" is an ugly word. We do not employ spies. We gather information such as may put us at an advantage.'

Beth paused before saying what she had come to believe to be true. 'Peter, you told me you just help out here and there. But I think you're in charge. Please tell me the truth.'

'Beth my love, it's not something we talk about.'

'Peter, do you know that spying for a foreign power is punishable by death in Australia?'

'You're not a spy. You're simply a girl helping out.'

'I'm not a girl. I'm a woman, in case you haven't noticed. I'm twenty-three.'

'Oh, he's noticed,' said Heather. 'Believe me.'

He took her for a walk around Grantchester, ending at the café in the orchard under the clock tower. Tea and scones. Without anyone in earshot, he nevertheless spoke quietly. 'Beth, I don't think you quite grasp what's happening in the wide world. You think of transition to communism in Australia, and no doubt elsewhere. There is going to be a war, Beth. The Soviet Union now controls the whole of Eastern Europe. Within two years there is bound to be a communist government elected in Italy and France. The Americans won't accede. They will bring on a war before the Soviet Union has developed its own atomic weapons. Not alone. Aided and abetted by Britain. The Americans already have nuclear weapons stationed in Britain. But they don't want to go it alone. They want Britain as an ally. It looks better if you intend to murder ten or twenty million Russians if you have the mother of parliaments supporting you. Do you follow?'

Beth gave him a dubious look.

'The Russians will test their atomic bombs in Kazakhstan. The Americans have the South Pacific. We in Britain, where do we go? North Yorkshire? We go to your homeland, Beth. And we happen to know that sites have already been chosen. In South Australia. This is what we want you to do. Photograph the sites. Come back to me with the pictures. We can show the world where Britain intends to explode atomic bombs before they are even detonated. We can whip up a frenzy of protest. Your Aborigines are living on those sites. Do you think they will be warned to clear off before the tests? Not likely. They are probably planning three years of testing. But let's start now. Let's get you and some colleagues over there with cameras.'

'If they catch me, they'll hang me.'

'Hmm. Unlikely. They'd probably barter a deal with the Americans and Soviets and MI5 and swap you for a Soviet agent. Of course, you'd be required to live in Russia for the rest of your life. Not the worst possible fate. Not the best, either. People are starving over there.'

She thought of Wes. That would certainly put an end to his hopes of courtship. The thought produced a pang. She had urged him to marry Franny with her bombshell figure and her looks and her hunger for sex, but the idea of Franny with her arms around Wes distressed her, for the first time. She had only ever conceived of loyalty as a loyalty to the people, to the program. But she had to concede that loyalty could also be loyalty to an individual person. Wes was loyal to her. Wasn't this worth something?

She said she would do it. Where were the cameras? Who would provide them?

'Di Porter.'

Transport? Also, when did Peter expect this to be done?

'Oh, the testing won't be for a couple of years. But we need the photographs taken as soon as possible after you get back.'

'But there's my speech to the Arts Faculty…well, that's okay. I won't mind missing that.'

'No? I understand you covered yourself in glory.'

'I'm not dressing up just to please a whole lot of self-important egotists.'

'There's a certain amount of egotism in refusing to, don't you think?'

Peter drove her to Heathrow in the Riley.

Chapter 11

HIROSHIMA WAS built originally on the delta plains of seven rivers, with dwellings and factories packed closely together on the compacted silt. All but a few buildings were timber and they burned as if soaked in petrol when the firestorms, which instantly followed the bomb's detonation above the city, spread north, south, east and west.

Patty dealt predominately with horrendous burns in her first six months in the hospitals of Hiroshima. Most of those she and the doctors tended died, often while being treated—more than three thousand. She worked in the Occupation hospital and also in thirty of the small, one-doctor Japanese hospitals, without permission from the Australian contingent of the BCOF officers and senior nurses. She wouldn't take leave, even when threatened with discharge. Her friend the major protected her from the menace of the more senior nurses, who couldn't abide her free and easy manner, but that wouldn't last forever. She also worked in the VD clinics and the official supervised brothels for the Australian troops. But every second house that was built on the delta plains by the surviving Japanese, using any debris that hadn't been incinerated in the blast, mere shacks, became a brothel if the household included daughters over the age of twelve. It was one of few ways of earning money. The Australians were forbidden to fraternise with the Japanese, but the rule was universally ignored. Australian troops could arrive in the morning and become infected with VD by the afternoon. 'Had the mother and the daughter one after the other,' the patients would boast to Patty.

'Well, aren't you a lucky boy. And now you have a painful reminder of your adventure to explain to your girlfriend. This goes on your record.'

She should have left but couldn't. It was years since she'd been home to Almond Tree. It had been George Fox Farebrother's belief that a certain trial is set for each person in life, just one, and that person knows that the trial is there and cannot evade it without harming his soul, her soul. All of the Quakers of Almond Tree accepted this belief of George's.

For Patty, it was Hiroshima. She couldn't leave. But nor could she stay, if the BCOF authorities had their way. She was forced to resign. She appealed to the Americans, who had the final say in everything in Japan; to an American colonel who had been a pal of the major. He organised for her to stay for a further year; 1949. He was one of the rare Americans who admired the huge strides the Japanese had taken to rebuild their city.

Patty had to confess that she didn't at all like the frenetic rebuilding supported by a flood of US dollars. The Japanese hurried about their business as if recovering from a nuclear blast was just another calamity, no different from an earthquake. She never met a single Japanese who harboured feelings of bitterness toward the Americans. Defeat meant next to nothing. Something like prosperity was coming to Hiroshima and the attention of the Japanese was on the houses being built, the businesses springing up overnight.

In five years, there would be a new Hiroshima, with the Genbaku Dome, what remained of it, left standing as a 'memorial'. She thought the only fitting memorial would be to do nothing to the ruins, to leave the reddened acres exactly as they were. In her heart, without too much searching, she could find hatred for those who made the decision to fly an aeroplane over Hiroshima and release a bomb that would kill in a second eighty thousand Japanese, the majority of them civilians. And then a week later, after a conversation that probably went no further than, 'Had enough? Okay, Nagasaki,' fly a second aeroplane over the city further south and kill some thousands and thousands more.

Banks were operating, housing construction was going ahead at a furious pace, factories sprang up overnight and people were returning in their tens of thousands to the city.

Returning to the irradiated soil.

Most of her work these days was with victims of radiation sickness. Patty and the doctors and the BCOF personnel ate only what was imported from Australia and America. But the Japanese ate what was now growing in fields on the fringe of the city and they came to the hospitals with their hair falling out and huge tumours in their throats and chests, too weak to walk more than a few paces without needing to rest. But the very air she breathed was toxic and she had accepted that she would develop radiation sickness in time.

She came to know all of the doctors who ran the small hospitals, but none better than Doctor Tanaka, who had worked for the military as a civilian doctor for the entire length of the war. He was forty, tall for a Japanese, with an engaging smile and a knack for irony that she had never met with before in the local people. He spoke perfect English with a slight American accent—he had trained at Harvard—and told her she was only ever to speak English to him because her Japanese was awful. She had lunch with him whenever she could, food that he prepared himself from American supplies. He liked her, so he said. He hoped she liked him. Did she? Yes.

And to tease, told him in her rubbish Japanese that he had 'kind eyes'.

'For the Americans,' he said at lunch one day, 'the war was an experiment.'

'How so?'

'They had a theory that America was the most powerful country in the world. The war was raging in Europe and Asia. But they could not join in and put the theory to the test because they had nothing against the Germans other than distaste, and nothing at all against the Japanese. Pearl Harbor was the catalyst for the experiment. They soon saw that they were likely to destroy Japan. The first Japanese bomb that landed on Pearl Harbor was the beginning of the end for the Japanese imperial forces. The further stage of the experiment was to do to the Germans what they had done to the Japanese. And so they did. The theory was proved. Next, of course, we have to consider the Soviets, who have a theory of their own. Several, in fact.'

'Poppycock.'

'"Poppycock"? What is "poppycock"?'

'Nonsense,' Patty provided, in Japanese.

'I love this word. Poppycock. Not only will I use it, I will speak it, as I so often do.'

Kado Tanaka had no sensible reason for being so cheerful, and in fact he was not. He was still in mourning for his wife and four children who had died when the bomb dropped. He was out of the city on that day and came back to find everything in flames. The children and their mother, Monica, had been at home when the bomb exploded, just beyond the immediate area of destruction but not beyond the heat. When Kado could get to his home, he found his family dead, their bodies an unnatural red all over and their clothing and flesh fused.

Monica and the children had all been Catholics, a conversion that went back generations. He dug a grave a little way from the house, then spent the rest of the day hunting down a Catholic priest, a German, Father Schlink, from the church Monica and the children had attended. He found the priest badly burnt but able to walk and had him officiate at the burial, in the one grave, of his family. Monica had given all of the children traditional Catholic names, just like her own, and had wanted her husband to call himself Joseph but he had declined. He had only converted to Catholicism to please Monica and had never attended mass. He asked Patty to explain what it meant to be a Quaker.

'Don't shout, do no harm,' she said.

'I have heard you shout in the wards.'

'Don't shout unless you're frustrated by bad nursing in a Hiroshima hospital.'

By degrees.

Her affair with the major had been ridiculous. With Kado, more important to her than the major, she'd move it along by degrees. Her better self had come to feel offended by the ludicrous bouncing about with the major. He was so brisk that she'd never had time to exercise her judgment. One of the things she so appreciated in Kado—well, she admired and appreciated everything— was that he left it all up to her judgment.

His affection for her wasn't in doubt. He smiled at her, seemed to welcome the times in an examination of a patient when their hands touched briefly. She allowed him to adjust his surgical mask. Over one patient, a boy of six, too sick with radiation sickness to survive, Kado stepped away from the bed and stood at the window staring out. She went to him and wiped his eyes with folded gauze. He took her hand and held it briefly.

It became part of the program of each day that she would put her arm around his back and hold him, only for seconds. One day, she said, 'You don't mind this?' He shook his head, smiling.

In this way, little by little, they reached a point where it seemed foolish not to kiss. The kissing was intended to be an introduction to greater intimacy, but it quickly went further and became passionate. Patty pulled away, looked Kado in the eyes, made her judgment, and kissed him again. The next day, more of the same, but with murmurs and endearments.

The US Marines, criticised for their 'anything goes' treatment of the Japanese, held a friendship gathering in a building outside Hiroshima with Japanese professionals to discuss what was happening inside Hiroshima. Kado was invited and asked Patty if she would accompany him. The Americans had little to say other than that plenty of people were dying. A Marine choir sang Cole Porter and Irving Berlin songs. In the middle of the evening, a Marine colonel, newly appointed to head the Marines in Japan, made an apology for the destruction of Hiroshima, Nagasaki and a big part of Tokyo.

'I apologise for war, on behalf of humanity, that we need to resort to war to settle an argument. You Japanese hit us hard at Pearl Harbor, and we did what Americans always do—we came back and hit you harder. But it gives Americans no pleasure to kill Japanese. It's just war, and as Sherman said, "War is hell." We will rebuild Hiroshima, but we can't rebuild the Japanese and American lives lost.'

Then a reprise of Irving Berlin's 'Always'.

On the way home in the taxi, Patty said, 'Shall I stay with you tonight?'

'Please, yes.'

Kado lived at his hospital in a small ward set aside, completely unadorned. His bed was no different than those of his patients. He and Patty showered together, then made love until well after midnight, the first time a little awkwardly, with more ease later.

In the morning, it took Patty a few moments to remember where she was. When she did, she laughed with delight, held Kado's face in her hands and kissed him again and again, until he was laughing too.

'That was heaven,' she said. 'Can you please tell me it was heaven for you?'

'Heaven, Patty. Better than heaven.'

She dressed and went to the nurses' quarters to change into her uniform. She kept three spare uniforms in her locker, and she needed to; patients were brought in bleeding from their mouths, their noses, from everywhere. They would be dead within hours, after leaving their blood all over her. She showered and dressed. It was all she could do during the day to stop herself kissing Kado and rubbing her body against his.

They were lovers. It was meant to be. Could things really be meant to be? No. Except this. Except this.

He spoke to her in Japanese while they were in bed, as if this more confirmed his feeling for her. In the narrow bed, they were always close, folded into each other. He told her in English that Monica had always been squeamish about sex. 'She believed God was watching, critically. I asked her, "Why?" and she said, "You don't pray." Monica prayed all the time we were making love.' He said that Monica paid no attention to the war and never prayed for the victory of Japan and Germany, as everyone else in the Catholic congregation did. 'She was a patriot of heaven, only. She wanted to see the victory of God on earth. She was childlike in her faith, but I loved her with all my heart.'

'Do you feel as if you're betraying her with me?'

'Patty, she is dead. We can't betray the dead, unless we're neurotic.'

A few days after this conversation, between treating one patient who died from radiation poisoning and another who died of the same cause, Kado asked Patty if she would marry him and bear children. She said: 'Yes, of course.' Then: 'I will be acceptable to your parents?'

'Yes.'

They married in a Catholic ceremony, to please dead Monica. The priest asked Patty if she was a Catholic and she said, no, a member of the Society of Friends. Father Schlink shrugged. 'In these times, who cares?' His face was brick-red from radiation exposure and his gabardine cassock, the only one still left to him, had been burnt here and there and patched, not skilfully, with red cotton fabric.

They lived in the ward until it could be arranged for the two of them to move in with Kado's parents, who lived outside Hiroshima but had nevertheless been burnt in the ferocious blast of heat that roared out from the immediate site of the explosion. The burns were not serious. Kado treated them himself. The parents, Shinsa and Maka, admired Patty for staying to help, but also found her odd. She understood nothing of the customary ways in which a daughter-in-law was expected to behave. She left her underwear on the clothesline in plain sight of Kado's father and kissed Kado on the lips no matter who was watching. Kado told her, with a smile, that his parents thought she was a barbarian, but nice.

'Have some babies,' he said. 'They will forgive you everything.'

She wanted to take him back to Australia, to Almond Tree, to meet her own parents. 'I haven't been home in years.' But would the Australians give him a visa? He had worked for the military, even though he'd never been in the army. There was no need to worry. The Japanese, who had elected their own parliament, the Diet, had so embraced American values, Western values, Australian values, that they wished to appear the best friend the West had in the East. Look at China, now communist. Look at us, we hate communists like lepers. They provided the Australian Consulate with a version of Kado's war record that exonerated him completely—he was a civilian doctor 'forced' to work for the military. They would leave for a month in Almond Tree, mid-1950.

Chapter 12

WES FINISHED the stables in October 1949 and the grand opening was to be in January, followed the next day by a special race meeting of seven events, including the Lady Mary Morecombe Plate for women, with prize money of five hundred pounds, and the Sir James Morecombe Cup of four thousand five hundred pounds, run over a mile. Wes was to be presented to the gathering as the architect and builder of the stables, which were considered by everyone who saw them to be a work of art, almost too good for horses, you could set up a table and chairs and eat dinner in any of them.

To Wes's surprise, Beth accepted an invitation to attend the grand opening, along with Di Porter. Her degree was complete and she was, in any case, home with her family in Almond Tree for a few weeks. He was amazed that she could spare the time. So far as he knew, she was running the communist parties of the world and was forever flying to Moscow and England on 'party business'. Considering how much it cost to fly to England, let alone Moscow, he was baffled at the local party's ability to pay the bills. It was also surprising that she was able to keep out of prison. ASIO kept tabs on her, no doubt hoping for some transgression that would land her in the clink. Franny still pestered him, off and on, but at least refrained from fondling him. Her expression now was a sly conviction that he would come across in the end. But that was also just off and on. Mostly she appeared downcast.

On opening day, Beth came as promised with Di Porter, both of them in beautiful summer dresses and high-heeled shoes. Wes commented on Beth's dress and was told, awkwardly, that Di had made her wear it. Di said: 'I had my way this one time. Usually she chooses dresses that make her look shapeless and frumpy. She thinks there's greater virtue in looking like a peasant than in showing off her looks. I think she looks gorgeous. What about you, Wes?'

'Yes, gorgeous.'

'So you built all this,' said Beth, escaping the subject. 'Hmm. Most impressive.'

'Impressive?' said Di. 'You're selling him short. It's a masterpiece.'

At the opening ceremony before a crowd of fifty or so, Jim Morecombe, in his favourite phrase, considering himself a speaker who avoided, always, boring the audience, started out with: 'Ladders and Jellybeans, are you bowled over by what Wes Cunningham has built for us here? The most glorious racetrack in Australia made even more beautiful with these twenty-two new stables.'

When it was Wes's turn to say a few words, the words were few indeed. Dressed in a dark suit and tie, he stood at the microphone and gave a brief bow to Sir Jim and Lady Mary. 'It was a pleasure,' he said, and that was it.

The next day, the day of the meeting, Wes didn't ride; all the jockeys were professionals and far below any weight Wes might make. Franny rode in the Ladies' Plate, and won. She ran to Wes from the mounting yard, pinned the blue ribbon to his suit jacket, put her arms around his neck and kissed him on the mouth. He reddened with embarrassment and put the ribbon in his pocket. Beth said: 'God, she's shameless. She'd ride naked if you asked her.' There was a note of grievance in her voice. Di Porter, who knew the story of Beth urging Wes to marry Franny, said teasingly: 'But dear heart, isn't that what you want, Wes and Franny to ride off naked together?'

Beth tossed her hair in irritation. 'If my sister is a trollop, it's not my fault.'

~

That evening, Wes came by invitation to Di's cottage for dinner. Di made a salad with pitted black olives, basil from Wes's mum's garden, and feta cheese she had brought with her from a deli in Collingwood. And a number of other ingredients. She served it with warm cuts of roast pork. Beth knew nothing about cooking and, left to herself, would have lived on ham sandwiches. During dinner, they talked about the recent testing of Soviet nuclear bombs, how much more powerful they were than the Hiroshima and Nagasaki bombs. 'But we have maybe ten bombs,' said Beth. 'The Americans have hundreds.'

'And this is a good thing?' said Wes. 'That the Americans and the Russians can fight each other with more and more powerful bombs? You know Patty is in Hiroshima, nursing people with radiation poisoning? She saw the city seven months after the blast. Said it left a wasteland.'

'Yes, but if we don't have nuclear weapons, we are at the mercy of the Americans. Now the Americans have to think twice before they drop a bomb on Moscow.'

'When you say, "we", you mean the Russians?'

'I mean the Soviet Union, which is where my heart is, Wes.'

'My heart's in Almond Tree.'

Beth said she had a favour to ask of Wes, a very big favour.

She explained that she and Di had to get to a region a long way off, and although they had a Land Rover they

100

could use—it belonged to a comrade—neither she nor Di could drive over the terrain they would need to cross.

'And where is this region?'

'The South Australian desert.'

'Dear God!'

'I was going to ask if you would drive us.'

'Well, yes. Why, Beth?'

'It's for work.'

'For the union?'

'Not exactly. I can't tell you.'

'For the party?'

'I can't tell you.'

Di intervened. 'Yes, for the party, Wes. Well, really, we're asking him to drive fifteen hundred miles, he deserves to know why. Beth didn't want to ask you, get you mixed up in party stuff. It's a bit dicey, Wes. I persuaded her, I must confess.'

Beth said: 'Wes, it's espionage. For Di and me, if we're discovered, too bad for us. But I care for you too much to put you in danger. You should say no.'

'And when you get there? What then?'

'We take photographs,' said Di. 'Lots and lots of photographs. I have the camera.'

'You shouldn't say that,' said Beth, with a censorial look.

'You expect him to shut his eyes while we're taking pictures?'

'And when do you want to go?'

'In a week,' said Beth.

Wes said he'd have to check out the Land Rover. He'd come down to Collingwood in a couple of days and go over the vehicle.

The next day, Wes came to lunch at the Hardys' to be on hand when the news was broken about the marathon trip to the South Australian desert. He had insisted that Bob Hardy and Lillian be told of the trip. If the women died in the desert, it shouldn't come as a shock to Bob and Lillian when their daughter's body was discovered in some parched wadi more than a thousand miles away. Gus and her husband Pete were at the table too, with the baby Sylvester (just called Vester) crawling around on the kitchen floor on a mission to torment one of the dogs, Bandy, a long-suffering bitser. Maud and her husband were having an argument at the far end of the kitchen concerning three missing jars of blackberry jam which he gave to Sue Tilly, so Gus claimed. 'Every time you see her, it's "Sue dear this" and "Sue dear that". You should get her to move in and make her tea and toast in bed in the morning.' Their two kids amused themselves at the table by mimicking their parents.

Sitting on the back porch after lunch with a cup of tea, Beth, in as casual way as she could manage, told her parents (and Franny, who was loitering nearby) of the plan. Bob Hardy scratched his head. 'Well, she'll be in your care, Wes. Can't think of anyone I'd trust more.' Lillian, who was not excitable, said: 'Bloody long trip—for what? That silly old party?—is all I can say.' The most volatile response came from Franny, who leapt to her feet, tossed the remainder of her tea on the ground where the chooks were gathering in case scones were on offer, and said, 'You're going to be four or five days with that boring bitch. Are you mad? I'm the one who cares about you, idiot. What's the matter with your heart? What's the matter with your head?'

She retreated into the house and let the screen door slam behind her.

'Hysterical,' said Beth.

Franny came storming out again, her cheeks wet with tears. 'I heard that. Maybe I am hysterical but at least I have a heart. I can love. You, what do you love? The people. Nobody can love "the people". The people are all different. Loving "the people" is bullshit. You love certain people for certain reasons. I care about Wes in a way you could never understand, you fool. And he's a fool, too, for not seeing.'

She went back inside. Among those left on the porch, an awkward silence took hold. Di Porter noticed that Beth looked a bit sickened, even if no one else did. Bob Hardy said: 'Wes, take a stroll with me.' They walked down to the back of the dairy. Bob scratched his head, his usual preliminary to saying something significant. 'Wes, here's the thing. Franny is never going to give you up. I know her. She's just as stubborn as Beth. It's a curse in the family. And Beth is never going to give up the party, bastard of a thing that it is. She thinks romance is for people who aren't serious about life. She's married to Red Joe. Beth doesn't know anything about romance. Mate, you're going to be better off with Franny, believe me. You'd have a queue of blokes in Almond Tree stretching from here to the Town Hall to get a kind word from Franny. It's you she wants. And hell, Wes, she'll make you happy. She can cook, she knows how to keep a house neat, that beautiful place you're building, it'll be full of kids. And listen, when it comes to how's-your-father, what in God's name would Beth know? Take Franny. And take the bloody rabbits, too.'

'Can't, Bob. I know Beth doesn't love me. But I care about her.'

'Then you're a mug.'

Chapter 13

THE VEHICLE. The Land Rover. When Wes came down to Collingwood, he took one look at it and let out a sigh. He lifted the bonnet and sighed again. Whatever love and concern the comrade who owned the Land Rover felt for his fellow man, it didn't extend to his fellow man's internal combustion engines.

Beth and Di stood watching anxiously while Wes investigated the engine.

'Can we help?' said Beth, pleadingly.

'No. It'll take me three or four days. Your comrade who owns this thing should be jailed. The neglect is horrible.'

'It's Bernard. He's hopeless.'

'Didn't you think of that when you made your plan?'

'We thought you could fix it.'

Wes closed the bonnet and gave a despairing shake of his head. 'Okay, I can fix it, maybe. Let me start it up and take it for a drive. At the moment, I doubt if it could get up Hoddle Street and back. Is the party going to give you some money to make repairs to this thing?'

Beth looked at Di with the question on her face. Di shook her head.

'No.'

'Well, they take good care of you, don't they? Wait here until I get back.'

Wes made a rackety exit in the Land Rover down Vere Street to Hoddle Street. When he returned in ten minutes, he leapt from the driver's seat as if the vehicle were a bomb with the fuse burning.

'It's junk. My God. The gearbox would have to be replaced, the timing belt, the steering linkage is barely holding on, the whole engine needs tuning, the spark plugs are worn out and the shockers have to be replaced, too. I need a hoist. Without a hoist, I can't do much at all.'

Beth said: 'What's a hoist?'

'Lifts the thing up so that you can work on it underneath.'

Di said she'd phone Jerry, not a comrade, just an acquaintance who was a mechanic. Jerry said to drive it over to his workshop in Abbotsford. At the workshop, Jerry and Wes leaned on the Land Rover, one each side gazing down at the disgrace that was the engine.

'Who owns this thing?' said Jerry. 'Must think an engine repairs itself. A mongrel.'

'A bloke named Bernie. Criminal what he's done to this engine.'

And then the inevitable sighs and shaking of heads and expressions of doubt common to tradesmen everywhere in the grip of disapproval.

'I don't know. Might be beyond saving.'

'Could well be.'

'And you say the shockers are buggered?'

'Completely, Jerry. And the steering linkage is only just hanging on. Gearbox needs replacing.'

'Bugger me. I'd take it to the wreckers.'

'Same here.'

'And you say the girls want to go two thousand miles in it? Might as well say they want to fly it to the moon.'

'Might as well.'

Jerry knew where he could get a reconditioned gearbox and some serviceable shockers. The steering linkage? Have to search around.

'Let's get it up on the hoist and have a frig about with the gearbox, get it out. And the shockers.'

As they worked together, Jerry asked what it was like to be a Quaker. And was told. Then: 'So now we've got Menzies. Pig-iron Bob, Wes. How do the Quakers feel about having a Tory as a PM?'

'We mostly vote on the left, Jerry. Pass me that three-eighth socket, will you?'

'There you go. Yeah, even in school at Christian Brothers down in Elsternwick, I thought there was something shonky about the whole business. Brother Marco, he had us memorising this what-do-you-call-it? Like a prayer. The Lord is my shepherd.'

'Psalm twenty-three.'

'Yeah, that's it. A psalm. "The Lord is my shepherd, I shall not want, so on, so on, he leadeth me by the still waters, so on, he prepareth a table before me and annointeth my head with oil." I'm thinking, "What the fuck?" Excuse my language, Wes. But that's what I'm thinking. "What the hell? He annointeth my head with oil?" For what? He pours oil on your head? Speaking of oil, have a look at the crap coming out of this sump. You think this bloody Bernie's ever changed it? Like hell.'

The Land Rover was just about roadworthy in three days. Di packed three sleeping bags, two tents and enough food and water to sustain the population of China for a year. Wes packed four spare tyres into the back, and he would need them. Car tyres after the war had all the hardihood of plasticine.

Di had worked out a route to Mildura with half-reliable maps, up through Bendigo to the Murray then on to Mildura. They would stay with two comrades for the night, Nettie and Deb, then next morning, down the highway to Adelaide, stay with Di's sister-in-law, Marsha. Then Marsha would tell them the best way to Maralinga.

Beth suggested singing. She launched into 'Click Go the Shears', then 'The Road to Gundagai'. Beth's singing voice was awful. She couldn't keep a tune. Di offered her a thousand pounds if she would stop.

They took the highway north to Bendigo, on Beth's advice—she was in the front with the maps—missed Bendigo after one of her shortcuts and wound up in Charlton, well north-west of Bendigo. By this time all three of their bladders were bursting and they raced for public toilets in the park. They ate their ham and cheese sandwiches at a bench under a jacaranda. Di went back to the Land Rover and fetched the maps.

'I'm taking over the maps,' she said. 'Honestly Beth, you couldn't find Myers if you were standing in the middle of Bourke Street.'

Wes had the car filled at a servo before Di called the way to Ouyen, taking a route that led them over shabby dirt roads from one highway that crossed to another. They passed towns they'd never heard of, four or five houses, a grocery shop with a red phone box outside.

But Di knew what she was doing and got them to Ouyen, then to Mildura on the Murray, chain-smoking her Dunhills all the way. Beth, in the back now, didn't stop complaining about the persecution that communists were enduring in Australia under Bob Menzies.

'Beth,' said Di, 'shut up about Menzies. You're boring the daylights out of me. And probably poor Wes.'

Deb and Nettie lived in the heart of an orange orchard to the west of Mildura. Di had the directions, and also some information. Nettie owned the orchard, left to her by her widower father, as his only child; Nettie's mother had died in her early thirties of something or the other. Nettie and her father had adored each other.

It was after six before they reached the big old federation house in the Land Rover. Nettie and Deb strolled out to greet them. Di, the only one of the three who knew Deb and Nettie, introduced Wes and Beth. Nettie tall and lanky, with short fair hair, dark trousers, a short-sleeved red cardigan; Deb shorter, older, with greying hair that reached her waist. She wore a sleeveless white summer dress, and, oddly, dark spectacles. 'You'll have to excuse me,' said Deb. She gestured at her spectacles. 'I struggle with sight every now and again. Optic neuritis.' She spoke with an American accent.

'We're ready to eat,' said Nettie. 'You're late.'

After dinner—a casserole and apple pie, cooked by Deb—Nettie showed them around the house, three bedrooms, vintage furniture. Matisse had a stranglehold on the walls, reproductions in every room.

'Deb's taste,' said Nettie. 'We happened to be looking at Matisse in the Met while I was visiting New York. We were strangers then. Not for long. Deb moved here with her two kids, Dad didn't make any fuss. He was puzzled, wasn't he, Deb?'

'Oh sure. And my husband, Harris. It's our task in life to puzzle people.'

Including Wes. 'And the kids?' he asked.

'Both at Sydney Uni. Happy with the arrangement. One mom and a spare. Except that Nettie is a commie and I'm a Democrat, tried and true. I'm praying that Adlai wins. Adlai Stevenson? You know of him?'

'Yes I do,' said Wes. 'Best of luck to him.'

'Nettie, you wouldn't tell me on the phone why you were going to South Australia. But it's the British, isn't it?'

'Maybe.'

'Everybody knows the British are making an atomic bomb. And they'll have to test it. A while off yet, but they'll have to test it. And where do they have the ideal test site? South Australia. Not so many Aboriginals to clear out of the way. Miles of desert. Am I right?'

'Nettie, you know we can't tell you.'

'It's the British. The bloody British. And Tom Playford—he's been the premier since forever—will let them do what they like. They could test a bomb on Glenelg Beach if they wanted to.'

Beth, changing the subject: 'I think I've seen that you have eight comrades in the Mallee branch,' said Beth. 'That's right?'

'Yes, eight.'

'Plus Nettie, who is part comrade and part mother hen,' said Deb. 'They come here for meetings. Anything Nettie says goes.'

'That's an exaggeration.'

'Darling, you peck them for the whole meeting.'

They chatted after dinner about politics before Nettie, who had forty pickers coming the next morning at seven showed Wes and Beth the route to Adelaide on the map, gave each guest two towels and went to bed.

'You have a foreman?' asked Wes.

'Yeah, me,' said Nettie.

'And believe me,' said Deb. 'She talks, they listen.'

Deb was up early to make Nettie and the guests some breakfast: bacon and eggs and her own home-made yoghurt. Nettie left her guests to deal with the pickers. Deb's final words to them were, 'Hope for Adlai.'

They drove to Morgan over a road rough as guts, then south through countryside so sparse in its vegetation that the sight of a full-grown tree was a novelty. Abandoned farms with decaying homesteads and corrugated iron sheds rusting away were visible from the road. What the farms would have produced was a mystery, unless it were sand and rocks.

While they drove, Di filled Wes in on her sister-in-law and brother.

'Brian writes a gardening column for the *Advertiser*, and Marsha runs a charity shop that benefits people suffering from arthritis. Their kids, son and daughter, can't recall their names, have left home. Marsha is fifty-five and very jolly. My brother is fifty-eight and quiet.'

'So,' said Wes, 'a pair of firebrands?'

'But comrades, in their way.'

When they reached Adelaide and finally found Marsha and Brian's house off Fullarton Road, the couple came out to the front veranda of their white weatherboard house to greet them. And Marsha, a woman with a robust figure, was indeed jolly, and Brian was quiet. Brian, who did the cooking, provided lamb shanks and roasted vegetables.

'Why Maralinga?' said Marsha, as they sat around after dinner, listening to 'American Jukebox' on the radio. 'There's nothing there, darl. A few blokes in tents scratching away for gold, best of luck to them.'

'Party stuff,' said Beth. 'A bit secretive. Sorry.'

'Well it's a bloomin' long drive, darl. You have to go up through Port Augusta, get onto Tarcoola Road for about a year, then across country to Maralinga.'

Brian, washing the dishes, muttered, 'Wouldn't do it for a thousand quid.' Then, lifting his head, 'Hey shush. Let me listen to this. Patti Page.'

They listened to Patti Page sing 'I Went to Your Wedding', Brian with a tea towel in his hand and a rapt expression.

'Beautiful voice,' he said, wiping a tear away.

Off in the morning, with directions to Port Augusta, and then to Tarcoola Road. Wes had changed two tyres on the track down from Morgan to Adelaide, and stopped to buy three more in Port Augusta. He paid for them by cheque.

'Sorry the party can't help out,' said Di. 'Worse than the most miserly bank in Australia.'

Finding Tarcoola Road was a chore. Wes pulled over and asked four people for directions. It was sealed in a fashion for a way, but tough going.

They pulled off the road at six in the evening and Wes set up the two tents. Beth and Di searched for firewood, found enough under the eucalypt bushes. It was gourmet night off the Tarcoola: baked beans on toast, and billy tea. They slept, at least, or Di did; Beth was kept awake by the cries of animals.

'They sounded like tigers.'

'No tigers in Australia, dear heart,' said Di. 'Dingos and possums. Calm your little self down.'

The countryside was barren—just the low eucalypt bushes. It was late afternoon before Wes found the turnoff, a metal sign riddled with bullet holes; kangaroo hunters exercising their jovial humour. The road was barely a track and the Land Rover lurched and threw the three occupants all over the place. Two hours of bumping along was enough.

'Will this do?' said Wes.

'There's no sign.'

'What do you expect?' said Di. '"Wait here for a few years and you'll see an atomic explosion?"'

Wes said that they should set up camp and take the

pictures tomorrow, and this was agreed.

He made a campfire; Di cooked omelettes and bacon. Wes set up the two tents again, with painstaking care. They washed and cleaned their teeth in a round enamel basin, said goodnight. It was freezing cold. The night was full of alien sounds; a deep humming cry that never abated; the howls of dingos; an intermittent chirrup that came closer then retreated; the hissing of God knows what, not snakes, surely, maybe lizards. Beth lay awake for a while, then brought her sleeping bag into Wes's tent. 'Di is sound asleep. I'm terrified.' She maintained a chaste distance from Wes, but kept him awake with questions: 'What's that? It's a snorting sound. Are there wild pigs here? They can kill you. They eat human flesh.'

By dawn, Beth had moved her sleeping bag up against Wes and had one arm stretched across him. Wes woke first and lay there in smiling comfort. When Beth woke, she saw what she'd done in her sleep and was aghast. 'It doesn't mean anything. Don't think it means something. I was unconscious.'

'Relax.'

The next day, Di took a hundred pictures of the barren landscape. Here and there, they found yellow stakes driven into the dry earth. Mining claims? The stakes were numbered. The heat of the day was intense and the cloudless sky a lazy, interminable blue. Dried-up water courses formed a network over the surface of the parched ground.

Wes, like Nettie, knew very well the reason for the expedition. It was widely rumoured that the British were developing their own nuclear weapons, and where else would they test them but here? He thought of what Patty had seen in Hiroshima, and that one day it might be seen in Adelaide, in Sydney, Melbourne. When he prayed—as he did each day, silently, with his eyes shut—he begged God to spare the world a nuclear conflict. At the same time, he did not believe that God had the power to stop war, to inhibit evil. He believed that God had given humans the power to love, but that was all.

Di's pictures showed nothing but desert. Bored, she asked Beth and Wes to stand together for a snap. Beth was reluctant, but she gave in.

'Put your arms around each other.'

'No!'

'Go on. It won't kill you.'

Wes circled his arm around Beth's waist. She managed a smile.

'Didn't hurt, did it?' said Di. 'Now me.'

She gave Beth the camera, then stood beside Wes with both arms around his waist. Then she kissed him on the mouth, a proper kiss.

'That's how you do it, Bethy. As if you're enjoying it.'

'Oh, so you want me to be cheerful? La la la la la, a billion people who live like slaves, la la la la la!' She walked off to be by herself, and was allowed to be alone, if that was the way she felt.

Di said to Wes: 'How do you put up with her?'

'I care about her.'

'Well so do I, but if I were a man, I'd be looking for someone less skinny. Franny wants you. Give Franny a try. She's gorgeous. Good natured. Fabulous bosom.'

'Di, I said I care about her. And I do.'

They decided to stay a second night to spare Wes the drive for a bit. The noises of the dark were even more frightening than the previous night. Beth again came into Wes's tent in her striped pyjamas with her shirt and trousers tucked under her arm. 'I can't bear the noises. Please don't touch me.'

'Of course I won't touch you. The noises won't hurt you. Rest. You'll be safe.'

In the morning, Wes rose early to make a campfire. Beth stayed deeply asleep. It was while he was setting the fire that he noticed, some fifty yards or more away, an Aborigine standing perfectly still, staring at him. His hair and beard were grey; he wore dark trousers and an oversize, rumpled blue jumper. He was shoeless. Wes raised his hand and waved. There was no response. The man continued to stare fixedly at Wes, and even over the distance, it was evident that there was nothing welcoming in his gaze. Wes raised his hand again, and again, no response. The man's gaze was not hostile, but it was as if he did not want Wes to be there.

Wes roused Di and Beth.

'We have to leave. I think we're somewhere out of bounds. There's an Aboriginal man here.'

The women dressed in the tents and emerged full of curiosity. The Aboriginal man remained motionless.

'We should go and say hello,' said Beth.

'Beth,' said Wes, 'he doesn't want to say hello. He wants us to go.'

They packed as quickly as possible, bypassed breakfast, but left oranges, apples and bananas for their visitor. After camping overnight, they reached Marsha and Brian's place at four in the afternoon. Beth argued most of the way that Aborigines were part of the proletariat and that Australians belonged to the proletariat, not to any tribe.

'And this was explained to the Aborigines by Arthur Phillip when he anchored in Sydney Harbour, was it?' said Wes.

'They were colonialists. In other words, crooks.'

'Beth, have you ever thought that within their tribes, Aborigines have been communists for thousands of years? They hold property in common. You know that.'

'Oh, come on. They have no politics. They have no theory.'

When they reached the Norwood house (finally,

ultimately, and dear God what a journey) they told Marsha about the old Aboriginal man.

'We have a Maralinga Tjarutja fella who comes and collects bags of clothes from the Port Augusta shop. But he's a young bloke. Wouldn't have been him.'

Wes encouraged the women to rise for an early start to Mildura.

Brian asked Wes whether he had enough tyres.

'As I hope,' said Wes.

'You look all done in, mate. Take some breaks.'

Wes didn't take any breaks on the drive to Mildura. Nor was there much talking. But Beth did say she was disappointed that they didn't get to Emu Plains.

Wes stopped the Land Rover and turned to Beth.

'Beth, has it ever occurred to you that the Maralinga people had their homeland stolen? And now they're going to have it blasted to smithereens. Have you thought of that?'

'Maybe we can stop it.'

'And maybe we can't. That Aboriginal man we saw, and the rest of his tribe, do you think they're going to pack up and leave? The British will clear out the white men. The Aborigines, they won't trouble about.'

'All the more reason we have to stop them.'

Chapter 14

THE DAY AFTER the return from the expedition to South Australia, Beth sent a letter to Peter Corning to say that she had the photographs, but only of the Maralinga countryside, not Emu Plains. Two weeks later, Peter Corning telephoned Di Porter's home and spoke to Beth. He gave instructions. The pictures were to be printed, all of them, and delivered to an agent whom she would call 'Ivan', a Russian, at a park that he believed was known as Fawkner Park. She was to take a bench near the tennis courts that he'd been told she would find in the park. At ten in the evening, Ivan would join her and take the pictures. He would have a document with him which she was to sign.

'And then what happens? With the pictures.'

'I can't tell you that yet.'

Beth was there at nine-forty-five. The park was lit with lanterns. She found a bench beneath an oak and waited nervously for the arrival of Ivan. She was carrying a shoulder bag with the thick wad of photographs inside. She was well aware that she was now engaged in espionage. Being constantly harassed by the police and having her politics vilified in the newspapers was bearable; years and years in prison, even at the scaffold—that was something else. She patted her chest and said, in a whisper: 'Courage, Elizabeth Josephine, courage.' She hummed 'The Red Flag' and thought of the many thousands who had given their life to the cause. She also wished Wes was with her. Just for the company. She was more comfortable with him than she'd ever been. He would have come if she'd asked him. Women had been assaulted, raped in this very park. And yes, she was on edge. Why did she have to hand the pictures over? Why not some junior in the movement, when she had so much to do? She was working as the coordinator of policy for the CPA, which meant settling disputes between the various CPA factions.

She was seated below a lamp that attracted moths in great numbers. It had been a warm day but was now cold enough to cause her to shiver in her brown cardie and her green linen skirt. At exactly ten by her watch, a man in an overcoat approached: short and portly, a grey hat, a tie, round rimmed spectacles. He raised his hat and sat beside her. He said, in Russian: 'I am Ivan. And you are Miss Elizabeth Hardy. I have seen your picture.'

Beth replied, in Russian: 'Yes, I am Elizabeth Hardy.'

He seemed completely relaxed. But his Russian was a little awkward, not native Russian. He had obviously been taught Muscovite Russian, with its soft sound and sibilance, just as she had by Di, and the peculiarities of the Moscow accent could never be mastered by those who hadn't grown up with them.

Beth took the thick envelope of photographs from her bag and handed them to him. At that moment a possum appeared, ran past them up the oak. Ivan swung his head around to watch the possum disappear 'Jesus Christ, what's that,' said Ivan in a distinct Irish accent.

'Just a possum,' said Beth.

'Oh.'

He produced from his inside breast pocket a folded sheet of paper and opened it. What was written on it could only just be made out in the lantern light. It read, *I, Elizabeth Hardy, acknowledge copyright of the photographs of Maralinga South Australia taken in March, 1950. I further acknowledge that I have provided them to a second party representing the Soviet Union to be used in any way he sees fit.'*

'Why exactly do you wish me to sign this?'

'Procedure.'

Since that was as much explanation as anyone ever got from the party, it settled all doubts.

For a time.

Later, back with Di, she spoke about her uneasiness. 'He wanted me to believe he was Russian, but he wasn't. He spoke Russian like I do, as if it was taught and when he got spooked by a possum—a possum!—he shrieked something in English that sounded completely natural. English is his native language.'

'We've done what we were supposed to do. Just leave the rest up to them.'

'I feel dubious, Di.'

Three weeks later, at the drab, windowless office of the Communist Party of Australia, six policemen arrived with a warrant for the arrest of Elizabeth Josephine Hardy.

They did not say why she was being arrested. Nor did they take her to a police station but to a room in a building in William Street as drab as the one in which she'd been arrested. At a desk sat a smartly dressed man in a relaxed pose, possibly forty, his silky fair hair flopping over his forehead. When Beth made to seat herself on the other side of the desk, a policeman growled that Mister Wagner would tell her when she could sit. Mister Wagner said, genially, 'Go right ahead.' Then: 'You will have perhaps detected that I am English, Miss Hardy. From Cambridge, where you visited not so long ago. That's right, isn't it?'

'I would like to know why I am here. And I would like to see a lawyer.'

Wagner closed his eyes briefly, perhaps to show how

deeply relaxed he actually was. 'Here's the thing, Miss Hardy. According to my Australian colleagues, we don't have to let you see a lawyer for twenty-four hours. And indeed, we will not so allow you. But another interesting fact is that you must answer my questions truthfully. Are you prepared to do so?'

Beth didn't reply. She was not nervous or anxious. She knew she would likely go to prison. She saw almost immediately what had happened. The parcel of photographs had been handed over to Ivan, and Ivan was a government agent, or an ASIO agent, or even someone from MI5 or MI6. This meant that Peter Corning was also from MI5 or MI6. It was a set-up. It was obvious that she would never get the chance to let the British party know that Peter Corning was a traitor. She said: 'It was Peter Corning.'

Wagner leaned forward with his hands clasped on the desk. 'I think I can share with you a fact of our own. Peter Corning has been taken into custody in Cambridge. For a political movement so practised in suspicion, your comrades can be extraordinarily naive.'

'And what am I supposed to have done?'

'You handed what you considered to be sensitive intelligence to a man you believed represented a foreign power. Essentially, a foreign power that has displayed animosity toward the Commonwealth of Australia and the British Commonwealth as a whole. You may well be found to be a traitor to your country.'

'And who says I considered it sensitive intelligence? They were pictures of the desert.'

'Well, I daresay the judge will decide. But when he learns that the photographs depicted what you understood was a prospective atomic testing sight, it may have an influence on his thinking.'

Beth was taken to the women's section of Pentridge Prison in Coburg. She had been to this section of Pentridge before, visiting comrades who had been locked up for weeks without charge merely for demonstrating. It was bleak, it was cold, and it was falling to bits, since a new women's prison was planned for Fairfield and no money was being spent on Coburg. The male governor's authority extended to the women's section, but he was content to leave it in the hands of two relatively junior female officers who did more or less as they pleased. One of the junior officers was Bev Hutchinson, a woman of stocky build with thick-lensed glasses that gave her the look of a good-natured toad. She chatted genially to Beth as she escorted her to her cell.

'So you're a commie, lovie. Got some sympathy for the commies. The ones we've had here—maybe a dozen or so—all been quiet and well-behaved. A little bit boring, you might say. Out on the street, as rowdy as a herd of goats. In here, practically silent, reading their tracts. Can give you a cell to yourself: bit light on for bad girls at the moment.'

Before they reached the cell, Bev stopped and faced Beth. 'One thing, darl. I'm not going to get any strife from you, am I? Because I'd have to give you a hiding. And believe me, it will smart.'

Beth wasn't permitted a phone call. She'd been arrested mid-afternoon. But Janet at the CPA office would have informed Pip Morton, the lawyer who regularly represented party members, and also notified a QC, usually Matty Lear. At five in the afternoon, she was visited in her cell by Pip in his dilapidated dark blue suit, which may have been the only suit he'd ever owned. The dark blue had faded to grey in places. His tie was always worn loose. His attire perfectly complemented his mangled face, which had been squashed in a car crash some years ago and inexpertly repaired. He'd left his teeth behind in the wreck and the false teeth that had replaced them were also the work of an amateur, the upper and lower teeth the same size so that it was impossible for him to close his mouth fully. He was always in a rage that his fixed smile contradicted.

'In her cell?' he said to Leonie Peek, the other junior officer who managed the women's section with Bev Hutchinson. 'Why aren't we in the interview room, for the love of Christ?'

'The roof fell down.'

'And who told this young woman, Betty, that...'

'Beth,' said Beth.

'...Beth, that she couldn't see a lawyer for twenty-four

hours? That Pommy ponce, was it? He'll be from MI5 or MI6. The British, they send these pooftas over here to tell ASIO what to do. And our blokes are so meek they do what they're told. "Ooh, MI5, how impressive." Makes me sick. Anyway, tell me what they're saying you did, love.'

Beth gave a thorough account of the Maralinga expedition, and of the meeting in Fawkner Park with Ivan. She confessed she'd signed a document at Ivan's request, and quoted word for word what the document said.

Pip covered his face with his hands, as if concealing briefly his despair. 'What a fucking stupid thing to do. You've given MI5 and our wallopers a signed confession.'

Leonie Peek was sitting in on the interview. She was a tall woman, over six foot, renowned for her strength, and was sometimes called into the male part of the prison when more muscle was required to subdue rowdy inmates. Otherwise, she was more benign than Bev, pitied the women who'd ended up in Pentridge, found magazines for them and handed out lollies. She was known to the prisoners as Santa. But that was the surface. Underneath, as hard as nails. She'd been known to bang heads together to the point at which hospitalisation was required. She said: 'Bloody hell, Beth, do you want to hang? You meet a man in the park and sign your life away?'

Beth held her chin up. 'I'm not ashamed.'

'I'm not saying you should be ashamed,' said Leonie. 'But dear God!'

Pip asked her who had accompanied her on the trip to Maralinga.

'No one.'

'What, a skinny thing like you drove over the outback alone? Do me a favour.' That was Pip.

Pip said: 'Di Porter was with you, right?'

'Just me.'

'And what was the brand of the camera you used?'

'Can't remember.'

'She's not going to lag,' said Leonie. 'Good for you, love. Can't abide laggers.'

'Well, whoever was involved, even if it never comes out, is going to be living underground after the referendum next year, you realise that?'

'What referendum?' Beth asked.

'Menzies is planning a referendum to get the Communist Party banned. Late next year. And it will pass. A case like yours? They'll flog it for all it's worth. Sweet country girl seduced by communist propaganda, becomes an agent for Red Joe. They're going to love this.'

'Well, let them. I'm a communist. I'm not about to deny it.'

She was given a shapeless grey uniform to wear, a dress no more ugly than the clothing she had chosen for herself when she was free. Other women prisoners came to stickybeak at her through the bars of her cell.

'Say they're gonna hang you, love. Zat right?'

'Maybe.'

'Just for being a commo?'

'For espionage.'

'Yeah? Fuck me. You must have guts.'

Beth was five days in the Pentridge cell before she was formally charged by the Crown with espionage and taken before a judge of the State Supreme Court who denied her bail, and told her that she would be tried by another judge of the Supreme Court, sitting alone, no jury, such was the sensitivity of the information that would be revealed. In two weeks' time—an astonishingly short period.

Another officer of the Crown, who looked about fifteen, had visited her in her cell to tell her that it had been discovered that Di Porter had travelled with her to South Australia and that the vehicle had been driven by Wesley Cunningham of Almond Tree, neither of whom had broken the law and would not be charged with anything. A dozen people in Almond Tree knew of the planned marathon journey so the information could have come from this person or that. As it transpired, the information came from Di and Wes, who had been questioned by the MI5 agent with the floppy hair.

Beth was allowed to see Di and Wes in company with Matty Lear, who would be taking care of her when she faced the judge. She hugged both of them, Wes first.

Di said, 'We told that creep from MI5 that we knew why you wanted the pictures. They don't care. Handing over the pictures to that pseudo-Russian was the offence, not taking the pictures.'

Wes was almost silent, but distraught. He reached for Beth's hand, and she was content for him to hold it.

Matty said: 'Deary, you're up that famous creek with a telephone pole for a paddle. Bob Menzies wants you punished. Look.'

He showed her a copy of the *Argus* with a headline: *Red Spy Girl to Face Judge*.

'And my love, you haven't got a defence worth the name. You signed a confession. Have you seen Jean Lee while you've been here? Probably screaming. She murdered poor old Pop Kent, tortured him. She, they'll hang. Right here, while you're eating your Weetbix. They won't hang you, my dear. Too young, no bloodshed, and your espionage wasn't protracted. But Judge Mitchell will give you ten years. He's as close to the PM as his Bonds singlet. Get set for a long stay.'

Chapter 15

JUDGE MITCHELL might have been any age between sixty and a hundred. He looked constantly on the brink of falling asleep as he listened to the Crown prosecutor and to Matty Lear. At one point he emerged from his torpor to discuss fly-fishing on the Upper Yarra with Matty—a shared passion. After an hour of listening to arguments this way and that, he raised his hand and waved it, signalling he'd heard enough. He displayed a document to the court, and read it aloud. It was the document that Beth had signed for the Irish Russian in Fawkner Park. He asked the clerk to show the document to Beth and asked her if her signature appeared at the bottom. Matty made a gesture of acquiescence, and Beth said, 'Yes.'

Two days later, she returned to court for her

sentence, which was, as anticipated, ten years. A further week later—a mere week—she was back in court for ten minutes to hear her appeal dismissed. Matty Lear was with her. After the announcement of the dismissal, Matty was permitted to make a statement for the record. 'Your Honour, these procedures have made a travesty of the law of the Commonwealth. This young woman was judged and condemned before she ever set foot in this courtroom. No jury. None of the elements of a fair trial. More like a star chamber. I protest the highly unusual rules that have obtained here in this courtroom. As I have said, a travesty, your Honour.'

Judge Mitchell nodded genially. 'Noted, Matty, thank you. Sunday week, Matty, Launching Place on the Upper Yarra?' Here he acted the casting of a line.

'I believe I can manage that, your Honour. Yes, I'm sure I can. Meet at the Home Hotel on the Warburton Highway, say noon?'

'And Matty, bring some of that Penfolds you brought last time. Superb. Lives in my memory.'

So the cell in Pentridge was to be her home for ten years, seven with good behaviour. She lay on her bunk as stiff as a plank and stared at the ceiling. Leonie came to console her. 'Seven years is nothing, sweetheart. Got women in here seeing out twenty-seven years. Stabbed their hubbies, throttled their kids. 'Course they had proper trials, not like yours from what I hear, which was bullshit, half the stuff they tried out on you wasn't even in the law books. Wasn't us responsible. It was the Poms, MI5. We do whatever they want, and they wanted you locked up and a DOD order slapped on the press. The papers can say you're a red spy, but nothing else. Pip told me what you did, going to South Australia and all, told me why. If I whisper a word of it to the press, it'll be you and me sharing this cell. Look love, I'll do what I can for you. Get letters to you from your near and dear, smuggle your own letters out. Don't you tell a bloody soul, okay? Not a soul. If you do, I'll have to give you a hiding, one you won't forget.'

Beth thanked her, surprised and grateful.

Later that night, she heard someone down the corridor bleating as Leonie laid into her for some infraction or other.

Beth's whole family had been in Melbourne for a week waiting for a chance to see her after the failed appeal, kids included. They were given permission to see her in Pentridge by the Governor, who told Bev, 'Yeah, yeah, wave them through. The whole mob of them aren't commies are they?'

The day of the visit was a day on which Beth felt sick at heart. She was not in the world anymore. Nonetheless, she smiled and tried to give the impression that she was coping nicely.

Bob Hardy wept for the whole visit. The kids asked

if there were any shops in the prison, lolly shops. Lillian held her daughter's hand and reminded her that she had a loving family backing her every step of the way. If they were allowed, one or more of them would visit every week. Gus and Maud called her a moron. Franny sat stiff and erect, unsmiling, knowing that Wes would never desert her in prison. Maud said: 'You're all over the papers. They're saying you were a milkmaid before Di Porter got hold of you and bent your ear with commie rubbish. A milkmaid? You've never milked a cow in your life!'

Gus said: 'All this ratbag stuff and this is where it lands you.'

'It's just politics,' said Bob Hardy. 'They don't like her politics. That's all. We're not at war with the reds. We just don't like their manners. Putting a kid in jail for ten years for her politics is evil.'

'But there it is and here we are,' said Lillian. 'It's all Bob Menzies and his referendum. Nice country girl got hold of by the Russkies. What nonsense. "Could happen to your lovely kids" is what he's saying.'

Beth said: 'Mum, it's MI5, the British. More so than Menzies. They want me to disappear.'

There was no exercise yard for the female prisoners, just an ancient building that had once been the laundry where the women could wander around and chat. Beth met Jean Lee in the old laundry, and one look at her made Beth think of a woman standing at the gates of hell.

Jean bailed her up in a corner.

'Did nothing. Didn't touch the stupid bastard. It was Kev and Bob. Do you believe me? You fucking better, because it's the truth. Did nothing.' She grabbed Beth by her arm. 'Get me out of here. You're still pretty. They'll listen to you.' She threw back her head and screamed: 'They made a slut out of me!'

Leonie strolled over to intervene. 'Calm down, Jeanie, just calm your little self down.'

Jean fell to her knees and threw her arms around Leonie's legs. 'Lon, don't let them hang me. Don't you let them!'

Leonie hoisted Jean to her feet. 'Don't go thinking about it, sweetheart. Read those magazines Bev got you. You've got a *Pix* there, a *Women's Weekly*. Read them instead of carrying on.'

Leonie led Jean back to her cell.

Another prisoner, Deirdre, shuffled over and gave Beth a hug, and she needed something of the sort, badly shaken as she was. 'Can't hang her too soon for me,' Deirdre said. 'I'm sick of her. Like this every day.'

She asked Bev for books and was told that she was denied reading material; then within an hour Bev returned with an armful of books from the prison library.

'Who makes up these rules? Got you some romances. Helga Moray. Heard of her? Beaut writer. Lots of sex, doesn't go too far. Funny thing. Got some girls here who try it on with each other, but what they like to read is boy-girl stuff.'

Beth read one a day: didn't like them but persisted. She wrote a list of titles and asked Bev to look for them in the library. But the library was devoid of political philosophy, except for John Stuart Mill's *On Liberty* and God knew how that had ended up in Pentridge. She had read it before, but read it again with less scorn. And there were two anthologies of poetry left behind by a convict who'd served the final thirty-one years of his life at the prison. He had no relatives so his anthologies ended up in the library under *Fiction*. Beth read both anthologies avidly and found she had to admit that 'The Rime of the Ancient Mariner' was her favourite, even with its twee ending. Also 'Sohrab and Rustum'. She feared she was growing sentimental.

When her dad visited she asked him to bring her a dozen of her books from home, but Bev couldn't allow him to leave them with her. 'We'd have to go through every page looking for messages from your commie buddies. So they say; means nothing to me.'

Wes, after great persistence, was permitted to visit her, or he wasn't, but Leonie waved him in. It was the first moment of pure joy Beth had known in weeks. They sat on her bunk, and it was she who reached for his hand. 'Don't tell me about anything in the newspapers, the way they're using me. I don't want to hear. Tell me about what you're doing in Almond Tree.'

He told he was building three houses, including his own, all with the help of his brothers, Teddy and Max, and all three houses were beautiful. 'The one we're building for Liam Murphy and his missus on Canterbury Creek near that old Chinese camp where the creek runs over the boulders, that's special, that's made from granite blocks, heck of a lot of masonry stuff. With a triple gable of iron, and a veranda that runs down four sides, big windows, mullions.'

She just wanted to hear him talk, hear his voice. She asked him to bring a book next time to read aloud to her. 'You choose.'

She came to know all the other women prisoners and their stories. Leonie kept Jean Lee away from her, but not out of earshot of her shrieking and pleading. Most of the women were where they were for crimes such as theft, fraud, soliciting, shoplifting (years of it before they were caught with a house full of merchandise).

She listened. Laureen had expropriated seventy thousand pounds from her husband's business accounts and spent it on nothing, just kept it hidden until one fine day she burned it. Gloria had shoplifted herself ga-ga, anything she wanted she took, until she discovered that she was under surveillance and stuffed everything she'd stolen under the house, where the police found it.

Acts of violence were few. Kathleen, a grey-haired woman of striking beauty, came to Beth and asked her what the commies had to say about sex. Beth told her that

Marx had said little about sex, except its commercialisation in prostitution.

'Meaning what?' said Kathleen.

'Capitalism commercialises everything. Even human emotion, human desire.'

Kathleen nodded slowly. Beth noticed that she had been allowed to keep her small gold earrings. 'Present from my granddaughter,' said Kathleen. 'So why am I here, lovely? Murder. Bit surprising? Caught my mongrel of a husband with his hand up my granddaughter's dress when I walked into the lounge room one time. She lived with us, Tessy. Her mum, my daughter Sue, died of breast cancer the year before. He's got his hand up her dress, her school uniform, she's got tears running down her cheeks. I knew he'd mucked about with Donna, too, my other granddaughter, or I was pretty sure. Donna never said. I told Tessy, I said, "You go to your room for a few minutes, sweetheart." I went to the shed and got the mallet, came strolling back in and stood in front of him, of Rupe. He could see the mallet but still looked smug, until I belted him over the noggin with it. Knocked him out cold. Dragged him out into the backyard, poured a bottle of kero over him, dropped a match, and poof! That woke him up. He went tearing around the backyard like a madman, crashed into the Hills hoist, burning like a candle. Dowsed him down with a few saucepans of water until he was just smouldering. Then I went out to the telephone booth in the street and called the police. Took

138

their time coming. Didn't bother with the ambulance. The coppers finally turned up, took one look at Rupe and saw he was dead. But they called for an ambulance. In court, the jury found me guilty—well, I said I was, didn't I? Donna, she told the jury that Rupe was always after her. Tessy said, "He made me do things I didn't want to." Found me guilty but with a recommendation for leniency. It was the kero that did for me. They said it showed "malice". Bloody right it did! The judge gave me five years, I've done three, I'll be out in six months. Good behaviour. My daughter June's been looking after Tessy and Donna. Hard for her. She's got her own two littlies. So there you go, Beth. You can write up my story to fill in time. Needs telling, you think?'

When Wes visited next, he brought *Anna Karenina*. He had read it a year earlier at Beth's suggestion. Both loved it, all over again. She had even explained to him how to pronounce Russian names, where to place the stress. He settled at a table in the old laundry. Bev pulled up a chair, too. 'Have to make sure you're not doing anything creepy with secret Russkie codes, don't I? No, my dad used to read the classics to me right up until I was fourteen, fifteen. *Treasure Island*, that was my best. And *White Fang*—all about a wolf up in the snowy bits of America, or Canada, can't remember. So go on. Read. I'll be quiet as a mouse.'

Wes raised his eyebrows to Beth, but she seemed content. He started with the epigraph: 'Vengeance is mine, sayeth the Lord; I will repay.'

'What?' said Bev. 'Is that the start?'

Beth said, 'No, no, that's the epigraph. Just a bit at the start that gives you some idea of what the book's about.'

'What's it mean, but?'

'It means only God has the right to punish. We mortal humans don't have the right.'

'Is that right? Too bad nobody told Jean that before she got to work with the carving knife on poor old Pop Kent. Go on.'

Wes read: 'All happy families are alike. Each unhappy family is unhappy in its own way.'

'Whoa!' said Bev. 'Is this another one of those epi-things?'

Wes said, 'No, this is the start of the story, Bev. The first line.'

'Read it again.'

Wes read it again.

'I don't reckon that's true,' said Bev. 'No, no. My family, we were happy. Proper happy. Some of my friends, not so happy in their families. Either way, they were all different.'

Beth said it was simply the proposition of the author. It wasn't a fact.

'They should have cut it out, well.'

Wes was allowed to read deep into the scenes of mayhem in the Oblonsky household without any further interruption. More women prisoners pulled up chairs to listen, attracted by the novelty of a man's voice. Wes read well, too. He never stumbled, and had found a way of slightly varying his voice for different characters without sounding affected. No one was more drawn to him and his reading of the great book than Beth. She glanced at his profile every so often and wished to God he could stay the night with her on her hard bunk and kiss her and hold her. She must have had rocks in her head when she rebuffed him. And when she told him to marry Franny.

And so a pattern evolved of Wes visiting each Friday, taking the train from Almond Tree and the tram from Flinders Street to Coburg, the book in his hand. Beth's family—some members, not all—visited once every two weeks. All of the women prisoners considered it a treat to listen to *Anna* being read each week. Even Jean Lee was permitted to sit in, having promised to be good. And she was good, no more than a murmur from her now and then. Expressions of disapproval were uttered on occasions, but brief. 'She's got a little boy! She can't be chasing that what's-his-face, Vronsky!' And: 'It'll end in tears, I can see it.'

Beth made a comment here: 'Well, he loves her.'

Bev said: 'No, no, don't give me that, Beth dear heart. You can look after your kids first thing, that's what you can do.'

In six weeks in Pentridge, mixing with her fellow

prisoners, listening to their tales, Beth had come to understand something she would have bitterly disputed in the past. She had barely grasped life in its complexity and danger before Pentridge. She had seen only the smugness of the bourgeoisie, never the heartache, the desperate struggle to keep a life going. If a woman walked into a room and found a despised husband with his hand up a beloved granddaughter's dress and punished him with a mallet and a bottle of kero, the class struggle wouldn't explain it. Nor would it explain Claire throttling her boyfriend's bit on the side. Human passion overwhelmed all theory. But politics had been her life for ten years now. She couldn't cast it aside. At least her politics addressed the great injustice of inequality. She held to that, even as these new recognitions rounded off corners in her heart, reshaped motives.

She learned what a slap from Bev felt like, too. She'd given one of the books that Bev had brought her from the library to Deirdre, and Bev confronted her in her cell.

'Who said you could give that book to Deirdre?'

'I just thought it did no harm.'

Bev slapped her. 'I say who gets favours. You understand?'

Beth said yes, she understood, and was slapped again, harder. 'Good. Keep understanding.' And a third slap. Beth had never been hit before, not even by her argumentative sisters. She backed up to the wall in shock, her hand to her face.

Chapter 16

CHRISTMAS IN Pentridge was surprisingly cheerful. The women made decorations—stars, chains of coloured links, a small Madonna and child in plaster donated by Leonie—and the women with children visiting were all given bags of lollies for the kids. The mothers were tearful when the kids had to leave. The two women with husbands still on the scene gave the hubbies big, sloppy kisses and told them to be 'good boys'. Beth's family did not bring gifts, at her insistence, since most of the women would be getting so little. Bob Hardy, as usual, wept for the entire visit. Franny came along on this Christmas visit and smiled as best she could. Lillian said: 'Christmas in the poor house, God what a sight. Still, good old Mister Marx, looking down on our daughter with pride.'

Wes came on Boxing Day, and gave the women what they really wanted, more of *Anna*. One of the women asked why Anna was so upset after she made love with Vronsky for the first time. 'It's what she wanted. She should just cop it if she's not sure.'

Wes was two-thirds of the way through *Anna* when Jean Lee was hanged in early February of 1951. Bev was required to witness the execution, the feeling being that a woman should be on hand. 'She fainted when she saw the hangman, poor thing.' The women had gathered around Bev to hear the story, just as they gathered around Wes to hear Anna's story.

'The doctor gave her something that pretty much knocked her out. So they had to carry her up the scaffold. Strapped her to a chair and stood the chair on the trapdoor. One, two, three—and down she goes! She's left hanging there not knowing a thing that'd happened in the last five minutes. It's not right. Just keep the poor silly creature locked up, but don't go around hanging people. Thirty-five minutes, they hang Bobby and Norm. How'd you like to go home to your missus with that on your mind. "What'd you do today, my darling husband?" "Oh, hanged three people, two blokes and a woman." "Well, you'll be needing a good strong cuppa, won't you?"'

Back in Almond Tree, finishing the last of the furniture for the house, Wes looked up from the kitchen chair he was fashioning to see Franny standing before him in a bad way, wet cheeks, eyes brimming with distress.

'Franny, what is it?' He hadn't seen her for a month; it had been a relief.

'I'm pregnant.'

Wes put down the sandpaper he'd been using on the shoulders of the chair.

'What the heck?'

'I'm pregnant, Wes. I've been to Doc Smith. He said I'm six weeks gone.'

'Smithy said that?'

'Six weeks.'

She began to cry and shudder. Wes tried to take her in his arms but she pushed him away.

'I'm okay. But I need your help, Wes. I have to have an abortion.'

Wes had to concede that he didn't know clearly what an abortion involved.

'They scrape the foetus out of the womb.'

'Kill it?'

'Yes.'

'Franny, is that what you want. To kill your baby?'

Franny struck herself on the head, two times, three times, hard.

'No, it isn't what I want, idiot! I have no choice. What, you want me to raise a child of a man I despise?'

'What man?'

Franny went quiet for a minute.

'Vern Alfred.'

'Vern who runs the caravan park?'

'That Vern Alfred.'

'Franny, he's twice your age. Married, with kids. How on earth?'

Franny said that Vern was starting a small zoo to please the customers and bought rabbits from her. He would sell them. She delivered them, explained how to care for them. Vern had a couple of wallabies as well, a very aged dingo, a blue tongue and a goanna.

'He asked me if I'd like a drink—this was two in the afternoon. I said yes. I don't drink much, but I knew what was going to follow and I was full of anger with you for going to see Beth every single week. We went into an empty caravan, had a glass of gin, I let him have sex with me. You know his reputation. Then I went home and chucked up. Four weeks, no period. I went to Smithy and he said I was pregnant. No doubt about it. I went home and chucked up again. I want you to ask Di if she knows anyone who can abort this baby. Di will know.'

Since Wes planned to live in the house himself, he'd had the telephone installed, mostly so that Beth could call him if there were an emergency. While Franny was still there, he called Di and told her the situation. 'Dear God, what a scatterbrained girl. Is she there? Can I speak to her?'

Wes handed the phone to Franny.

'Franny, if you want to do this, you have to be sure. Completely sure.'

'I'm sure.'

'Hand the phone back to Wes.'

Di said that there were a hundred or more abortionists in Melbourne, nearly all of them medically unqualified and dangerous. When schoolgirls came to her pleading for help—always to Di—she told them that their parents would have to be informed because the one doctor she could recommend was formidably expensive with a practice in Toorak. He had a certain commitment to termination—he wouldn't have done it at all otherwise—he also charged three hundred and fifty pounds. In Almond Tree, it was once possible, before the bushfire, to buy a house in one place and another from Hoong Li, now dead, for one-hundred and fifty pounds. The doctor—Doctor Child, an irony—considered himself a communist by some convoluted reasoning and would turn up at branch meetings every so often, listening sternly in his suit and white shirt and tie, never saying a word but raising his hand when votes were taken.

Di would make an appointment for Franny. She would find one hundred pounds. Franny had to find the rest. Wes still had his discharge money untouched; he told Franny he would provide one hundred and fifty pounds. Could Franny find the rest? She could, from her rabbit savings.

The doctor kept the patients in bed at the clinic for twenty-four hours after the procedure, and required a reliable friend to take the patient home. Wes would be the reliable friend.

When Wes put the phone down, he pushed his hands through his hair and shook his head. 'Fran, this is going to be horrible for you. I'll be there, but what a foolish thing to do.'

'Don't you think I know? Don't you?'

When the family was told, sitting around on the armchairs and sofa of the lounge room, Wes was there to support Franny. For Bob Hardy, two choices: take the 12-gauge down to the caravan park and fill Vern's gut with buckshot, or whack him in the chops. Bob opted for the shotgun, and murder, but Lillian chased him and confiscated the weapon.

'What are you going to do? Shoot the other dozen men in the town who've enjoyed our Franny? The women of this town all think of Franny as a slut. Not me. She's got some sort of appetite for sex that's practically a handicap, but she's no slut. And haven't you seen the way women steer their husbands clear of Franny down at the shopping centre? I've bought condoms for her at the chemist. You'd think I'd done some good, then she lets that vile Vern take her into a caravan, no condom. You want to slap Vern about, go to it. But I'm not having two family members in Pentridge.'

Bob Hardy drove down to the caravan park and found Vern replacing a tap washer. His man took off, and Bob, with his bad leg, couldn't catch him. It was two days before he came across Vern down in Brewster's the bakers, tapped him on the shoulder and smacked him all over the shop. 'No need to thank me. It was a pleasure.'

The appointment was for a Tuesday in April. Wes had to cancel a couple of appearances at which he was speaking with Doc Evatt, the federal opposition leader, on the issue of the constitutional banning of the Communist Party coming up in September. Wes was asked to speak at these gatherings in Progress Halls in the region because people loved to hear his voice. Not so much Evatt, who tended to badger and roar. Wes made it clear that he was not a communist, but communism was politics and you couldn't ban a party because you didn't like it. 'They don't blow up bridges, they don't shoot people. It's just politics. If you don't like them, don't vote for them.'

Wes took Franny to the city by train, then to the clinic off Orrong Road by tram. She kept the same grim face for the whole journey and barely spoke a word. But she held Wes's hand and frequently pressed it against her cheek. The clinic was at the back of a stunning mansion with an extensive garden planted with elms. Wes handed Franny over to a nurse, middle-aged, unsmiling. Later Doctor Child came out to the waiting room and sat beside Wes. He spoke in a deep voice, almost a baritone. Considering how spick and span he kept himself, Wes was surprised that Doctor Child had let the black hairs in his ears grow rampant.

'Never speak about this, Mister Cunningham. If it becomes known what I sometimes do here, I will go to prison for five years, Franny will go to prison for three years, and you, as the facilitator, will go to prison for one year. You may think that the amount I charge is exceptionally high, but half of that goes to a certain detective sergeant who protects me. I only ever abort unmarried women and girls; the married women have to find their own way of coping. We understand each other? I know, incidentally, that you are not the father.'

The doctor left Wes in the waiting room and told him it would be two hours before he could see Franny. The walls were ornamented with posters: *Drink your milk! Two glasses a day!*; *When you visit the toilet always scrub your hands*. Magazines were provided but Wes had no appetite for the *Women's Weekly*, the *National Geographic*. Two other patients joined him, a mother and a daughter as it appeared. The girl looked barely fourteen, fair-haired and pretty, but downcast, her eyes brimming with tears. The mother, stylishly dressed in scarlet, seemed seized with an unremitting anger and glared at Wes as if he deserved rebuke simply for being male. She slapped the daughter on the hand at intervals and hissed at her to show some sense. 'They're not going to cut your throat.'

When Wes was finally permitted to see Franny, she

was still emerging from the anaesthetic in a room painted white and spotless in every detail. He kissed her on the forehead and she said, 'Woo, oh Jesus...'

All she could talk was slurred babble. Wes told her he would be back the next afternoon to take her home. He stayed the night with Di Porter in Collingwood and helped out by reading aloud the speech she was going to give at the Melbourne Town Hall in a couple of days, 'Say no to the ban!'

Di came the next day in her husband's Chevy. Franny was in a fairly good state, but in some pain. Franny thanked her for everything, but winced as she spoke. 'Right-o,' said Di, 'you're not going home on the train in this state. I'll drive you.' They stopped at Collingwood so that Di could tell Beau that she wouldn't be home until midnight.

Franny slept stretched out on the back seat. The conversation between Di and Wes was sparse. Di drove fast but smoothly over the Black Spur, negotiated all the twists and turns without disturbing Franny. A little about the referendum.

'If we lose, then what?'

'God knows. We become more secretive,' said Di.

'Even honorary communists such as me?'

'You're not a commie, Wes. You're a Quaker. And a very good Quaker, I must say. A Quaker with a red tinge.'

'In the Quaker community, I'm considered an embarrassment.'

'Anyone who wants to muck about with the world is an embarrassment. You have to be an embarrassment before you're even noticed.'

Franny was delivered into her mother's care at ten at night. She turned up the next day while Wes was hanging the front gate of his new house.

'How are you feeling, you poor thing?'

'Awful. I have a request. I want to stay with you here. No romance. Just stay here in your spare bedroom. I can do housework, cook. I'm good at it. But I want to be near where you are.'

Wes sighed deeply and put down his screwdriver. 'And what do you think Beth would say about that?'

'She wanted you to marry me.'

'She's changed.'

'Ask her, then.'

On Wes's next visit to Pentridge, he read the scene in which Kitty draws letters in chalk on the surface of the card table and it is up to Levin to decipher her declaration of love. The scene pleased all the women listening. 'He'd be good at crosswords, that Levin,' said Bev, who enjoyed crosswords herself.

The women always allowed ten minutes at the end of a visit by Wes in which he and Beth could be alone. Beth knew about the abortion from a letter Wes had sent her via Bev, who accommodated them in this way.

'So Franny's all right?'

'Yes, but she has a request.'

'I'm sure she does. What is it?'

'She wants to live at the house I'm just finishing. In the spare bedroom. No romance, she says.'

Beth slapped her hand down on the table and her pale complexion turned scarlet. 'No! No, no, she cannot! Are you mad? Did you tell her it all depends on me? Why didn't you say no yourself? I can't believe you're asking me this. No! She'd be in your bed in ten minutes.'

'Beth, she's in a bad way. I thought we might give her a break.'

'She cannot live at your house. No—not now, not ever. God in heaven, any woman who would have sex with Vern Alfred isn't right in the head. You know what she's like. And she's sly. It would be, "Oh, Wes, I just need a cuddle. Oh, Wes, I just need to take my pyjamas off for a few minutes."'

'Okay, okay.'

'What? Why are you smiling?'

'You no longer want me to marry your sly sister?'

'Please yourself.' Then: 'But you'd have to be as stupid as her.'

It took nine months to finish reading *Anna*. The women were left disappointed. 'Would you call that a happy ending? Anna's dead.' 'Yes, but Levin and Kitty are married.' 'So?' 'The thing is, Anna went nuts. She needed medication, in my opinion.'

Anna was succeeded by *Middlemarch*. Not quite the hit that *Anna* was, but still, not bad. Everyone liked Dorothea, but once she'd gone nutty over Casaubon, she was also considered a candidate for medication. 'That old stick! He'd never get it up. And Dorothea, she's so gorgeous. What a waste!'

Three weeks into *Middlemarch*, and ten months into Beth's sentence, she came to know that Bev could be bribed. Twenty pounds for a private hour with your husband or boyfriend. Beth mentioned it in as casual a way as she could manage to Wes on his next visit. Wes said, 'Is that something you could agree to?' Beth shrugged. 'Might be nice.' On Wes's next visit, he passed an envelope to Bev, who led Beth and Wes to a cell separated from the other cells by a gated corridor, which Bev locked behind her. This was the cell in which Hilary the Poisoner had been held, Hilary who claimed she could make lethal poisons out of air and dust and whom nobody would share with. It was a cell in the same derelict condition as all the other female cells but Bev had left three blankets on the bunk and a pillow.

'You two cuddle up. I'll lock the corridor off. Nobody will come down for an hour. Use these.'

She handed Wes two condoms in their sealed blue packets.

They stood apart, shyly, until Wes took the initiative

by spreading the blankets on the bunk. 'Sit beside me.'

Beth sat beside him, not too close.

'Well,' she said. 'Now what?'

Wes turned her face to him and kissed her on the lips. Then lay down and urged Beth to do the same. Before she did, she removed her prison uniform, and beneath the blanket, her underwear. She told Wes to take off his clothes.

'All of them?'

'All of them.'

'Stand there,' she said nodding at a place on the floor close to the bunk. As he did, naked, her gaze wandered all over his body. She said, 'I just want to look at you.' Finally she reached out to him and drew him to the prison bunk. Holding him naked was the single greatest pleasure of her life.

She was different afterwards. It was as if her body had been stingy and mean with her about what it could yield up, resentful of the sheer delight that it harboured. When Wes was gone, the other women stared at her and smiled. 'Sweety, look at you. Better than porridge, isn't it?'

Beth blushed, but didn't deny anything. Only there was Franny. If she laid a finger on him, she would cut her throat so help her God. From ear to ear. And enjoy it.

Chapter 17

PATTY AND Kado made their two-week visit to Almond Tree in August of 1951. The entire Friends community came to the station to greet them, including Wes. They were fascinated by Kado's perfect English, and the ghost of an American accent in his speech. They knew the story of the loss of his family in the atomic explosion from Patty's letters, and they knew of her nursing in the hospitals of Hiroshima. Patty's mother, Daisy, did her best to prepare Japanese dishes, without access to perhaps half of the ingredients. They stayed in Wes's old room in the Cunningham house.

Kado was warned by the Friends, and by Patty, that anti-Japanese sentiment in Australia, even in Almond

Tree, was intense, and that he had to expect abuse and insults. He was sanguine about the prospect and when he encountered anger and hatred, his strategy was to smile broadly, or if the opportunity existed, to apologise for the grief his country had inflicted.

Patty drove him about the shire in her mother's little Austin.

She stopped in the car at the cenotaph, which was being cleaned, as it was 365 days of the year, by Daph Sawyer with a small red hand brush. The cenotaph honoured and named in bronze relief the soldiers of the town and region who had died in World War I, but now also those who had died in World War II. Kado wanted to get out and inspect the monument but Patty said no, no, not while Daph was there. 'I'll be courteous,' he said, and left the car to look. Daph, on her knees sweeping the two steps at the foot of the cenotaph, glanced up when Kado approached. And frowned. 'I am sorry to interrupt your work, madam. I have stopped here to honour your soldiers who died in the war.'

'Really,' said Daph. She shaded her eyes from the sun, still on her knees. 'You're not Australian.'

'No, in fact I am Japanese.'

'I'll be buggered. A Nip.'

By this time, anticipating strife, Patty had joined them.

'Jesus Christ, Patty Cunningham!'

Daph got to her feet, still holding her red hand brush.

'Give us a hug, pet. Haven't seen you in a thousand years. Where've you been?'

'Nursing in New Guinea while the war was on. Then I volunteered to carry on nursing in Japan after the war was over. I've been there ever since. In Hiroshima.'

'What, where they dropped that big bomb? That atomic bomb?'

'Yes, there, but seven months after.'

'I thought it killed them all.'

'Many thousands. Not all. I've been nursing survivors. Alongside my husband.' She nodded at Kado.

'Your husband. This is your husband? How did this come about, Pats?'

'He's a doctor. I was working in his hospital. He wasn't in the army during the war, Daph.'

Daphne gazed at Kado more with curiosity than disdain.

'And so you got married. Well, a woman can marry who she pleases. Are you going to live in Almond Tree, then? Lots of people here have a poor opinion of the Japs.'

Patty said no, they wouldn't be living in Almond Tree, but in Hiroshima where Kado's parents dwelt. And she added, because she thought she must, 'Kado's wife and four children were killed by the bomb.'

Daphne nodded. 'Come here for a bit, want to show you something.'

Kado followed her to the far side of the cenotaph.

She placed her finger on one of the names listed there, the names of the dead from World War II. Corporal Nicholas Sawyer.

'My son. He died on your railway you were building in Burma. Cholera.'

She kissed the name. Kado, risking it, also kissed the name. 'I have sorrow in my heart for your son. Soldiers of my country did terrible things.' He did not add: *Perhaps as bad as exploding an atomic bomb on my city, where we are still struggling with the damage.*

The sightseeing tour took in Mulga Bill's original bicycle, welded into place outside the shire offices—Mulga Bill, immortalised in Banjo Paterson's poem. Next to the rickety, ancient bike the first two lines of the poem were quoted: *It was Mulga Bill of Eaglehawk who caught the cycling craze and turned aside the good old mare who'd served him many days.*

Patty explained that Eaglehawk was a town to the west in the gold-rush country, and also that the people of Eaglehawk wanted the bicycle back. There was not the slightest evidence that Mulga Bill had ever existed, or that this was the bicycle in the poem. It had been purchased by a council man from Almond Tree decades past from a second-hand shop in Eaglehawk, advertised as Mulga Bill's original machine. The welding had been reinforced to prevent rogues from Eaglehawk stealing it, which they—the rogues—had attempted more than once.

Wes came along with Kado and his sister to show him the trout under Rusty Creek. The timber bridge was so dilapidated that you took your life in your hands driving a vehicle across it but people did, without concern. The three of them stood in the middle of the bridge while Wes pointed out the brown trout turning lazily in the clear water below. They were waiting for the insects that found some obscure nourishment in the rotted pylons of the bridge.

'Watch,' said Wes, and within a minute a big brown trout leapt clear of the water to take an insect from the air.

'Big brute, that one,' said Wes. 'Two pound, more.'

Then another trout leapt high enough to make a splash when it hit the water again. Kado said, 'Hoo!'

'Fly fisherman come here, climb down the bank and take usually two or three browns.' Wes had to explain fly fishing to Kado, the hook, the feathers, the tapered fly line, the manner of casting.

'Do you come?'

'Sure. But I'm the only one in my community who eats flesh.'

Wes led Kado down to the river and along the bank to a shaded pool. 'Wait,' he said, and in a short time a platypus appeared in the pool, came to the surface and floated for a few seconds, almost as if it were accommodating the visitors, then dived down out of sight. 'Ai! What is it?'

'A platypus. You saw that it has a bill like a duck? Very unusual creature.'

Over the rest of the outing, Wes was able to show Kado a wombat, big mother of a thing that sat hunched outside its burrow, and kookas, currawongs, magpies, rosellas, king parrots. No koalas to be found. It all delighted Kado. 'The strangest country.'

The next day, Wes was off to Pentridge and Patty took Kado to the Victory mine. At the entrance to the mine, Patty told Kado a story from her childhood. 'We came here when we were kids—me and Wes and Teddy my brother and another girl from the Friends community, Charlene. We played a game that was partly a ritual. We had to go into the mine one at a time, without any light, feeling our way along the walls to the end. We were pretending that the mine was the road to hell. The idea was that we had to find the end of the mine, knock three times on the rock, and cry out loud, "Hell, I defy you in the name of God!" then find our way back. We did this maybe twenty times, and always emerged back into the daylight exhilarated. And now you and I are going to do it together.'

She took Kado by the hand and led him into the mine, cautiously, feeling the wall, avoiding the openings that had functioned as exploratory offshoots, further and further, breathing in the moist reek.

'This is the end,' said Patty. 'Put both hands against

the stone. Now knock with one hand and say, "Hell, I defy you in the name of God."'

Kado did as he was told, but even in the pitch dark, she could tell that he was grinning. Patty said the same words.

'You know what is behind this wall?' said Kado in the darkness. 'Nothing. A place of no feeling either way, that's hell. God is variety without end, everything in multiples, and then the multiples multiplied again and again. In hell, nothing, not even the feeling of lacking, just nothing.'

'Really?'

'Is this poppycock?'

'No, my darling, it isn't poppycock. But what about evil, what about Hiroshima?'

'About evil I know nothing. Destruction, yes, that I witnessed, but evil is a mystery. Perhaps there is no such thing. Just ill-will.'

'Sounds plausible.'

They kissed in the darkness at the gates of hell.

For three years husband and wife had discussed pregnancy, but used condoms from the hospital while the discussion was unfolding. It was finally agreed that there would be no babies. For five years, Patty had seen exactly what radiation poisoning did to babies whose mothers had survived the bomb. The cardiac and pulmonary problems, the horrible disfigurements. Six months ago a woman had given birth to a baby girl with no eyes. Blindness was common. And Patty had to assume that radiation levels in her body were high. There would be no babies.

'It is a sorrow for you, and a sorrow for me. No babies. Just Hiroshima. Even adoption seems futile. There are more than one hundred thousand orphans in southern Japan alone. Could we pick out one, two, and give them a better life, but not the thousands upon thousands left in orphanages? I couldn't do that, and I don't think you could either.'

Patty wasn't all that sure. But she wouldn't harp about it. His point was difficult to argue against. Two babies out of a hundred thousand?

She took Kado to three meetings of the Friends, in three different houses. Wes sang at two of them. At the third, the gathering sat in silent prayer for an hour. Kado didn't pray. He kept his eyes open. Beside him, Patty sat with her head bowed. Occasionally her lips moved. Kado knew what she was praying for: a child. All the discussion back in Hiroshima proved futile. Sleeping together in Wes's old room, they had made love a number of times without condoms. There was no argument. Patty had simply decided to risk it. That was her prayer. That a baby would come and would not be blind or deaf or deformed. Kado took her hand and kissed it. A wish, unspoken.

They carried that wish with them back to Hiroshima.

Chapter 18

ON 22 SEPTEMBER the referendum to ban the Communist Party of Australia was held, and it lost narrowly. The news made its way into Pentridge a few days later and Beth danced on a table in the laundry and sang with gusto, 'The Red Flag', just as she had in Red Square. Leonie was the only other woman who knew the words, and joined in. 'My old man's a commie,' she said, 'in an on-again, off-again way. Taught us kids the song.'

But when Wes made his next visit with *Middlemarch*, months after the lovemaking in the cell of the poisoner, Beth was gone.

Bev took Wes into her office. 'Two blokes from Canberra came and took her away. Not coppers. Bureaucrats in daggy suits. They had a warrant to move her to—wherever. Wouldn't tell me a damned thing. Wouldn't tell Beth anything neither.'

Wes felt sick. 'Who *can* tell me?'

'Don't know. I'll find out what I can. Leave me a number and I'll ring you if I hear anything.'

Wes stayed with Di. She phoned a friend in the Department of External Affairs in Canberra, who knew nothing. She tried ASIO, but nobody answered the phone. None of the comrades had any information. Finally Wes phoned Bob Hardy, told him Beth had been moved from Pentridge and asked him to call Di if he was contacted by anyone.

No news came from any source. Wes rang every prison in Victoria. He allowed ludicrous scenarios to play out in his imagination. Beth secretly executed. Beth tortured for information. Lillian came to Melbourne and waited outside the office of the premier while staff came and went for hours, only to be told that the premier would not see her. Bob Hardy went to the office of the local federal member in Burforth, Terry Mills, and pleaded with him to do something. Terry represented the Country Party, in coalition with the governing Liberals, but served on the backbench, no influence. Nonetheless, Terry was outraged and got into the ear of the Minister for Supply, Olly Beale, a friend, who would see what he could do. No promises.

It was three months of intolerable distress for Wes and the Hardys before Terry Mills telephoned with an address in Canberra where something might be learnt. 'Just go to reception at the Department of External Affairs. You can take one family member or close friend of your daughter.' He gave a date and time in March 1952.

They took the bus to Canberra and arrived well in time for the two o'clock appointment. The receptionist called an assistant, a young woman, to show them to an office on the second floor, utterly featureless, nothing on the desk other than a blank nameplate, nothing on the walls.

'Won't be long,' said the assistant, in the manner of assistants who have no idea how long the wait might be.

It was an hour. At five past three, a man of about forty buttoning up a blue shirt came through the door. His full head of auburn hair was wet. He unbuckled the belt of his trousers to stuff his shirt inside, apologising all the while. 'I've been in the minister's pool, do apologise for not watching the clock. It's not Bondi, which I adore, but at least I was able to put in a few laps. If they offered me a job in Sydney, I'd take it just for Bondi. In your country, I must say, the best beaches in the world. I'm from Cambridge. The only time you ever get in the water is when you fall into the Cam.' Then he remembered to shake hands. 'Bob Hardy, is it, and this is?'

'Wes Cunningham. I'm a close friend of Beth Hardy.'

'Oh, so you're Wes. You're the Quaker. You look remarkably like anyone who isn't a Quaker. I won't give you my name if you can bear the incivility. Or if you like, call me Bill. Now, we have some documents for you to sign.'

He called loudly, 'Naomi!' and the young woman who had shown Wes and Bob Hardy to the bland office popped her head in the door.

'Those two documents I drafted last week, fetch them in, sweetheart.'

Naomi returned in less than a minute with a thin manila folder.

Bill opened the folder, pushed one document across the table to Bob and one to Wes. A third he kept for himself. What the documents recorded was brief. Bill (as he wished to be known) allowed Wes and Bob a couple of minutes to read the document.

'Now let me summarise so that we all understand the same thing, the same facts. If either or even both of you divulge anything from this meeting, other than the destination of Elizabeth Hardy, you will be arrested and charged and will certainly go to prison. Please sign in the appropriate place, in just one moment. Naomi!'

Naomi reappeared, as rapidly as if she'd been waiting poised on the other side of the door for this very summons.

'Naomi, my love, you will witness the signatures of Robert James Hardy and Wesley Cunningham.'

Wes and Bob signed, because there seemed no alternative. And Naomi witnessed both signatures. 'Do you have a comb in your kitbag, sweetheart?'

Naomi left the room and returned with a green comb. Bill combed his hair back, then asked Naomi if he looked 'the goods'. Naomi said that he looked fine.

'Pardon my vanity,' said Bill, 'if you can find it in your hearts.'

Everything he said was impeccably polite and completely insincere.

'Back to business. Your daughter, Mister Hardy, is in Moscow.'

Bob rose out of his chair. 'In Moscow? In Russia?'

'Yes, the Moscow that is in Russia.'

Wes, who had remained calm outwardly, asked simply, 'Why?'

'We traded her and seven other Soviet agents for one Briton taken in East Berlin. As you may surmise, this one Briton is extremely important to us, much more important than the Russians realise. They think we want him back because he is the son of a lord and related to the Royal Family, in a distant way. Not at all. But they have driven a hard bargain. The seven agents we could muster—mostly misfits and yahoos—were not enough. Then one of our people remembered your daughter, and the Russians accepted her, I think to forestall us dragging in one of their diplomats to make up the numbers. So there you have it. She's in Moscow.'

Wes said, 'Did she choose to go?'

'No. But she had no say. We sought and were given

the approval of your prime minister and his cabinet. To what extent he relied on his cabinet's endorsement I couldn't say. I think he enjoys the authority to do whatever he wishes. He could propose building a bridge from Canberra to London and he'd certainly have his way. And a relative of the Royal Family? Well.'

'Why were we not told of this months ago?' said Wes. Bob Hardy was too upset to say anything.

'Not possible.'

'And how long is she there for?'

'For as long as they wish. But my experience with people like Elizabeth—which is to say, what the Americans call chicken feed; she's unimportant—is four years. About four years. There's something about four years that makes the Russians feel that justice has been served. Three years, too soft for the NKVD. Now for some good news—we have not cancelled her Australian citizenship. If it is four years, as I suggest, they will put her to work translating, since she speaks Russian. Then she can apply to emigrate to Australia. If she does, we will be urging the Australian Government to view the application sympathetically. You can write to her, but your letters will be heavily censored by the Russians. She can write to you, but once again, the letters will be subject to rigorous censorship. However, once every three months she will be visited by a British diplomat, confirming her welfare, and he can smuggle a letter out that will not be censored. And he can smuggle a letter in, which will go uncensored. It's the only consolation we can offer.'

Wes wanted to know if he could visit her in Moscow.

'Alas, no. Her correspondence with her family for these coming few years will be epistolary.'

'Will be what?' said Bob Hardy.

'By way of letters. Cup of tea? While I answer any other questions you have? And provide an address for you in Moscow for Elizabeth. Naomi!'

The ever-reliable Naomi was there in a few seconds.

'I'm going to have Naomi prepare Earl Grey all round. Trust me, you'll be in raptures. No milk in Earl Grey, so I won't ask you, and better without sugar. Pardon me while I void my bladder.'

Left alone, Bob Hardy dried his eyes with his handkerchief.

'Poor kid. Poor Beth. This bloke is a born bastard. I'd like to wring his neck.'

Wes said, 'Bob, my feeling is that most of what they've done is illegal. But we wouldn't be able to do a thing for Beth at this stage.'

Wes was right. Within a month, the news of Beth's exile had made its way into the newspapers, but discreetly. *Red girl spy traded to Soviet masters.* The article in the *Argus*, a handful of column inches on page 22, said that Beth had gone to Moscow, 'of her own free will' and the deal had secured the release of an 'innocent diplomat held by the Soviets'. Beth's comrades in the unions were not about to make a big deal out of a fellow comrade being sent to live in the flourishing heart of communism. *Middlemarch* was on hold. Four years was shorter than Beth's remaining prison term in Pentridge (with good behaviour), Wes reasoned, but he wouldn't see her, kiss her. He felt at times on the frontier of insanity with grief.

The whole of the Hardy family, less Beth, were brought together to reinforce the need to be tight-lipped about Beth. Pete, Gus's husband, in charge of a thousand sheep now that his wife was occupied with kids in a reluctant way, and Algy, Maud's husband, who worked with the Ayrshires, were both bad drinkers and had spread a story in the Victoria pub that Beth had been kidnapped by the Russians, and had to be reprimanded by Bob.

'Beth's in Moscow, she was traded, and that's all you can say to anyone. Got it?'

The meeting was, as usual in the daylight hours, on the back porch. The kids, the three of them, were faring for themselves, also as usual. Lillian kept an eye out for anything dire, a brown snake in one of the kids' hands, Billy steadying himself to brain Jonathan with half a house brick—these things had happened in the recent past. Gus and Maud restricted their interventions to half-hearted calls of 'Keep it down!'

Franny said, 'What do you prefer, locked up in Pentridge or free in Russia? Probably loving it.' It was accepted that Fran was only too glad to see her sister spirited off to the other side of the world. The longer the better; forever best of all.

Pete said that he'd be prepared to go to Moscow and find Beth and smuggle her back to Almond Tree. He had an appetite for fantasies of triumph, always backed by Algy with, 'That's the shot,' and ridiculed by Gus, with, 'Pete, shut up.' This time Gus asked him if he intended to take on the entire Red Army.

'We'll do nothing,' said Bob. 'We get her letters, as we hope. We reply. We wait for four years and bring her back here.'

'And don't go blabbing in the pub,' said Maud. 'You kids, quieten down or I'll be out there with my smacking hand!'

Chapter 19

SO FAR AS he could, Wes distracted himself from his distress by accepting building projects willy-nilly. His own house, 'our house', was finished, but he was working on two other houses with his brother Teddy, and also installing a sunroom for Jolene and Jimmy Kemp out on May Pole Street next to the fire station. He was at the Kemps' when Bob Hardy pulled up in his Dodge with a letter from Beth. The letter had taken much longer than three months—it was June when it arrived. It was in an envelope of coarse-grained brown paper, redirected from the British Embassy in Berlin and bearing a number of stamps, one depicting Comrade Lenin and a British one depicting HMS *Victory*. The letter inside, written by Beth, was nonsense. It read: 'I am living among the heroic people of Moscow in happy circumstances. Do not be concerned about me. My quarters are very comfortable. I am translating English into Russian. I hope you are all well, including Wes. Love, Beth.' These were the remaining sentences. Three-quarters of the letter had been blacked out.

'Not much to go on, is there?' said Bob. 'But I was glad to see it. We have to hope and believe that we'll get something through the diplomat that the Pommy spoke about.'

Wes was happy at least to see Beth's name at the bottom of the letter. And his own name mentioned.

Three weeks later, a letter was forwarded from the Department of External Affairs in Canberra.

Dear Family, How in God's name did this happen? I understand I was in a package that brought about the return of a British goon being held by the Russians. But why me? A nothing from Australia. At least I can tell you the truth in this letter. I live in a squalid one-bedroom apartment close to Gorky Park, but I can't see the park because the windows are so filthy on the outside. I share the place with a complete moron from Yorkshire called Eva who migrated to Russia two years ago. She talks about nothing but Marx and the superior power of Soviet weapons. God, this was me! How did you put up with me? But I can't say a word in criticism because she would inform on me and my salary would be cut. I have to live on the equivalent of around one pound a week, buy all my own food. The apartment is free, though. My job is translating American textbooks into Russian. My Russian grammar isn't all that good, but it's better than my supervisor's. Nearly all the textbooks are about oceanography—dear family, I can't tell you how tedious it is. I have each Monday off work and I am allowed to go to various sites in Moscow. But I have to get permission from the police and fill in a form. There's a police station on the ground floor of the apartment block, and a week ago on a Monday I filled in a form giving my destination as Gorky Park. A policeman read my form and said, 'There is no such place in Moscow.' I told him it was just across the road, but he said again there was no such place in Moscow. I said, okay, I'll go to the Pushkin Museum. He said, 'To get to the Pushkin Museum you must cross Gorky Park.' I said okay, I'll cross Gorky Park. He said, 'There is no such park in Moscow.' So I stayed home and listened to Eva babbling on about the Yorkshire Workers Collective.

The second personal letter didn't come until February.

Christmas has come and gone. They still celebrate Christmas in Russia, but wherever you see a Christmas tree on display, there is always a portrait of Comrade Stalin set up at the base. And there is no holiday. People give gifts—some people—usually homemade things, like tablecloths and handkerchiefs. Quite a few Christians about. You notice that they cross themselves in front of shops that have a Christmas tree, very secretly. Now here is something that the Soviet Union can boast about (and believe me, I have come to see that there is not much)—public transport is free. I can easily get a police pass to go to the shops, and if I take a bus—free!

I am forced to go to parades. This is a city of parades. Marx's birthday, Lenin's birthday, military parades showing off new missiles, there's always something. I attended a celebration of I don't know what outside the Kremlin and Stalin himself stood on the balcony with five generals wearing so many medals, each of them, I thought they'd overbalance and fall over the rail. I shouted out: 'Hurrah for Comrade Stalin, the guardian of the Soviet people!' thinking, 'What an ego.' I think I have attended ten parades and celebrations in five months. The people around me always clap me because I speak Russian when they know, somehow, that I am not Russian.

Dear family, what a mess I have got myself

into. I apologise to you all. The other, folded page is a private letter for Wes. Can you give it to him Dad? I will get through this.

Bob Hardy took both letters to Wes's worksite at the house he was building for the O'Connors on Federation Drive. 'All the family has heard the letter, but this other one is just for you. I'll leave both of 'em with you.'

Wes called to Teddy to leave him be for half an hour. He took the two letters down the back of the new O'Connor house to Sandy Beach, which was not a beach and was not sandy, only a place where the bank sloped into a creek that didn't have an agreed name, just 'the creek'. A big willow overhung the creek with one huge bough so low that it sat just above the water. Wes sat on the bough and read first the family letter, then the one Beth had written for him alone. It was brief.

Wes, I miss you desperately and love you with all my heart. If you can wait for me, I will marry you. If you can't wait and meet someone else, tell me. I will be okay. I will throw myself under a tank at one of the parades I have to attend, but otherwise, I will be okay. Only not Franny. You cannot marry Franny. I'm not having you with my sister. That would be too much. Write to me. Dad knows where to send letters from you and the family. The British fellow who comes to see me now and again is pretty decent, but he has tiny teeth like a little child and I can never stop staring at them. Sometimes six months go by before he can take a letter from me. It's exasperating. Marry me.

Wes read the family letter twice, and his letter five times. The water purling against the bough seemed to harmonise with his rapture. *Marry me.* He needed to find out if he could visit Beth in Moscow. But a Qantas flight would be far too expensive for him. He would have to borrow from the community. The community had kept a fund for many years for Friends and it would be no trouble. He left Teddy to work on alone while he went home and wrote to Beth.

Can you have any doubt that I will wait? I'm going to find out if I can visit you in Moscow. That is, if the Russians will give me a visa. They should be sympathetic, since they will know that I was involved in your so-called espionage expedition to South Australia. I will do everything in my power to get to Moscow, my darling. Until your letter came, I was half-mad with worry. Moscow sounds dreadful. The house is finished and ready. I've left the elms in the backyard, and also a huge red gum that the currawongs and the ravens love. I have been growing cauliflowers in a plot in the backyard, also cabbages and the most beautiful tomatoes you've ever seen. Beans too, and capsicums. Along the back fence, a grapevine has been growing for years and years, and I keep a blackberry vine along the side fence full this year of big, plump berries that I picked and made into jam, much more than I can use. Most of the caulis and tomatoes and cabbages and grapes and blackberry jam go to the community, and the capsicums. I don't know whether you'll be interested in what I'm growing, but maybe when you see the garden you'll be happy to roll up your sleeves and get stuck into the digging and weeding. One day a few weeks back we had our meeting outdoors in the backyard. Everyone prayed for you, which probably means nothing to you, being a communist, but we weren't praying to God to look over you but Stalin, asking him to protect you. Then my grandmother, who was born in England, asked the gathering to pray for Queen Elizabeth as the coronation approaches. I am building two other houses and adding a sunroom to Jolene's place. One of the new houses is granite blocks, a lot of work, and one is red brick, much easier. I was working on three places to take my mind off worrying about you, but it didn't stop me. As soon as I get the houses finished, I will apply for a visa for Russia. About three months. Do you want to know what I'm reading? *Hard Times*. A lot about trade unions. Enjoying it. I'm only allowed one page for this letter, so I'll sign off now with all the love of my heart. And may Comrade Stalin protect you. And God.

Stalin died in March. Beth's next official letter read: 'You will have heard that our beloved Comrade Stalin has passed away. He was the guardian of the Soviet People and his kindness and generosity brought joy to the lives of everyone in the USSR. I wept for him, as did all the Soviet People.'

Two weeks later her letter from the Department of Foreign Affairs arrived:

Yes, Stalin is dead. He was, I suppose, an egomaniac and perhaps a worse mass murderer than Adolf Hitler and there was a time when I loved him as if he was a second father. Eva wept for three days without stopping; she wanted to know why I wasn't. I told her that the agony in my heart was too great. (Eva, by the way, has a boyfriend who is forty years older than her, an administrator in Soviet Rail. He asked me once if I'd like to join them in bed and I told him with a big smile, in English, that I'd rather walk barefoot over broken glass.) His funeral was a festival of crying and lamentations. He was laid out in Lenin's mausoleum and we all filed past, it took three hours. Eva was in line with me, sobbing continuously. She kept saying Beth can you believe it? See, this is what I can't do anymore. I can't worship people. I have heard stories of Stalin giving Beria permission to do anything, murder anyone.

We had the day of the funeral off but then it was back to work on the tedious oceanography. The room I work in is a frightful dump. Here's an irony: it's a converted laundry, just like the recreation room in Pentridge. If you asked me which I preferred, I would say Pentridge. Oh God, just let me be a wife and not a translator of oceanography texts and people every day being sent to the Gulag—that's a whole world of prison camps, mostly in Siberia. One of my fellow workers told me about them. She's very subversive, Kristina, a Russian girl. When Stalin died, she took me aside and whispered in my ear: Ha ha! The other letter, as usual, is for Wes alone. Love you all.

Dearest Wes—If you could only get here I would be delirious. The loneliness is unbearable. Before our time together on the poisoner's bunk, I didn't know anything about physical feelings. Now, day and night, I think of me in your arms and have such an avid desire to be with you. It must have been in me all this time, this desire, but I somehow squashed it flat. Please don't touch Franny. I know I have said this before, but it tortures me to imagine you with her. You don't know how crafty she is. I don't mean to be unkind to her, but maybe you will have to be. I wish you could do something about me being here. What they have done to me is not even legal. You can't deport or swap Australian citizens just for convenience. But I understand about the document you were forced to sign. I don't want you in jail. I want you taking care of your silly old vegetables. And Franny will have her stupid rabbits in your backyard before long, but that doesn't mean that she lives there, remember that. Does she cook you meals sometimes? I bet she does. Don't let her. If you want someone to cook you meals, do it yourself, you're not paralysed, or if you have to, get some of your people from the community to come in and cook for you, or even Mum. But most of all, borrow that money, finish building your stupid houses, come here to me in Moscow. Darling love, please, please don't forget me. I keep having these morbid thoughts of you thinking it's all too difficult. I know it's difficult, but believe me, it's more difficult in Moscow. Come to me, please, please! Don't touch Franny. Remember how crafty she is.

Not so crafty. Wes didn't see her for a month and when she came around one evening it was to tell him that she was going to get married to Ricky Devon. They were sitting on the front porch, Wes reluctant to let her inside. He'd made her a cup of tea. 'His wife died three years ago, you'll remember, they still don't know what killed her but something to do with her kidneys and it only took three months. Two little kids, Davie and Sue-sue, they're four and five now. So I'll be looking after them.'

'Wonderful, Fran.'

Her eyes were full of pain.

'Is it? I don't love him but he's a good man and he loves me. You know who I love. You know. But you don't care, do you?'

'I'm fond of you, Fran.'

Franny threw her coffee mug a fair distance onto the lawn. 'Fond? That makes me sick. You love that nut case in Moscow. She can't cook, she knows nothing about housework, nothing, and she's probably hopeless at sex. But for me, there's no hope. I can do everything, cook and sew and make your house beautiful and make you so, so happy in bed. But there's no hope for me, is there? Is there?'

Wes lifted his hands in a gesture of reluctant agreement.

'Even if Beth vanished from the earth, you wouldn't marry me, would you?'

'No, Franny. I wouldn't marry anyone.'

Franny nodded, got to her feet and fetched her mug. 'Will you come to the wedding? It's in three months.'

'I'll be glad to.'

'How charming. "I'll be glad to." I won't come around again.'

Chapter 20

THE ARRANGEMENTS to visit Moscow and Beth became complex. Wes wrote to the Department of Foreign Affairs in Canberra, explaining what he wished to do—visit Russia to see Elizabeth Hardy. Much later, he received a note in the mail directing him to come to Sydney and meet up with 'Bill'. Where? 'At Bondi, 3.00 in the p.m. At the Sun and Surf Café.' On such-and-such a date.

Wes took the early train to Sydney and the tram to Bondi. He was at the Sun and Surf a half-hour before the appointment and drank tea in the outdoor area where patrons still attired in their togs could find a table—a shirt was also required. It was summer and the beach was packed, big canvas umbrellas, blankets, kids running riot, women stretched out for a tan. Most of the patrons in the outdoor area didn't bother with a shirt, except for the women. At a little past three, Bill appeared, smiling, old-fashioned black woollen togs, a towel around his neck. He was tanned all over, a perfect deep gold. Wes stood to shake hands.

'The only time I could meet up, Mister Wesley. I have to make the most of the sunshine while I'm here. I've been back to London twice since I last saw you. Only too happy to get back to your charming land. Darling,' he called to the waitress, 'nice cup of Earl Grey, if you can manage it? Yes? And one for my associate. I've been on Coronation duty, Wesley, than which you cannot imagine anything more tedious. Clerics and choir boys costumed as if nothing had happened since Richard the Lionheart. And Her Majesty's Windsor accent. It grates on my teeth. I was only two yards away when they plopped that bloody great creation on her head. Skinny little thing that she is, twenty pounds of jewels supported by a neck as thin as a pencil. Pardon?'

'I asked if you are in MI5.'

'Now, as close as we are, Wesley, I must with humble apologies give you no answer to that. I am in the service of Her Majesty, suffice to say. In a certain capacity. Odd situation for a republican, but it's the only work I'm suited for.'

He leaned forward on the table and lowered his voice. 'You spoke in your letter to a colleague of mine on the subject of travelling to Moscow to see Elizabeth

Hardy. You would be required to apply in person for a visa at the Soviet Embassy in Canberra. The application would then be followed by a six-month wait, and you wouldn't know if your application had been successful before those six months had passed. The Soviets do not encourage tourism. They don't rule it out, but they certainly don't go to any lavish lengths to attract people. If you wish to go ahead, the Australian Government will not rule it out, withdraw your passport, for example.'

Wes lifted his hands in resignation, and let them fall. 'What can I do? I'll apply for a visa, wait six months, then finally see Beth.'

'So you hope. I admire your tenacity, Wesley.'

'It's not tenacity. I love Beth. I have no choice.'

'Well then, I admire the love you have for her, I should say. Never experienced whatever is in your heart, dear friend. It baffles me. But what do you say to a plunge in the surf? I do hope you brought your trunks.'

Wes went by bus two days later to the Soviet Embassy in Canberra to apply for a visa for the Soviet Union. A security guard asked him in terrible English if he was carrying a weapon, 'under apron'. A large portrait of Stalin framed with black crepe paper was still displayed behind the reception desk. The man at the desk directed Wes to the first floor, where visas were dispensed. He was accompanied up the stairs by two men, one on each side, wearing identical loose-fitting dark suits, shown to an empty desk, told 'Sit, wait.' Nothing on the desk other than a buzzer to occupy his attention, but the upholstered chair behind the desk was as spacious as an armchair. Finally a very tall man in a suit identical to those of the two men who'd shown Wes to the visa desk came strolling across the garish purple carpet and lowered himself into the chair.

He said: 'Good afternoon. You have come for a visa to visit the Soviet Union.'

His English was clear and perfectly enunciated.

'Why?'

'To see my girlfriend, Elizabeth Hardy. She was expelled to the Soviet Union.'

'Yes? Write please for me on this pad her name.'

Wes wrote Beth's name, and the visa officer rendered it in Russian, then pushed the buzzer on his desk. A middle-aged woman in a heavy woollen skirt and jacket, far too hot for the summer weather, came out of a door some distance away and shuffled across the awful carpet. The visa officer gave her the page of the notepad on which Beth's name was written.

'I will see her file. I think I remember her name.'

Not so much for the visa officer to do during the day. He sat gazing about for ten minutes then stood and repaired the black crepe paper around the portrait of Stalin, which had come loose in two or three places.

'Comrade Stalin,' he said when he sat down again. 'He passed away this year. Terrible, terrible sadness for all the Soviet people. Now we have no leader. Maybe Comrade Khrushchev. Maybe Comrade Malenkov. Both of these men are excellent.'

'I am sure,' said Wes. 'Both excellent.'

The woman in the woollen suit returned with a thin red folder and handed it to the visa officer. She said something animated to him, then departed.

'Red folder is good,' he said. He opened the folder and leaned back in his chair to read the contents, which amounted to three pages. He made sounds of mild pleasure and approval as he read, encouraging to Wes. When the visa officer had finished, he closed the folder and lay it on the desk. 'Miss Elizabeth,' he said, 'is a hero of the Soviet people. Is this right for a woman, hero?'

'Heroine,' said Wes.

'Yes? Heroine? Same like the drug?'

'Yes, same as the drug.'

'Huh. Strange. Miss Elizabeth is a heroine of the Soviet people. I salute her. Maybe we can make visa for you to see her in Moscow.'

Well, good; except that Wes was instructed to take the visa application away and bring it back completed in one month. Wes said he would do it on the spot. 'Not possible,' said the visa officer. Wes asked, already despairing of the answer he would hear, how long it would take for the visa application to be processed. 'Six months,' he was told. Could it be done quicker, by any chance, for a heroine of the Soviet people? The officer lifted his shoulders and let them fall. 'Not possible.'

Wes had to tell Beth in his next letter that it would be at least six months before he could get a visa for the USSR. Her reply came in October, three months after he had returned his visa application to the Soviet Embassy.

Wes, that's dreadful. I was counting on seeing you so much. My only solace here is music. I met a young couple in the Pushkin, Oleg and Bessie. Bessie's real name is Svetlana but she calls herself Bessie after Bessie Smith, a great blues singer of years ago. They have Bessie Smith records smuggled in, and Billie Holiday, and Woody Guthrie. They only have six records but we listen to them over and over in their apartment. It's forbidden to listen to jazz and blues and American folk music, but Oleg and Bessie live on the fifth floor of a block in which the fourth and sixth floors and all the other apartments on the fifth floor are too much of a shambles for habitation. So Oleg can play the records on his little turntable without anyone hearing. I'd never heard this music before. It thrills me, Wes! It's the only time I'm happy. Our house has to be full of jazz and blues and folk. Blind Willie McTell—have you heard of him? When you do finally get here, my darling, I'll introduce you to Oleg and Bessie. She'll say, 'What a gas.' It's her response to anything she likes—she picked it up from a Canadian tourist. Wes, is there no way you can get here sooner? We only listen to the music two hours a week—if Oleg uses more electricity, the authorities will notice. Two hours of happiness in a week is not enough to live on. Sick of the Soviet Union. I haven't entirely lost faith in communism, but it has to make a better society than this drabness everywhere and in everything. What hope is there for a society that bans Woody Guthrie? He's a communist himself. Do you know what they have against him? That song 'This Land Is Your Land'. They say it invites the bourgeoisie to participate in the building of America, instead of only the proletariat. Don't they listen? 'This land is your land, this land is my land.' Where is the beauty, Wes? The beauty in material things, the beauty in thought. I heard Katherine Susannah Prichard talking once and she said the only real beauty in the world was in the poetry of equality. I have to tell you, Wes, there's no poetry of equality in Moscow. And it's so cold! Winter is early this year. Eva's boyfriend gave her a little electric radiator but she hogs it and won't even let me warm my hands with it. I spend the whole day and night shivering. I was out in the street the other day and an old man died on the footpath, just dropped dead, and the ambulance came. The medics took his overcoat off to listen to his non-existent heartbeat and when they put him in the back of the ambulance they left his overcoat on the ground. About a dozen onlookers tried to grab his coat, fighting for it, and Wes, I was one of them. Shameful. When you finally come, bring me a big woolly overcoat, my darling, and I will love you even more. Everything is a mess in Moscow right now. We have no leader. Khrushchev and Malenkov are fighting for the leadership. Khrushchev has more support in *Pravda*, but Malenkov is fighting back. The thing is, nobody wants another Stalin. That's why they shot Beria, who had murdered thousands and thousands. People are tired of living in fear. I'm sorry my writing is so small, but I'm trying to fit in as much as I can. Oleg and Bessie introduced me to a fellow by the name of Anton, a bit crazy, quite young, about eighteen. He's in college. He asked me to take up what is known as samizdat, which means self-publishing in Russian. Many writers in Russia are forbidden from publishing and the only way they can get their books to the public is to copy them out by hand. One person copies out a manuscript and hands it on to another person, who also copies it out and gives it to someone else to read and copy. It's illegal, but it works. And I'm doing it now. I go to Oleg and Bessie's flat and spend two hours each night copying manuscripts. It's Oleg who passes them on. Darling, it's arduous but exciting!

I've used up my page, dearest Wes. I can't write

on the back because my family will be able to read what I say to you. Dad said Franny is married. To what's-his-name Devon the ranger. Glad to hear it. May she get pregnant immediately and stay pregnant for the rest of her life.

Chapter 21

WHEN PATTY became pregnant, Kado's mother, Shinsa, who had lost two sons and six grandchildren to the bomb, was overjoyed. Patty explained in her best Japanese that what they were doing was fraught with danger. Kado's mother did not understand radiation and thought Patty was being neurotic. Kado took over and spoke about radiation and the problems it caused not only for pregnant women but for everyone in Hiroshima. He told her of the thousands of births over the eight years since the bomb that had revealed deformities and other problems. Shinsa told him he was being melodramatic. Nothing could impede her happiness.

Kado's mother and father took it for granted that the child would be raised in Hiroshima. They didn't know of the long discussions between husband and wife on the issue of continuing to live in Hiroshima after the baby's birth. Kado said his parents would never leave Hiroshima and move to another part of Japan, far less to Almond Tree. 'From hell to paradise,' said Kado of the Almond Tree option. 'But we cannot.'

'Then we have to accept whatever comes,' said Patty. 'The women who have children here have no choice either and they have to deal with whatever they give birth to. We have to accept that we're in the same boat with our patients. We stay.' But all through the pregnancy, she was worried sick. She prayed for the baby a number of times a day, standing still with her eyes shut, not making a sound. She asked her mother to enlist the community in praying for the baby. She had seen the worst that radiation poisoning could do to a child and had to lecture herself to be content so long as the baby was born alive. If there were problems, deformities, whatever, the baby would be loved and cared for. But so much better if it was born whole and healthy.

Her mother-in-law couldn't keep her hands off her. Shinsa would have Patty lie down with her tummy exposed and massage the bulge with an ointment she had obtained from a Zen monk. The ointment had a pleasant aroma, like rosemary, and had to be left on for an hour. As she massaged Patty, she chanted a prayer over and over, not in Japanese, that sounded to Patty like, 'rub-a-dub-dub'. Kado's mother said it was from

Nepal. Religious rituals from all over were being invoked to overcome the possible harm to the baby of the atomic bomb. Patty was happy to receive assistance from any deity at all. But the baby's heartbeat was not entirely regular, a concern. Kado listened to the heartbeat himself and confessed himself a little worried. He outlined five possible causes and thought the most likely cause was ventricular septal defect—a hole in the wall between ventricles. A frantic note came into Shinsa's chanting.

The baby, a boy, was born on time at Kado's hospital. Kado delivered it himself. The baby howled as he ought and displayed the right number of fingers and toes. Kado listened to his heart and detected the same irregularity as in the womb. Patty, the rigour of birth already forgotten held out her arms, 'Gimme!' and cradled the baby to her breast. She wept with happiness and cooed the baby's name, Francis, in keeping with Kado's dead wife's family tradition of giving Catholic names. Patty's mother-in-law and father-in-law called in as soon as they were permitted, twenty minutes after the birth. Shinsa was besotted with the baby instantly and kissed his cheeks. Kado's father, Maka, produced the first genuine smile Kado had seen on his face since the bomb, and the death of his sons and daughters-in-law and grandchildren.

Patty didn't ask if the defect in her baby's heart could be fixed. She expected it to be, without question. Kado had to tell her that Francis wouldn't be ready for surgery for two years and that it was possible that he could die in that period. Patty said that if he let the baby die, she would cease speaking to him. 'You keep him alive. Then get Haru to fix him.' Haru was a surgeon, a friend of Kado's. She alarmed herself with the way in which she held her husband accountable for the baby's survival. As tender as she was with Francis, she could look up from his face to Kado and something almost savage would come over her. He was a doctor, he must make the baby live.

He did have some good news after a month. Haru had examined Francis and reported that it was possible that the gap between the ventricles might close by itself—he'd known this to happen. But if it came to surgery, it would be difficult. 'We would have to patch. Very awkward.'

Patty's mother-in-law, besotted with the child since twenty minutes after his birth, seized on this possibility of the gap closing by itself. But the baby needed help in the healing. When Patty returned to work six months after the birth, the baby came with her in the care of Shinsa, and Patty would slip away to the nursery at intervals to breastfeed Francis. She wanted to stay with the baby, but there were so many patients at Hiroshima's hospitals and so few nurses willing to work in a radioactive atmosphere that she was forced to make the sacrifice. The hospitals were no more radioactive than anywhere else in Hiroshima, so exposure was no greater. The baby seemed well, except that he wasn't.

~

Patty took a day off to go with the baby and with her mother-in-law by train to a Zen temple fifty miles north of Hiroshima. Fast, modern trains ran on a meticulously observed timetable. Everything in Hiroshima was fast and modern. Nobody spoke about the bomb. Nobody spoke about the war at all. Whatever humiliation the Japanese had experienced in defeat had been buried almost too deep for recall. It was as if the humiliation had been altered and expressed as a devotion to industry, to construction, especially. Even where Kado and Patty lived, five miles from the booming city, new houses were being built. People from the south were moving to Hiroshima, rather than away from it. Crowds turned out on commemoration days, but all they heard—Patty had attended three—was the mayor speaking in public language and platitudes about the need for the world to embrace peace. People listened but they didn't believe anything that was said. What they believed was that the Americans and Russians were building more and bigger nuclear bombs and were likely to go to war with each other. It was widely believed that the British were developing nuclear arms and that the French and Chinese were also working on a nuclear bomb (they were). They believed that soon six or seven countries would have nuclear weapons and that these bombs would be used against Japan if the Russians and Chinese wished it so. They listened, went home, woke up the next day and continued industriously building Hiroshima into a glistening city, one of the most prosperous in Japan. They took pride in what they were achieving. They took pride in their fast, modern trains.

The temple was five miles from the station. There were no taxis so they had to walk, taking turns to push the pram uphill along a dirt road. At the temple they were met by a novice with a shaven head who greeted them courteously and told them he would convey their request for an audience to the abbot.

The master, it transpired, would be only too glad to receive them.

They were shown not to the temple but to the stables, where a tiny man in a robe and apron was using a pitchfork to clean out one of the stalls. A huge grey horse was standing motionless just outside the entrance to the stall. The master or abbot, for so it appeared that he was, put the pitchfork aside, wiped his hands on his apron and bowed to his guests. 'You are asking yourself why I don't get a novice to do this. But the horse is my friend. He works for me, I work for him. You have a baby to show me.' He reached down into the pram and lifted the baby, cradled it in his arms like a mother. 'You are worried about the child. You can stop worrying. This child will be here on earth after we are all gone. You are not Japanese,' he said to Patty in English that carried a strong accent of the southern states. 'Not American, I think. Not English. Are you Australian? Yes? I have been to Australia many years ago. Brisbane. I wanted to learn from your Aboriginal people. I spoke to Johnno, a wise man. Johnno knew much more about the world than me. Please excuse me while I continue my work.' He returned the baby to the pram.

Shinsa said, 'Welcome news, much thanks, master. May we leave a donation for the temple?'

The master cackled. 'One million US dollars.'

'Ai, too much for us to afford, master.'

'No? Then stroke the horse. His name is Hero. He pulls the wagon up the hill and down. This you can afford? The time to stroke the horse?'

Both Patty and her mother-in-law stroked with pleasure the horse's smoothly brushed neck.

'Come again,' said the master.

Over the next two months, the baby's heart gave evidence of repairing itself; of the ventricle gap closing. It was as if Francis's tiny body had consulted a blueprint and noticed a defect. Haru came to the house to examine the baby and confirmed Kado's diagnosis. 'He is fixing his own heart. It is not common, but it happens sometimes.' Shinsa applauded with joy and Patty burst into tears. She picked Francis up and held him tight. 'You clever chap. You little champion.'

Elsewhere in Hiroshima, less good fortune. Babies died in their thousands. Graveyards on the outskirts of Hiroshima were so crowded that new plots of land had to be set aside as cemeteries every month. The cemetery industry rivalled the construction of factories, apartment blocks, houses, roads and highways, shops. The mayor was deeply concerned at the death rate and wanted to call a day of community mourning. But he was talked out of it by his deputy. Morale in the city was high. Why risk damaging it to draw attention to something that could not be changed?

Patty became pregnant again. If the baby was born with troubles to contend with, she would take it to the master. He would hold it and say: 'No need to worry.'

BEFORE WES'S six-month wait for the visa was up, Vladimir Petrov ruined everything. Petrov was a second-tier diplomat in the Soviet Embassy in Canberra who owed his appointment to Lavrentiy Beria, the head of state security and the most feared man in the Soviet Union. Following the death of Stalin, a struggle for the leadership of the Communist Party broke out with Nikita Khrushchev and his supporters on one side, Georgy Malenkov and his gang on the other. Beria also wanted the leadership, but nobody on either side wanted Beria. Everyone in the Politburo had a relative or a friend who had been murdered on Beria's orders. Without the support of Stalin, who had been happy to permit Beria to murder anyone at all, his influence was diminished.

The appeal of Khrushchev to his supporters was that he had no charisma. What, another Georgian psychopath like Stalin, who could do anything he pleased? Best not. Khrushchev and his allies organised the arrest of Beria, and his execution in December 1953 was bad news for Petrov in Canberra. He feared, not unreasonably, that he would be called back to Moscow and shot. People tainted with loyalty to Beria were being shot every day. Petrov allowed himself to be cultivated by ASIO agents who promised him security, a house, access to Bondi, a pension, and what amounted to a bag of lollies whenever he asked for one. All this if he brought them evidence of Soviet espionage in Australia. Petrov took the bait. He didn't tell his wife, Evdokia, who also worked at the embassy, what he was planning. He was prepared to leave her to whatever fate the Soviet state might have in mind for her.

Once news of Vladimir's defection reached Moscow, Soviet security agents bundled Evdokia on a flight back to Russia, but were prevented from leaving Australia by the Australian police, who took her off the flight at Darwin. The prime minister of the day, and of many, many days to come, Bob Menzies, cheerfully exploited the Petrov defection and the attempted kidnap of Evdokia to stoke up the simmering hatred of communists in a big part of the electorate to melodrama and hysteria. He ordered a royal commission into Soviet espionage in Australia, conducted at lightning speed, and the commission found, so it said, plenty. The commission's findings were not made public, just the conclusion. Menzies, outraged by the look of him, red in the face, broke off diplomatic relations with the Soviet Union and ordered the embassy closed.

Wes's visa application disappeared in the helter-skelter of packing papers into tea-chests and cardboard cartons. He had no need to be told in any official way that his visa would never be heard of again. He'd followed the Petrov drama with sickening foreboding. But he had a plan. His grandmother had been born in London and he was entitled to a British passport, which Doris, his grandmother, had secured for him so that he could carry it with him to New Guinea. Her motive was to protect him if he were captured by the Japanese, who, she reasoned, would treat him more leniently if they thought he was British rather than a crude Australian. Wes thanked Doris, but left the passport with Teddy when he departed for New Guinea. Wes still had it. He intended to go to London and apply for a visa at the Soviet embassy with his British passport as a British citizen. Doris, in her application, had entered Wes's full name, Wesley George Fox Heavenly Grace Cunningham. In his Australian passport, the authorities were content with plain Wesley George Cunningham. So he might be thought a different Wesley Cunningham, as he hoped.

~

Wes wanted to tell Bill at the Department of Foreign Affairs, or wherever, what he intended to do, so he sent a letter to the DFA, Canberra, simply addressed to 'Bill'. Astonishingly, in three weeks he received a reply, short. 'Come to Canberra on October 2nd, ask for me at reception, 3.00 p.m.'

This time Bill hadn't been in the water. He was wearing a stylish green suit, close-fitting, with gold buttons. His hair was cut to leave some length and brushed straight back. His tan had faded, but he was as cheerful as if he'd come straight from the beach. Espionage seemed a source of delight to him, like a thrilling game he had mastered in all its nuances. The office was the completely blank little place in which they'd met before.

Bill sat down and rested his folded hands on the desk. 'I've just come from lunch with your prime minister. Amiable fellow. Appetite on him like a famished jackal. Now, one or two things, Wes. Oh, and if you're wondering why I've given myself over to your case, it's simply because I admire you. And your love and loyalty to Elizabeth. You know, I was home recently— England—and Mrs Bill and I were having one of our customary chilly episodes. I asked myself, what would my life be like if I felt the way about Mrs Bill that Wesley Cunningham feels about the prospective Mrs Wesley? But I don't have your heart, Wes, alas. And if you scooped my soul out with a spoon, you could probably fill an old marmalade jar with a substance the colour of tar. Enough of the sorrows of Bill. You want to go to London and apply for a Red visa on your British passport. That would probably work, and in London you can obtain, generally, a visa in six weeks. When it comes to your interview, do not mention that you are a Quaker, or a believer in any sort of "supreme being". The Russians don't welcome Quakers.

'But there is an issue, Wes. As you no doubt suspect, I read the letters that go back and forth between you and Elizabeth. You do so suspect?'

'Yes,' said Wes.

'Better to suspect me. You won't always be right, but more so than wrong. Now, in her last two letters she spoke of samizdat. So you know what that is, don't you? Wes, what she is doing is dangerous. If she is detected, they will charge her and imprison her. For years. If she is arrested, we will know. And I will tell you. Russian prisons, Wes, very, very harsh. Warn her.'

'I'm worried. She is a fanatic by nature. She is likely to be as crazy about opposing the Soviets as she was in supporting them.'

'Wes, you have it right. She is indubitably crazy. But her craziness is about justice, at least. You will have noticed what is happening in the United States, with Senator McCarthy. That's a craziness that is placed at the service of injustice. In America, your Elizabeth would have been locked up for twenty years, or even executed.

My sceptred isle has already tested atomic bombs on your red soil, and the Soviets are not in the least interested. In any case, we are not in competition with the Russians. We merely wish to stay ahead of the French. If it comes to another Agincourt, an atomic bomb will be our English longbow. When you get to London, come into Scotland Yard and leave your address and the Scotland Yard people will get it to me. "Bill" will be adequate. And please to remember, Wes, that this conversation is bound by the terms of our agreement. I may well see you in London in a few months.'

Teddy Cunningham was a competent builder, but he needed instruction. Wes couldn't leave him in charge of finishing the two houses and Max, his other brother, was busy elsewhere. Wes himself had completed Jolene's sunroom, but he had to ask the owners of the two new houses for a two-month break. To have Wes Cunningham agree to build a house for you was a privilege and the owners, the O'Connors and Davises, were happy to allow Wes the time to do whatever he needed to do, go where he needed to go. (Russia? Really?)

In December 1954, Wes arrived in London and stayed, by arrangement, with a fellow Quaker, Professor Michael Kemp in a Georgian villa just off Russell Square. The professor, now retired, had taught at the London School of Economics, close to the British Museum. He had visited Almond Tree twice with his wife and stayed with the Cunninghams. His wife was now dead, and his eldest son had moved away. The huge house was home to the professor and his two younger sons. He gave Wes a room on the upper floor with a view down to the square, once the room of his eldest son, Japanese prints on the wall, left behind by the son, Spender, who'd had a passion for Asian art. The professor's three sons, born in the late 1930s and early 1940s, had each been named after a poet—Spender, Auden and, a little awkwardly, Sassoon. The two boys were away visiting their aunt in Ottawa, so it was just the professor and Wes.

The professor's wife, Marigold, Wes remembered as loquacious, the professor as a man who preferred to sit and listen, posing an occasional question. All that had changed. Perhaps it was the death of his talkative wife that had freed something in him, or the need to express certain views knowing that he was likely to be dead of cancer in two years, but he was full of opinions, the most alarming of which were to do with atomic war. He welcomed it. He said it would give the world a chance to start again, a clean new beginning. 'Look at the people in the street, Wes. Their hearts and souls are exhausted. They have lost the capacity to honour life.'

Wes told him of his sister's experience in Hiroshima. 'She saw with her own eyes what an atomic bomb can do. I don't want that for anyone. The many thousands of people who died had hopes and plans. They had children. And now my sister is nursing those left sick by radiation poisoning. A hundred thousand. I don't think she believes that an atomic bomb leaves everything clean for a new beginning.'

Most days he left the house early and walked about London. He called at Scotland Yard to leave his address. The police officer he offered the address to said, 'Bill? Who the bloody hell is Bill? Bill Bumfluff?' He called another officer, more senior, who said, 'I'll take care of it.'

A letter came from Bill to the address off Russell Square. It enclosed Beth's most recent letter. 'Forward this on to your parents,' said the note with the letter. 'The page that is meant for them. Complex nonsense, isn't it? I sometimes think I'll take up dealing in stamps. I collect stamps, you know. Incidentally, if you happen to bump into Guy Burgess in Moscow, give him my regards. It could happen. We were friends before he flew the coop. You would know about Don McLean and Guy, would you not?'

Beth's letter to him was wildly affectionate in the first paragraph. Then it concentrated on samizdat. 'I'm writing out the poems of a wonderful poet, a woman who signs her work Radost, which is the Russian word for joy.' And much more about Joy and her work.

He went each day to the British Museum, and to the National Gallery in Trafalgar Square. Saw all the sights. But he couldn't give himself to tourism because his heart, each day, each hour, was coiled in longing for Beth. He had stayed in Almond Tree long enough to attend Franny's wedding. He doubted there had ever been a more beautiful bride in the world, in a dress painstakingly sewn by her mother. Franny took him aside at the reception and said, 'You could have had me.' He didn't know what to say, so he kissed her on the cheek and wandered away. And now he was where he was, gazing up at a huge Rubens canvas and yearning for Beth.

When the six weeks had passed, he called in to the Soviet Embassy and was shown to the office of a small, corpulent woman with greying hair permed in a helmet-like style that hadn't been seen in Australia since the 1940s. She was not friendly.

'Here is your visa. It is for two weeks. You must obey all the laws of the Soviet Union.'

'Two weeks. I requested one month.'

'Two weeks. You are for seeing your friend. She cannot leave Moscow. Two weeks is enough for Moscow. You will stay at Gorki Hotel. It is near to where your friend is living.' He left with his two weeks.

Two days later he flew from London to Vienna, then after a six-hour delay, to Moscow. He took a grubby state taxi with a damaged gearbox to the Gorki Hotel on Nicolskaya Street and checked into a room the size of an auditorium with a single bed against one wall. He had sent a telegram from Vienna to tell Beth where he was to stay, and at six in the afternoon, after the end of her working day, she burst into his room without knocking, smothered his face in kisses, stripped him of his clothes, and herself, and bustled him into the single bed. She didn't allow him to get the condoms from his suitcase. She barely gave him time to recover between sessions before renewing lovemaking and clung to him with such force that he winced with pain, but without protesting.

'Are you really here? I mean really here? I've wanted you and wanted you. You have to do this every day, every, every day. Except when I'm showing you about. First we're going to the Pushkin Museum because it's open late. But darling, I still have to work. They won't give me any time off. You have to stay here in bed all day while I'm working just waiting for me. Reading a book or something. Did you bring *Middlemarch*? Good. You have to read it to me from where we stopped. I'll tell you something. I want to get pregnant. You see what's happened? I'm crazier than Franny. Was she beautiful in her wedding dress and was it low-cut, her tits all over the place I bet? Well you can't marry her because you're going to marry me. Me! Whisper when you talk, darling, they're listening.'

The experience of Beth whispering to him with her lips against his ear was exquisite, and her body clasped to him so that her pulse beat against his flank was like a language being spoken each to the arteries of the other. Bizarrely, Bill's friend Guy Burgess popped into his head.

He asked in a whisper if Beth had met him.

'Burgess?' She laughed. 'Yes, I met him at a reception for a field marshal who was retiring and had asked for me to be there because he liked foreign girls. I was a big disappointment, I think. Guy wanted to know about the cricket and I didn't know anything and he liked dirty jokes and I didn't know any so he told me a whole lot of filthy jokes of his own and I laughed but I hated them. The field marshal wanted to sleep with me but I said no, of course, but he followed me around the whole evening, squeezing my behind. Grotesque.'

'And if he hadn't been grotesque?'

'You mean if he was young and handsome like you? Well I'd have let him enjoy me in the broom closet. You wouldn't have minded, my darling?'

'I would have had to kill him. Going against the teachings of my faith.'

'Would you, dearest? Would you have killed him?' She tickled his ribs. 'For me? How romantic. Until they hanged you.'

She introduced him to Oleg and Bessie and showed him where she worked on the samizdat. Oleg and Bessie had put together a beautiful dinner, a stew with rice said to have originated in Afghanistan, and even produced some American wine from California they'd been saving for an occasion like this. After dinner, Wes drew from his shoulder bag two 78 records he'd purchased in a

second-hand record shop near Foyles in London. He'd
been advised that one by Robert Johnson and the other by
Louis Armstrong were blues classics. They'd almost been
confiscated at Moscow customs but after a fight between
three customs officers, the most senior, who appeared
to revere Louis Armstrong, prevailed and the 78s were
allowed to enter the Soviet Union. When Bessie saw the
gift she screamed and jumped up and down, threw her
arms around Wes and kissed him on the mouth. She said
in English, which she spoke well, 'I bless the ground you
walk on, beloved comrade.' They sat and listened to both
records. The music was alien to Wes but left Bessie, Oleg
and Beth ecstatic.

Beth had to be back at her apartment by eight, and
so she was, with Wes. The cops didn't mind men visiting
the apartments, or staying the night, but with Eva there,
it was impossible to make love. Eva said, 'You can fuck
her, I don't mind.' Wes kissed Beth and they parted. It
would be six o'clock the following day, after Beth's day's
work finished, before they could meet up again. She asked
him if he had any American dollars, and he did. 'Bring
them with you tomorrow. I have a plan.'

Wes's huge room at the Gorki was silent at night. Hardly
any traffic noise, no sirens. He was in the bed in which he
had made love to Beth again and again. He could smell
her body, and it kept him awake. Smiling. God in your
heart was an inventor. He used the materials at hand.

Beth waved to Wes that day in Almond Tree, and from Wes's response He made something that had years in it. The tinsel lilies, the beach daisies, the sheepskins for Russia posters, the long road to the Gorki—all imagined by God, down to Louis Armstrong and Robert Johnson.

In Russia, a US dollar was paper gold. The police on duty on the ground floor of Beth's apartment were prepared to sign her out for the night, 'to attend a sick relative' for ten US dollars, which Wes handed over without subterfuge. They walked to Oleg and Bessie's apartment and before eating anything went straight to bed in the spare room. This time, they used condoms, at Wes's insistence. 'Beth darling, you can't get pregnant now. You know that.' Outside, Louis Armstrong played. Then Billie Holiday. Bessie called out in English: 'Please! We're starving!'

They went each night to Oleg and Bessie's, but kept the lovemaking until later, after dinner, after the blues, after Beth had completed an hour of samizdat, after responsibility. Wes gave Bessie and Oleg a thousand rubles to cover the cost of the extra food. Beth was never permitted to cook, since she didn't know how. Once dinner was over, and conversation (a third world war) and the blues, the apartment was hot; the one thing that could be relied on was the heating.

Beth no longer spoke of her pride in Russia's nuclear weapons, but of her fear of them. Bessie, in spite of years of trying, had not yet become pregnant, and now had to ask herself if she should be thinking of children when the total destruction of the world was a genuine possibility. Wes told them of his sister Patty's experience in Hiroshima. 'She and her Japanese husband had a child, even though they'd been living with radiation in their bodies for eight years. She's pregnant again now. I admire her courage, her and her husband, Kado. They could easily move away from Hiroshima. But that's where their work is, thousands of sick people, sick babies. She thinks that's where God wants her to be, and if she wants a baby, that's where it has to be born.'

'God?' said Bessie. 'He made the people who made the bomb too, no?'

Wes didn't answer. But he might have said that God had nothing to do with the bomb; that God only hopes that human inventiveness will find a better destination. That God despairs, in the same way as us, and has no power to intervene.

Wes, free to wander about Moscow while Beth was at work, walked along ordinary streets, looking at ordinary people, none of whom seemed capable of smiling. The older buildings were attractive enough, maybe in need of a coat of paint and some close attention to the woodwork. The newer buildings, three-storey concrete blocks, were unwelcoming. Down one narrow street he found a boy of about sixteen working alone on the construction of the upper half of a red brick wall that had been destroyed, perhaps in the war. The boy, probably an apprentice, was attempting to split bricks in half with a mallet and a cold chisel, and having no success. Wes watched for a few minutes then suggested to the boy in sign language that he allow him to have a go. The boy shrugged and stepped back from the bricks. Wes knelt down with the cold chisel and hammer and cut a shallow groove on the four sides of the brick at the exact halfway point, then mounted the brick on another, put his knee on the grooved brick and struck it with the mallet. The brick broke along the groove perfectly. He gave the boy to understand that he would break as many half-bricks as were needed for the wall, and the boy indicated that he didn't know. Wes stood back and judged the number of half-bricks that would be required, then set to work and fashioned twenty half-bricks. The boy was delighted and shook Wes's hand vigorously. Wes then helped the boy make mortar of the right consistency, cleaned his hands on a rag and said goodbye. The boy said: 'America?' Australia, said Wes. 'Ah, Australia,' said the boy. 'Good!' It was the one English word he knew.

On Beth's day off, she came to the Gorki at eight in the morning with bread and cheese and she and Wes made love until midday. She made him sing 'The Water Is Wide' and had him read from *Middlemarch*. 'Can this be our life? Making love and reading and singing?'

215

'What about the people, Beth?'

'The people can make love and sing and read, too.'

He laughed, and she sat up in bed abruptly and looked down at him.

'Don't make fun of me.'

'I'm not. But it's funny, the change in you. Once the people were your idols.'

'And now it's comical that I'm a bad communist.'

She threw back the covers and climbed out of bed, picked up her clothes from the floor and went to the shower, the only modern feature of the huge room. It was a round glass cylinder with bright new stainless-steel taps that worked in a complicated way. She didn't close the bathroom door. She emerged naked and dried herself in front of Wes, watching him all the time. And dressed herself. 'My modesty has gone, thanks to you. Have a shower and get dressed. I'm angry with you.'

She took him, unspeaking, to the visitors' entrance to Red Square at the Kutafya Tower and then past three- and four-storey buildings until they reached an area in front of the home of the Supreme Soviet. She turned to him and said: 'I once danced here. I sang "The Red Flag" and people applauded me. I was a good socialist then. But I fell in love, Wes. You made me a bad socialist, so don't laugh at me.' She was sobbing by this time. Tourists stopped and stared at her as Wes held her in his arms. Soldiers stopped too, and puzzled over her tears. One called out: 'English?' Wes said, in the Russian he'd been taught by Bessie, 'No, we are Australians.' Three of the soldiers came forward and embraced them both. One sang a ragged version of the opening of 'Waltzing Matilda'.

'This, an Australian taught to me.'

Beth took him outside the Kremlin walls again, and showed him St Basils. 'Wacky, isn't it? We're not going inside. It's extremely ornate and very depressing. Just the opposite of your faith. That lovely simplicity.'

Wes paid ten dollars each evening for permission for Beth to stay out all night at Bessie and Oleg's apartment. They ate dishes that did not vary much from one evening to the next. The Californian wine was finished after two nights, but then there was vodka, which knocked Wes out after one glass so that he had to be put to bed. After that he avoided the vodka. Beth could throw down one glass after another and became merrier the more she drank. She had Wes sing English folk songs, and also recite 'Mulga Bill's Bicycle', translating it for Oleg, whose English was scratchy. Beth asked Wes if he knew 'The Man from Snowy River'. He did, all of it, and after some brandy, stood and recited it, in a halting way, with Beth translating. This was likely the first time the poem had been recited in the Soviet Union.

On the second-last evening, Beth insisted that all four of them sit in a circle on the floor while she revealed a plan. Beth and Bessie and Oleg threw down vodka from small glasses, while Wes sipped from a glass of brandy, which he seemed able to tolerate. Judging by the stern expression on Beth's face, this was serious.

'Now, we three are Marxists, or have sympathy for Marx. But it was spoilt. This is not Marx, it's totalitarianism. It's terror. Right?'

Bessie and Oleg nodded. 'It's shit,' said Bessie.

'So we have to resist. With samizdat. By getting the truth to the people. Wes, I want you to take Joy's poems back to Australia then send them to a Russian language publisher in Paris, so that they can be published and hundreds of copies, thousands, can be smuggled in and sold in secret. It's been done before.'

Wes raised his eyebrows. 'That's going to get this Joy lady into a lot of trouble.'

'She's ready for it. The Russian version can be translated into English. If she becomes well known in the West, it will be harder for the authorities to victimise her.'

Wes told her of Bill's warning. 'And if the poems are found in my luggage at the airport, I will never be allowed back into Russia.'

Bessie said, 'Not in your luggage. Sewn into the lining of your overcoat. We have someone who will do an excellent job.'

Beth read aloud three of Joy's poems, translating into English as she went. They were terrible. There was no joy in them, and no poetry. She wrote about the leaders of Russia as ravening wolves who fed on the flesh of newborn babies.

Wes could see disaster. 'I know you have to do something. Your country is ruled by tyrants. But is the tiny influence you'll have worth jail? I'll help, but I hate the risk you're taking. Also the poems are not good.'

'She's taking a chance. It's a statement.'

'Yes, but Beth, a statement is not a poem. Wolves eating babies. It's not Pushkin.'

'You have read Pushkin?' said Bessie.

They slept together at Oleg and Bessie's apartment on his last night in Moscow; talking, not sleeping. 'I know the poems are not good, Wes. But they might publish them as politics. I have to help her. It's all she's got.'

'It's okay. Only don't get caught. Please, Beth.'

'And be without you? Never.'

He picked up the overcoat on the day of his departure and it rustled like a Guy Fawkes bonfire. He couldn't imagine how the noise would go unnoticed. He carried the coat. Beth was not given leave to visit the airport, but Bessie and Oleg were. They farewelled him before he entered the departure lounge. Russian security waved him through, no interest in his luggage or his person. On the aeroplane, when he stowed his coat in the baggage locker, it crackled again. But the stitching survived to Vienna, to London and, ultimately, to Almond Tree.

Chapter 23

SOMETHING WAS wrong. Five months into her second pregnancy, Patty had developed a sense of foreboding. Kado said everything was fine, but it wasn't. She went with Shinsa and Francis to see the master again, making the long hike over the dirt road.

He was not in the stable this time, but sitting cross-legged in a garden with a fountain, among a strange type of orange bamboo. He remembered both of them perfectly, even their names. He was smiling.

'No more bombs, so far,' he said. 'Good fortune.'

Patty and her mother-in-law sat before him on fine gravel, not cross-legged.

'Master, I have a feeling that something is wrong with the baby in my womb.'

The master roused himself and lifted Francis from the pram, bared his tummy and rubbed his nose against it until the baby squealed with laughter.

'A happy baby,' he said. 'In the world, nothing is so happy as a baby. Nothing with such love. When the baby takes milk from you, that is love. Come with me.'

He led them out of the formal garden into an orchard, where apples hung from the branches of the trees, bright red. 'Tomorrow the novices pick them. Today, take one apple each for Hero.'

Each carrying an apple, the master led them back to the stable. The master held the apple out to Hero and he took huge bites from it avidly. To his guests he said, 'Drop them on the ground, or he might bite your fingers.' Patty and Shinsa dropped the apples at Hero's feet and he fell to them with gluttonous delight.

'Pat him,' said the master, in his singing voice. And so Patty and her mother-in-law patted Hero's neck while he munched. 'He has been waiting for you. He said to me, "When will our guests return with a million dollars?" I said, "On March the tenth."'

He had Patty stretch out on the straw of the stable and knelt beside her. He felt not the bulge of her baby, but her feet, after removing her shoes. He rubbed his cheeks against her bare soles. Then sat up. 'Some trouble,' he said. 'Some trouble for you and your baby. It is a daughter. She will live, but some trouble.'

'What trouble?'

'This I cannot say. Some trouble. The baby will count on you. The daughter already loves you. She will count on you.'

This time, the master asked for ten million dollars, and laughed with a giggle like a young girl when told it was much more than Patty could afford.

'Do not give me ten million US dollars,' he said. 'But only love your daughter, whatever the trouble. I will give you some apples to take with you for your table.'

Patty's worry was unrelenting. She told Kado, repeating it over and over, 'Whatever the trouble is, we will overcome it. Anything, we will overcome it. Okay?'

'Yes, Patty. Anything.'

She went to work until the eighth month. A special hospital had been built in Hiroshima to cater to people suffering from radiation poisoning, and to Hiroshima women giving birth. That was where she worked. She saw, and had already seen, frightful deformities. The worst was a baby born with its brain exposed. Any—all—of these deformities could be in her baby. She said: 'We will overcome it.'

When her baby daughter was born—Esther, a biblical rather than a Catholic name, but acceptable to everyone— the 'trouble' the master had spoken of was immediately evident. The baby's fingers were tightly joined by a type of webbing. It was a condition Patty had seen a number of times before, and she didn't despair. The procedure was to surgically separate the fingers at six months, then break them and reset them. When the fingers were reset and healed, the baby could require a type of therapy to restore independent movement in the fingers. It would all take a year.

Francis's cardiac problem was not necessarily caused by radiation poisoning, but the deformity of Esther's fingers was. It made Patty's heart ache to see the baby's clumps of fingers unable to grip. Esther howled in exasperation, as if she knew what her hands should do, but couldn't. Patty and Kado took the risk. The consequences had to be accepted. Patty stroked the baby's head and said, 'It will be okay. Wait, just wait.'

Haru operated on the baby at six months, separated the fingers, broke them, reset them. When the baby recovered from the anaesthetic, she screamed with pain for two weeks. Haru gave her painkillers, a little too powerful for a baby, but not dangerously so. Her hands were bandaged for a month. When the bandages were removed, it took a further two months of manipulation for the fingers to move independently, and without pain. They looked ugly, with scars on both sides of each finger and the thumbs. But they were functional. Haru said to Kado and Patty: 'No more babies.'

~

The bomb and its poison had not prevented Patty and Kado from having children. This was, in its way, a victory, and when Esther's fingers were fixed—so far as they could be—Patty exulted. She stood one day with a child in each arm and wept for joy.

'Take your bombs to hell,' she called to the Hiroshima sky, 'and never come back, you bastards!'

Chapter 24

TWO MORE letters came from Moscow to Almond Tree, full of affection and enquiries about the fate of the poems Wes had posted to Paris. The address was not, after all, that of a publisher but that of a comrade in Paris who would forward them to a publisher then notify Wes of the outcome. He heard nothing from Paris in two months. A letter came for Wes from Bill, to say that he had business to transact in Melbourne during a short stay; would be driving down from Canberra and hoped to call in at Almond Tree to visit Wes for an hour or two on the way back.

Bill (his name had been Bill for so long now that it was accepted) arrived at Wes's house in the middle of a Wednesday morning, driving a polished red Cadillac convertible. He hopped out and spread his hands towards the car. 'A monster, isn't it, Wes. But something magnificent about it. Do you want a drive?'

'No. Do you want a cup of tea? I don't have any Earl Grey. Bushells.'

They stood before the house, Bill admiring the workmanship.

'I'm hoping you'll have some news for me.'

'If I were you, my dear Wesley, I'd be hoping I don't. Your girlfriend is risking her neck copying out these verses. I would assume that these poems, like the majority, are frightful. You've read them? You told me you carried them back in the lining of your overcoat. Lining overcoats is the best possible use they could be turned to. Your contact in Paris sent them to a colleague in Paris, who advised me. I didn't read them but he said they were shockers.'

'Yes, I read them. Shockers, as you say. What brings you to Melbourne?'

'The Labor Party split, Wes. A chap by the name of McManus who's gone berserk. Those of us keeping a watchful eye on the wide brown land don't like it. We want the anti-communists all in one place, under the one umbrella. And we don't like rabid anti-communists at all, Wes. We prefer our anti-communists to behave like gentlemen. Far easier to get on with. So I went along to a meeting with Frank Mac, a Catholic. Dear God, defend me from the Catholics. They're still attracted to burning heretics at the stake. No reasoning with them. The kindling, the crackling of the fire—it excites them.'

Bill wanted to know where the original almond tree of Almond Tree was located, and had to be told that it no longer existed. 'Almond trees only last for thirty years, Bill. But I can show you an almond orchard that started from the original almond tree. It's two miles away over those pasture paddocks. Want to see? We can take your Cadillac. Down the dirt road.'

The orchard, Perce and Lotte Cornwallis's, lay below them as they rolled to a halt in a cloud of dust, spread over five acres and all in vivid white bloom. Further away to the west stood Carl Braun's pears—Carl, a German immigrant before the war used to wander up and down in the shopping centre giving out leaflets. *The Nazis are the enemies of all civilised people, especially my mother-in-law who is Jewish. Please my wish don't be for blaming me!!!* No one did. To the north, the hills began and reared to a fair height without stupefying anyone with their elevation, a regal blue under the brilliant sun. Somewhere in the side of the biggest hill, called, without much imagination, Big Hill, the Champagne Falls descended for eighty feet.

Outside the car, sitting on a stump, Bill said he found it hard to conceive how a girl like Beth, hemmed in by beauty on each side, had developed such a gaunt vision of life. 'If you hail from some fetid hell-hole on a Russian estate, perhaps you have an argument. But here, Wes?'

'Beth wanted justice, that was all. But you're not

going to squeeze much justice out of the Soviet Union.'

Bill left in the afternoon, with a wave from his shiny Cadillac and Wes went back to rebuilding Chinese Town.

When Hoong Li died in the horse trough on the day of the spur fire, nearly all of his houses in Chinese Town went up in the flames. They were insured by Hoong Li with canny care for more than they had been worth. John Li, his eldest son, who inherited the insurance bonanza and the land on which Chinese Town stood, intended to rebuild everything. All the houses on the forest side—the charred forest—would be brick. All of those further from the forest would be timber. Altogether, twenty-three houses; and Wes Cunningham would, by agreement, oversee the entire project, which would take three years. Migrant workers would be brought in, mostly from Italy, to work on the project but they would take all their directions from Wes. The migrants, mostly from Italy, would be boarded with families and in vacant houses all over the shire. The attraction of the project to Wes was the money he would make, and the attraction of money was that he would be able to afford another airfare to Moscow in nine months. It cost a fortune and he couldn't borrow again from the community fund.

He informed Beth of all this. He also told her that the Paris publishers, according to Bill, said that they would publish the poems as a political statement, even though they had misgivings about the quality. 'At least they've got guts,' she wrote. 'But it will make big, big trouble here, and I'll have to be especially cautious. Oh God, nine months Wes. Nine months. It will kill me.'

Wes had Clarrie Carpenter draft the plans for the first three houses and went to work on the foundations, carting everything he needed down the spur road with a couple of Italians, Luca and Antonio, driving the trucks: stocky workmen from Naples who barely spoke English but could be made to understand what was required. He worked faster than normal to be sure that he had the money he needed by December. But his commitment to craft was so ingrained that he hardly made much of an impression on his schedule. The foundations still had to be a foot deeper than average; the uprights still had to be no more than eleven inches apart; all the gables had to be reinforced with lengths of hardwood. These were the timber houses; the brick houses had to wait on four brickies from a village in Umbria. The discipline he needed to keep his occupational life separate from his emotional life was taxing. He stopped work a dozen times a day to think of the animation in Beth's face when she spoke of 'striking a blow' against the Soviet state with the same vehemence that she'd spoken of striking a blow of the same sort for the Soviet state. Completely mad.

At the same time that Wes was rebuilding Chinese Town, the Victorian Government was building an entire township to house the athletes who would attend the

Melbourne Olympics of 1956. Wes included news of the preparations for the Olympics in his letters to Beth and was told in her reply not to waste space. Instead, tell her about politics. Did Menzies still reign supreme? (Yes.) Had the Petrov fiasco hurt party membership in Australia? (Yes.) When he came to Moscow again, could they stay in bed all day and all night? Could they make love until they collapsed and had to be taken to hospital? Say yes! (Yes.) And she said that Joy had been arrested. This turned out to be the most significant piece of news in any of Beth's letters, according to a note from Bill.

> They will torture this Joy for the sake of her poetry-cum-political statement. There is a rather unyielding faction in the KGB, as state security is now known, that wants to hang anyone found guilty of samizdat. The faction won't get its way just for the moment. But the torture will go ahead. We have to depend on this Joy woman's wherewithal. If she implicates Beth, nothing will save her.

This division between the emotional and occupational was no longer possible. Wes worked all day with a heart suffering blow after blow, like a hammer striking an anvil. One of the four new Umbrian bricklayers looked him in the eye one day and placed his hand over Wes's heart. 'Pain,' he said. 'Sorry to you.'

⁓

In October, Hungarian students in Budapest marched in the streets to protest the Soviet Union's dominance in Hungarian politics. In the manner of student protests, no one was in charge and there was no agreed program of reform. Just frustration with the Russians, and with the doormat status of the Russian-approved Hungarian Government. Once the protests gathered momentum, attacks on the police escalated, the throwing of projectiles ranging from smashed cobblestones, bricks and, finally, Molotov cocktails. Workers joined in and all at once there were leaders, a number of them, and the clashes were now with the military. Initially, the Russians left it to the Hungarian regime to restore order by shooting protestors, but when not enough were shot, the Russians took over the shooting themselves. Also, the protestors had begun to call what they were up to a 'revolution', and this the Russians would not abide. The Russians considered that they had copyright on the term, at least in the twentieth century. They crushed the uprising in a week and appointed a new government and ordered the Hungarian Olympic team to swallow its grievances and keep its collective arse down in Australia. The first the Hungarian team knew of the Russian invasion was what they read in Australian newspapers.

Bill telephoned Wes in early December of 1956 and said he was in Melbourne, without the Cadillac, and urgently needed to see him. He would meet him at a big restaurant known as the Russell Collins, unsurprisingly located downstairs on the corner of Russell Street and Collins Street, at midday on the Wednesday. 'I was supposed to get a letter in late November from Beth. Is this to do with that?'

'This is a face-to-face matter, Wes. On Wednesday.'

Wes got a lift to the city with Lenny Chapman, who drove the smallgoods van all over the shire and was off to Victoria Market to restock. No need to think of what to talk to Lenny about; he had the conversation covered: football, cricket, fishing for trout in Jewel Creek. Wes was dropped off right on the corner of Russell and Collins. The restaurant was stunning; so many booths, so many customers. Where he would find Bill was a puzzle, until a tubby man in shirtsleeves approached him, introduced himself as Georgio, and asked if he was looking for Bill. 'Bill is what you call him,' said Georgio. 'A mysterious man, yes? He saved my life in Cyprus in the war. From a firing squad. You think I don't love this man?'

Georgio led him to the back of the restaurant and through a swinging door to a private room, with a beautiful frieze of mermaids and dolphins. Bill, sitting in a booth, stood to thank Georgio and shake Wes's hand.

'A drink?' said Georgio. 'Macallan for you, my friend, of course. And for your guest?'

'Nothing,' said Wes.

'No, a Scotch for Wes, too. You'll need it.'

Georgio said: 'The two most handsome men in

Melbourne, hidden away. You should be out there where the customers can see you.'

When Georgio departed, Wes and Bill sat facing each other on either side of the booth.

'Wonderful place, isn't it, Wes. Art deco. Only a few in the world like this. I'm here in Melbourne fairly often, you know; vetting the defectors from the Hungarian team this time. Lots of them. You saw they played a water polo match against the Russians the other day? A bloodbath. Usually I come here to train spies and dear God, do they need training. Your people's idea of a subtle, probing question to the Hungarians is "Are you a secret Russian agent?" There would be one or two or three, but it seems unlikely that they would confess on the spot.'

'You didn't ask me here to talk about spies and Hungarians, Bill. I haven't heard from Beth for seven months.'

'Indeed, no, Wes.'

At this moment, Georgio returned with the drinks, bowed theatrically to Bill and departed.

Bill sipped his Scotch. Wes left his untouched. When Bill put his glass down, he spread both of his hands on the table. Something that Wes had not noticed before: Bill was missing the nail of each middle finger. Noticing Wes's glance, Bill said, 'Gestapo. 1943 in Vichy. I was rescued by the Maquis. Wes, Beth is in prison. The poet and maker of political statements betrayed her. Under torture, one assumes.'

Wes bowed his head with his hands over his face. 'Jesus God,' he said.

'She's in remand. Held in Butyrka prison for eight months. She will face a tribunal in prison, be found guilty and, according to our information, be given a two-year sentence, down from six in recognition of her former status as a friend of the Soviet people.'

'I should never have taken those poems. What was in my head?'

'Wes my friend, what was in your head was love, apparently. Wisdom, no. Simple common sense, no. Despite all you've learnt about the Soviet state, you still don't comprehend what you're facing. Wes, they draw the line precisely nowhere. Butyrka prison is hellish.' Bill sat back in his booth and crossed his arms. 'Beth had two further years to endure before she could return to Australia. Two years as a heroine of the Soviet Union. She would have survived. But two years as an enemy of the Soviet people in Butyrka prison, living on starvation rations, subject to terrible abuse, no, she will not survive, Wes. A skinny little thing like her. I am sorry. I've been to see the head of your security, asking if Australia could intervene. He has not the slightest interest. The Russians could hang her in front of the Kremlin without him being in the least exercised.'

Wes wanted to know if Beth could receive visitors and was told that she could in theory, after she was found guilty next week, by joining a line of around two hundred people outside the prison gates, all waiting to see husbands, sometimes wives, sons and daughters and friends inside. The guards allowed three people through each day for a sixty-second visit. 'We can get you a visa for Russia for a price. We are close to a greedy little fellow in the Soviet Embassy in London, extremely shrewd, who could get a visa for the czar, should he come back to life. We provide him with money and pretty young women, tickets to Ascot. As a known friend of Beth, you are regarded with suspicion. Nevertheless, for five hundred US dollars in cash he can get you to Moscow, where you can join the line of two hundred. Unavailingly. Then, of course, you have to find the air-fare. The air-fare is dramatically lower as of a month ago, more competition, an endorsement of capitalism.'

Wes allowed his gaze to wander the frieze of dolphins and mermaids. Then he drank his Scotch in one swallow. 'If I find the money, can you arrange the visa?'

'Really, Wes? Two hundred people? Some have been coming to the prison gates for a year.' He shook his head. 'Yes, I can arrange the visa, if you provide your passport. I'll be in Melbourne for another fortnight. Get your passport to me, and five hundred dollars. Leave it at police headquarters in Russell Street, addressed to Bill Jones. I'll speak to the police commissioner. By the time I get the visa settled, it will be early February. You can fly to Moscow on the tenth. I'm going to give you an address in Oxford Circus in London. You fly to London on your Australian passport. When your flight reaches London, come to the address. The passport and visa will be at the front desk.'

Wes went directly by taxi to see Di Porter at the printing works in Collingwood. He met her in her office and told her the story—Beth in prison, unlikely to survive. She pushed her hands into her massy dark hair and groaned. 'She's determined to die a martyr, isn't she? In Australia, she martyrs herself to the party. In Russia, she finds a way to martyr herself to freedom of speech. Of course she wants justice, but would a little sense hurt?'

Wes told her he had to get to Moscow to see her, if it was possible. He needed one thousand pounds. The other half of what he needed he would get John Li to advance him on the building project at Chinese Town. Di wrote him a cheque for cash drawn against the company's account and said if it wasn't enough, she would find more. 'You have only a slim chance of seeing her?'

'Yes, slim, but I have to try.'

'Wes, I resigned from the party after the Hungarian invasion. I talked Beth into becoming a communist. Now I've abandoned them.'

John Li lived in one of only three houses still standing in Chinese Town after the spur fire. Wes called on him on the Thursday. John wished to know the whole story before offering the money Wes was asking for as an advance on the project. And he heard it.

'Miss Hardy was communist, now she is against the communists?'

'In a fashion, John.'

'The communists want to kill her?'

'She's not under sentence of death. But the prison she is in is so brutal that she will quite possibly die.'

'Okay. Communists, I hate. Bastards. But I will help your friend, Wesley. She has seen the mistake she made in becoming a communist. You are a Christian, Wesley, not a communist. I have been to your meetings, Quaker meetings, Society of Friends. As you know, Wesley, all my family is Christian. I went to Scotch College. Communists, I disdain.'

Chapter 25

WES HAD never seen snow. He saw it now, before the gates of Butyrka prison. It settled on his overcoat shoulders and on his hair. He wasn't wearing a hat. He did as the many, many others in the line of hopeful visitors did, and stamped his feet and hugged himself. The fortress-like prison with its single tower was a long way off. Guards shuffled rather than marched up and down the line, too bored to look menacing. The ordeal was too great for some of the older people in the line. They collapsed and ramshackle ambulances carted them away, four at a time. The ambulances only departed when they had the full complement of four patients.

The majority of those in the long line were fairly aged, but there were some in their twenties, thirties.

Young or old, they didn't converse, but stood stoically gazing straight ahead. A toilet was located by the wall halfway along the line. The protocol was that if anyone had to leave the line to use the toilet, that man or woman would be allowed to rejoin the line at the point of leaving it. Wes used the toilet—it was filthy—and was welcomed back into the line. The aged lady behind him tapped him on the shoulder in the first hour of waiting. 'English?' she enquired. Wes said: 'Australian.' He heard this interesting information passed along the line, forward of him, behind him. A little later, the old lady tapped him on the shoulder again and offered him a hunk of bread, which he accepted. He stupidly hadn't thought to bring anything for himself to eat. The bread was delicious.

Standing still for hours at a stretch, the mind soon exhausts anything original that might crop up. For periods of a half-hour, he would pray for Beth, attempting to convey telepathically that he was near. But then he would find himself puzzling over the type of tree that stood by the prison's wall. An elm? No. Unless it was a species of elm he'd never seen before. A type of oak? It was difficult to tell without foliage. But this was not what he was here for, to distinguish between different sorts of trees, and he would return to prayer, unable to stop himself imagining that Beth might at that very moment being tortured.

No miasma of hopelessness had settled over those

waiting. It looked to Wes as if everyone in the line somehow expected to see their relatives and friends one fine day and would wait even if it took ten years. Their loyalty—yes, he saw that he shared it with the Russians around him. He would wait however long it took to see Beth. The woman in front of him, aged, short and frail, turned to him and smiled and patted his cheek. She said something in Russian, perhaps encouraging, and he put his arms around her and hugged her.

But now the snow was being driven by a bitter wind, and some of those in the line had to retreat to the shelter of the wall. The guards abandoned their patrols and sought their hut, a chimney on top releasing black smoke. One of them called something loudly in Russian, waving his arms in a 'go home, get the hell out of here' motion. Few withdrew. Wes, like all those who remained, doubled himself over and shuddered in the blizzard. It was now the middle of the afternoon and the sky was darkening. The guard came out of the hut again, shouting even louder. He fired two shots into the air and the line of people became a mob, hurrying to the gates. Wes was one of the last to retreat, together with a tall, thin woman of about fifty or more. She said in distinct English, 'Come with me.' He allowed her to lead him into the blizzard along a street that he happened to know was called Novoslobodskaya Street. The woman was wearing a thick red knitted cap, which she held onto her head with both hands. She signalled to him to follow her off the main street into a network of much narrower streets and alleys lined with apartments dowdy and long in need of repair. She unlocked a door and ushered him in.

It was dark inside; a bare light bulb hanging from the ceiling of the foyer wasn't working. Inside the small apartment, though, a surprise. Once she turned on the light switch, brightness and warmth; maybe a hundred-watt bulb overhead and heat was given off from a coal stove.

'My neighbour comes in and adds coals to the stove while I'm out during the day. The light bulb, I stole. My name is Anna—Anna Rothstein.' She held out her hand to Wes, who shook it after removing his leather gloves.

'Your name I know. Wesley. Take off your coat and scarf.'

'How did you know my name?'

Once Anna had removed her heavy grey overcoat, she revealed a slim figure, almost too slim for health. But she was beautiful, and would once have been much more beautiful.

'I have been going to the prison for two years, hoping to see my son Andre. I became friendly with one of the guards. He knows the story of the Australian girl. He was at her first two interrogations. He pronounced your name 'Visli', which I assumed was Wesley. She speaks excellent Russian, I was told.'

The walls of the apartment were entirely covered in

arresting paintings, each canvas filled with tiny human figures, naked, hairless, male and female, exquisitely drawn, some bending, some kneeling, some upright hugging themselves as if against the cold. On each canvas maybe one hundred figures were painted, all in flesh tones. The expressions on the visible faces were bleak, demoralised. The setting was identifiably Red Square.

Anna said: 'My son's pictures. Those we could save. He's in prison for painting decadent art, far from socialist realism. He would have simply been banned from any further exhibitions, but at his hearing he made some shocking comments about Soviet society and politics and was locked up for five years. He's unrepentant. I go each day to see him, but no success. Will I make us some tea?'

When they were sitting in a pair of threadbare armchairs with large cups of tea, she continued. 'I wanted you to come here to tell you something you won't discover by yourself,' she said. 'You will have noticed that the guards now and again take people out of the line and lead them to the top of the queue? Good. Those people have paid the guards. One hundred US dollars. Most of the people cannot afford the bribe. They sell everything without raising enough. I have one hundred US dollars. I could bribe the guards. But Andre would refuse to see me because he would know I bribed the guards. I wait out of love and loyalty. Knowing all the time that Andre is being abused. He has a terrible temper. What I have to accept is that they might very well hang him. Each week a KGB squad comes to the prison and beats the prisoners. Not the murderers, not the thieves, not the rapists. Just the anti-Soviets, like your girlfriend, like my son. You, Wesley, I could arrange to see your girlfriend. That is why I brought you here.'

The tea was rich and strong, no milk. Wes now noticed something odd: Anna's eyes were purple. Not a deep blue but a distinct purple. She was smoking a cigarette, powerful. She'd asked Wes if he'd like one but he'd declined. He smoked every now and then, but the packet Anna had offered him, with a portrait of Lenin on it, didn't seem appealing.

'I have a problem with offering the guards money,' said Wes. 'I have the money, but most of those people don't. It seems unfair.'

Anna asked quietly: 'Do you think all the other people think it is unfair?'

'I think they would, yes.'

'They do not.'

'No?'

'No. They think good luck to anyone who can find the money. Russia is not a place where we think of "fair" and "unfair". That is too innocent. You have enough to bribe the guard, Yevgeny, bless your good fortune. They have all seen you in the snow. They were impressed. Wesley, right and wrong is in your head. In your heart is Elizabeth. You may not see her alive again.'

Her purple gaze was gentle and piercing at the one

time. She stubbed out her cigarette in a large, overflowing porcelain ashtray shaped like a dove with its wings raised.

She said she was a poet, who published under the name of Anna Rosen. 'There was already an Anna Rosenberg, a regime stooge, and I didn't want to be confused with her. She writes what amounts to hymns in praise of Comrade Stalin and the courageous Soviet people. She's very pretty, I think she probably slept with Comrade Stalin. But if I awoke one morning and found myself writing like her, I'd kill myself.'

'What do you write?'

The tea, as if it weren't strong enough already, had been fortified with brandy.

Anna stood and went to a tall set of bookshelves. On the middle shelf she pointed out a row of volumes. 'These are mine. And I did not sleep with Comrade Stalin to have them published.'

She handed him a volume in English with the title *Selected Poems of Anna Rosen*. 'Read some, while I prepare us some borscht. You have tried borscht. Of course! At the Russian border they make you eat a litre of borscht. If you can't, they throw you out.'

He read: a conversation between Anna and John Keats on the subject of his odes, very elegant, and more intimate, more bawdy than anything Keats had suggested in his odes. The fourth one was about Catherine the Great; how she had brought a robust peasant sensibility to the Russian throne.

Anna called him to the table for the borscht.

He said the poems were very good, and she said they were actually better in English than in Russian. 'I translated them myself. My mother was English, and my sensibility is more English than Russian. My mother came to Moscow during the revolution. She was a communist. And she stayed. She met my father here, who came from Odessa. They fell in love. They were happy. All the communists were happy, for a time. You know the Wordsworth lines, "Bliss it was in that dawn to be alive, to be young was very heaven"? No? No matter. That was what it was like for them. I know because I was there, with my mother. I was fifteen.'

'She didn't think it would be dangerous for you? A revolution?'

'Eat your borscht, Wesley. You must eat borscht hot. And eat the bread with it. When you finish you will be a Russian. No, she didn't think it would be dangerous. She was a romantic. In any case, she couldn't leave me behind—my father had abandoned her years before. My aunt was ill and my uncle was an alcoholic. She didn't think she would return. At first we lived in luxury. We found a huge room in the palace with a kitchen attached to it. We ate off silver plates. In the kitchen, a huge amount of food. Then the looters came and cleaned everything out and we had to move to an apartment not far from here, on the park. Still attractive. We found money in drawers, gold coins from the czar's anniversary. But then the Whites counterattacked and my mother's friend was drafted into the Red Army, sent to Ukraine. And we starved. He never came back. We survived on the charity of the People's Committee and lived in the basement of an old church with forty or fifty other families. The reds were always fighting among themselves. Factions. I saw people shot every day. My mother was about to be shot because she had stolen the people's food from the palace years before, then at the last minute a new faction stormed in and shot those who were about to shoot my mother. They put my mother and me to work sewing buttons on uniforms in a factory that had once made soap. I was twenty-two. We had both lost our love of communism. The whole thing was a terrible mess. We never knew who was in charge. Then I met Maxim, a beautiful boy and I became pregnant. He was in charge of exterminating rats in our district. The rats carried plague, and he caught it and died in eight days.' Anna's voice faltered. 'But at least he saw Andre. At least he saw our beautiful Andre.' She turned her face away. Her eyes were wet.

'And now,' she said drying her eyes with a small handkerchief from her sleeve, 'my beautiful son is going to die for painting pictures, and your beloved is going to die for writing poems. Wesley, what a country!'

The next day was as cold as the previous one. The snowflakes were larger, but the wind as powerful. Wes stood in the line with Anna. She shouted at him when she wanted to be heard, and he shouted back. At least he was wearing a woollen cap today, a red one like Anna's. She showed him how to wear it, pulled down to his neck so that it covered his ears. At ten in the morning, when she caught sight of Yevgeny, the guard she knew, she took the hundred dollars from Wes, stuffed the money into one of the coarse-grained grey envelopes used in Russia and took it to the guards' hut. When she returned, she shouted to him: 'He doesn't know when!' An elderly woman from a few places ahead left the line to put her arms around him, and kissed his cheeks three times. She shouted something in Russian that went on for a minute or more. Anna said: 'She is telling you that you came all the way from Australia to see your wife. She says you are a good man. May you and your wife be together again.' Wes asked her to thank the woman, who nodded and went back to her place in the line. Other women came to him and patted his shoulder.

He wasn't selected to see Beth that day. He stayed until the guards turned away all those waiting. Fifteen people collapsed and Wes himself almost froze to death. Anna rubbed his back to keep him upright. 'You don't want to go to hospital,' she said. 'Hospital is worse than this.' When they left the prison, Anna took him to a restaurant at the end of her street. 'The name means the People's Kitchen.' Inside, it was warm and noisy and on the walls portraits hung of famous Russian writers, world famous, Tolstoy, Dostoyevsky, Turgenev, Pushkin, also a number that Wes didn't know. But in the midst of those he did not know was one he knew very well: it was Anna, some years younger, with longer, darker hair and a slightly sardonic expression. Her lips were parted and the purple of her eyes gave her an erotic charm. 'Yes, it's me. Andre painted it. On the right side of me is Osip Mandelstam, and on the other side, Nikolay Gumilyov. You have heard of them?'

'No.'

'No matter. And this gentleman is Vasily.'

Vasily, not a portrait but a living man the size of a bear with a massive black beard, first kissed Anna on the mouth, then threw his arms around Wes. He stood back and held out his open hands to Wes, as if asking Anna, 'What gives?' She told him, five minutes of chatter, Vasily shaking his head, slapping his forehead, letting out howls of what seemed indignation. Everyone in the place was alert to what Anna was explaining—she was talking loudly, as if to include all listeners—and when she was done, one person after another, men and women, came to Wes and hugged him, kissed his cheeks. Some had a few words of English to offer. 'Your sweetheart in Butyrka, bad for you.' One young woman kissed him on the lips and was lightly slapped by Anna and chastised. A record was playing, the soundtrack of *High Society*, somehow, Frank Sinatra and Celeste Holm singing 'Who Wants to Be a Millionaire?'—'A friend from England gave it to him. Vasily loves Frank Sinatra.'

'Okay,' said Anna, 'we will have pelmeni, and then for pudding—you say pudding in Australia, yes?—for pudding, pirozhki. And some Odessa red wine.'

She asked about being a Quaker, and how he reconciled drinking alcohol with his faith, and about Almond Tree, which she knew was where Beth came from. He told her of the river and the lake and the orchards, the sheep, the dairying, and of his rebuilding of Chinese Town after the bushfire, and she told him of Maxim. 'Two marriages after Maxim. They lasted two years each. I seem to be attractive to men with bad taste in women. But God knows, I cooked, I cleaned, I'm said to be good at sex. But two years, and they packed their suitcases and wandered off. I'm a suitcase widow. I think it was the poetry. Neither of them read my poetry, or anyone else's. Konstantin said, "All you do is write, what's the use of it?" I told him it had no use. I think they felt the poetry was more important to me than they were. And then, they didn't get along with Andre. They sensed that he was more important to me, too. So he was. Love, Wes. It gives you no relief.'

The next day was Saturday, and the weather, the snow, was murder. Only half the usual number of visitors showed up, including the tiny woman of about eighty who hoped to see her grandson. She came draped in a blue blanket and shivered for the whole of her futile wait. Wes brought bread for her because he'd never seen her

249

eating. Anna told him she'd been coming for five years. It was only when the old woman parted the blanket to accept the bread that Wes saw she was carrying a wooden cross, not small. She demonstrated something she wanted him to do, which was to kiss the cross. And so he did. Anna explained. 'Her grandson is in prison for life. He's a devout Orthodox Christian and he was arrested putting up posters that called Comrade Stalin the anti-Christ and said he would go to hell. Beria wanted to hang him but Stalin apparently liked the poster. Now that Khrushchev has denounced Comrade Stalin, there's some hope he will be released.'

Mid-morning, when visitors were leaving the line in some numbers to save their lives, the guard Anna knew came stumbling through the blizzard and gestured to Wes to follow him. He was wearing two overcoats, so that it was impossible for him to wear his rifle slung over his shoulder. He carried it pointing at the ground. Wes was led under the stone arch of the older part of the building, when it was a castle, and into a more modern section, along one corridor after another all painted a moribund green with countless heavy metal doors. From over a distance, he heard screams, not those of prisoners being tortured, as he judged, but the screams of madmen. Two yellow lines were painted along each corridor and Yevgeny made Wes understand that he was to keep between the lines. Everything was clean, the floors mopped, the brass doorhandles shining, as if, like sailors, the prisoners spent half of each day swabbing. From a window, Wes saw down to a small courtyard where a scaffold stood. Yevgeny allowed him to stop and look, then acted out a noose around his neck being pulled taut and laughed.

They reached a corridor on the left that led into a part of the prison with ancient stone walls and cobble-stoned floors. At the end of the corridor, they reached a cell closed with thick wire mesh. Yevgeny rapped with his knuckles on the timber division between the broad areas of mesh and called a name loudly and waited. On the wall hung a portrait of Khrushchev, smiling. He made Wes think of Elmer Fudd. The portrait left an area around its perimeter fresher in its green than the rest of the wall, and Wes guessed that the portrait of the new leader had replaced a slightly larger portrait of Stalin.

Yevgeny called again and a door at the back swung open and a beefy woman, far from young, shuffled in and shouted something in Russian that must have been along the lines of, 'Hold your horses.' She wore an opaque plastic patch over her left eye and had a cane to support herself in an upright position. She called something over her shoulder and Beth entered. Wes inhaled deeply. His joy at seeing her was overwhelmed by the appalling look of her. She was wearing a pale blue uniform with long sleeves, mere cotton, okay for hot summer days but absurd for winter, and a brown cardigan from which all the buttons were missing. On her feet, slippers no more substantial than ballet shoes, black. She was shivering with her full body. Her hair had been cropped shorter than a boy's. Her face was bruised all over, and some stitches had been used to close a split in her upper lip. She was as thin as a pencil. She didn't look at him, but at the floor. She called to him after a minute of silence, 'Don't look at me. I'm ugly.'

Wes took two fifty-dollar notes from his pocket, handed one to Yevgeny and gestured for the woman guard to come and take the other one. She moved to the small locked window in the mesh more rapidly than would be thought possible, unlocked the window and quickly pocketed the banknote. Wes used hand signals to indicate that he wanted her to open the heavy iron-and-timber door to the cell and let him in. After a minute of what seemed casual conversation between the woman and Yevgeny, she produced a huge ring of keys and opened the door. Yevgeny, resting on his rifle, shrugged.

Wes put his arms around Beth, but gently; he was afraid she would break. He kissed her dry, stitched lips, stroked the stubble of her hair. Both were weeping.

She said: 'I shouldn't be here. This is insane.'

'I know, darling, I know. I'll do everything I can. But it will be six months before I can come back, you have to hold on.'

'Pardon my lips,' she said, and kissed him all over his face.

The woman guard separated them and pointed at

252

her wristwatch. An argument broke out between her and Yevgeny. Beth translated. 'He says I should give us five more minutes. He says you've been waiting four days in the snow. Is that true?'

'Yes.'

Beth again kissed his whole face. 'We love each other. We have to be together. Pray for us to your silly old God.'

'I pray all day. The whole gathering prays for us.'

'God bless the Quaker God.'

Then it was over. The woman guard led Beth away, and Yevgeny took Wes back to the line. He told Anna he'd seen Beth and Anna relayed the news to the hopefuls, who cheered and applauded. Wes had been staying at the Gorki, in the same room he'd first occupied, but that night Anna persuaded him to stay at her apartment. He slept on the sofa. In the morning, they exchanged addresses. She came with him by taxi to the Gorki, where he picked up his suitcase and paid his bill. His ticket was good for all the days of his visa, and since visits were restricted to once a month, there was no point in him staying in Moscow. When they parted, he kissed Anna on the cheek.

'Lips,' she said, and he kissed her again, on the lips.

Chapter 26

KADO DIED in March of 1958. A type of brain tumour that revealed no symptoms until it killed him in ten seconds. In May, Patty went to see the master again, by train and on foot, as ever, taking the two children because the master enjoyed them, but not her mother-in-law; she was too demoralised by the death of her one remaining child. It was a long walk for Francis but he skipped along without complaint. A novice showed Patty to the master in a room she hadn't seen before, at the side of the monastery, very small with split bamboo walls and plaited rush flooring and ceiling. He was sleeping, his head on his chest. In the five years since she'd first seen him, he had aged ten. He was snoring and had to be woken by the novice. But once his eyes were open, he was instantly alert.

'Missus Patty, Francis, and this baby one is—don't tell me—Esther? Yes, Esther. Let me hold her.'

Patty lowered the child into his arms and he cradled her expertly. 'Are you having another baby?'

'No, but I need your advice.'

'Do you mind if we speak in English? I need the practice.'

'Of course.'

'Advice,' said the master. 'My best advice is sleep. But since I am awake now, what can I say that might help you?'

Her husband had died suddenly, said Patty. Together they had made a commitment to remain in Hiroshima and help those who were suffering from radiation sickness— many thousands. Now she was thinking of returning to her home in Australia, Almond Tree. Other mothers and children in Hiroshima looked aghast at Esther's hands. They thought it was the punishment of heaven for something Patty had done wrong, a superstition. If she stayed in Hiroshima, Esther would have to endure being tormented at school, indeed all through her life. No such superstition existed in Australia. Compared to Hiroshima, Almond Tree was paradise.

The master listened as he rocked the baby and smiled. Still smiling at the baby, he said, 'Paradise is nothing.'

'Nothing?'

'Nothing. Your town of Almond Tree is paradise, you say. I heard on my radio that the Americans have

255

three thousand atomic bombs on rockets. The Russians have one thousand. Together they could destroy the whole world. They could destroy your paradise. Any paradise that can be destroyed is nothing.'

'You listen to the radio? I am surprised. I thought you would disdain the world.'

'I live in one small part of Honshu. I want to know the world. Zen is the world, Missus Patty. Your great poet, Blake, said one can see the world in a grain of sand. No. In a grain of sand, what you see is a grain of sand. Unless you have Mister Blake's imagination, which none of us do. Paradise? Here.'

He took an apple from a basket beside him and bit out a mouthful. 'Now you.'

Patty took a bite from the apple.

'That is paradise. An apple. The tree made the apple from earth and air. The apple tree is God. Come.'

The master, still holding the baby, led Patty to the stable, where Hero the horse was enclosed. He opened the gate and beckoned Patty in. Then he lifted Hero's tale, rubbed his rump, and Hero produced three clumps of dung.

'That is paradise,' said the master. 'What do you call this in English?'

'Dung. Or more crudely, shit.'

'What we turn away from is closer to paradise than what we study closely. Dung is Zen. The apple is Zen. You cannot leave Hiroshima.'

She didn't know. It was possible that the master was mad. Dung was Zen? At the train station, a woman came up to her and looked at Esther waving her ugly hands about in her pram and whispered into Patty's ear: 'Accursed.' In the mood she was in, it was too much. She reached out and grabbed the woman's throat and squeezed until the woman fell to her knees. 'Apologise, you bitch!' She spoke in Japanese. The woman couldn't speak because she was being strangled. Patty relaxed her grip on the woman's throat. 'Apologise!'

The woman coughed out, 'Sorry! Sorry, madam!'

By the time she reached home, Patty's mind was made up. She would stay. The children would stay. Esther would suffer, but she would survive. Patty would continue to run the hospital, which was now hers.

Chapter 27

THE NAZARETH channel ran south-east from the lake and irrigated orchards all the way to Tom Kennedy's apricot spread twenty-seven miles away. Tom had recently acquired Sammy Limerick's neglected spread down by the Hutchinson billabong and wanted to plant it with apricots, which were making him a fortune, but needed a channel running due south. Tom was an intelligent man and drew up a proposal for the shire that proved that it would recoup the cost of the channel in rates in five years. He argued his case to the council and won approval. The issue was, who would grade a channel eighteen miles long? Tom had the answer to that, too: Wes Cunningham. Well, not Wes himself, who was rebuilding Chinese Town, but Wes could oversee it. Tom had run into Wes in town a week after he got back from Moscow, where he was visiting his nutcase girlfriend in the clink, and Wes had told him that he hoped to go back in six months if he could find the dough. So Tom had a pretty fair idea that Wes would accept the channel job. The whole thing was supposed to go out to tender, but the shire said Wes could do it if he agreed with the oversight fee of eight thousand pounds—after all, nobody better in the shire or the state to get a job done properly. Tom drove over to Chinese Town and found Wes at work on the frames of the wooden dwellings further from the forest, while his brothers and the Italians were erecting the brick houses closer to the timber. He put the proposition to him, told him the fee, and Wes accepted immediately. It was a different Wes these days—all the mirth was gone from him, never a smile. Tom said he'd bring him the contract from the shire the next day, and the specs, and arrange for the dozers. Flat land all the way, no big problems.

It was true that Wes had become a stranger to cheer. All he could think of was Beth and her suffering. He found some relief in concentrating on his craft, in problem-solving. Beth had been beaten, and would likely be beaten again. Whatever information they wanted from her, he prayed she would give them. But he thought it likely she was being beaten for the sake of it. Even prayer seemed futile. Had prayer helped any of those in the war at the gates of Auschwitz? Had it helped those in New Guinea,

Australian soldiers, Japanese soldiers, their torsos ripped open, him praying over them while the surgeons, cursing, laboured to stitch them closed? Not once. God watched on, sorrowing, in the same way he sorrowed, and could not save a man for all his power if a wound had let too much blood flow away or had destroyed a body's physical integrity.

He spent each day, seven days a week, racing between the starting point of the channel, at the orchard site, to Chinese Town. He had to arrange a powder monkey to blast out some of the stumps, and didn't always take the care he should. The backdraft of one blast tore his shirt off. People worried, his parents especially, even Franny who came to the Chinese Town site with a couple of doorstopper sandwiches and hot tea in a thermos. She had a baby now, and was all goodwill and affection, without any further strategies.

He was way too busy, and he knew he was pushing towards madness. He hired a blaster who was willing to work on Sundays, Bobby Burton, whose competence was questionable. When Wes drove over from Chinese Town, he found Bobby fifty yards from the stump being blasted but his son, Roy, right beside the stump setting the explosive. Wes looked down at the case of explosive that Bobby was using. It was out-dated dynamite.

'You're using this?'
'Yeah.'

'It's fifty years old. The fuse will burn through in thirty seconds. Get that kid out of there!'

Wes didn't wait for the fool of a man to act but ran to the boy himself. The fuse was burning. Wes grabbed the boy and dragged him ten yards, then covered him with his own body. The explosion lifted the stump and sent it flying over them. A rain of earth fell, but at least they were alive. Wes brushed himself down, and the boy, who could only have been fifteen or sixteen.

'Are you completely insane?' he said to Bobby. 'Nobody uses this stuff anymore. Don't you know the older it is, the quicker the fuse burns? You should be using jelly. This stuff is suicide, you fool. Send in your invoice to the shire, but you'll never work for me again.'

The boy looked distressed.

'It's not your fault, son,' said Wes. 'Don't be upset. You're alive when you should be dead.'

John Li was not rebuilding Chinese Town for the Chinese. No Chinese would come to live in the town again. It was considered unlucky, not unreasonably, after so many people died there. John was building the new houses for the immigrant workers from Italy, Greece, Lithuania, who had come to work on the huge Eildon Weir hydro project. Now that the project was finished, John had won a concession from the Victorian Government to clear-fell a thousand acres of timber in the hills twenty miles from Chinese Town, and would lease the houses to workers.

Chinese Town would no longer be an appropriate name for the town.

He asked Wes's advice on a new name. 'Working People Town? You think?'

"No, John. Too awkward.'

'Italian Town?'

'What about all the people who are not Italian? The Balts, the Greeks? They might feel insulted.'

'Do you think "Europe Town"?'

'No, John. That's awful. Do you know the story of the mythical bird called the phoenix? Who rose from the ashes and was reborn?

'Yes! In Scotch College. The phoenix!'

'Call the town Phoenix.'

'Yes! Yes! Phoenix Town! This is genius!'

'No, just Phoenix.'

'Just Phoenix. Yes! I thank you with my heart, Wesley. But with *f*. Easier for people.'

Three days later, a billboard had been erected at the exit of the spur road into what had been Chinese Town: *FEENIX. SAFE!*

Wes kept up the seven-days-a-week schedule but didn't bother with the channel on the Sundays when no expert blasters were available. He never let the quality of his work lapse. Every frame was solid, every measurement was true and square. He watched over the plumbers with an eagle eye and made the carpenters reset an entire gable when he found it was a quarter of an inch out on the down side; a quarter inch would ruin the line of the spouting.

His mother, Beth's mother, Franny and even sometimes Gus cooked for him each day. He didn't have the heart to do anything away from the channel and Feenix. He wandered the house he'd built, pining, fretting. He slept fitfully.

Letters arrived for him each fortnight from Anna in Moscow, sent by a friend in Leningradsky Prospekt because anything Anna wrote had to go through the police and would be censored. They always began with: *Your Elizabeth is alive.* Each time he read the opening words, he sighed in relief. She told him the Moscow news. The KGB, a faction of it, a law unto itself, hated Khrushchev and wanted to get rid of him. Spring was coming. Moscow was glorious in spring, he should see it. And the satellite! Russians who hated the regime are still singing its praises. Everyone smiling. *My son is still alive, too. Thank God. If he survives, I will become a Christian.*

Finally he invented some relief by reading *Anna Karenina* aloud in the way he had read the book to Beth and the other women prisoners in Pentridge, imagining Beth beside him, her thigh against his, stopping him every ten minutes to kiss him, and the jeers and hoots of the women, who one time made him kiss them all, giving exaggerated orgiastic groans. And the women leaning forward avidly as he read, and their comments, like that of Jinxy Nash: 'All of this for a root. I've never met a man I'd give a packet of Smarties to for a root.' It gave him some comfort, a little.

Over the months, Wes was able to repay the community and John Li, and took an advance on the channel project allowing him to plan a trip back to Moscow. In October 1958 he sent his British passport and five hundred dollars to Bill, care of Scotland Yard, and asked him to arrange a Russian visa.

Bill returned the following message to Wes's address in Almond Tree.

> First, some candour, and I blush to reveal how infrequently candour emerges in my correspondence, my dear friend. I am at MI6 these days, and have been for some time. The deepest of mea culpas for the subterfuge. Now, I want you to meet me in London on October 10th at eleven in the morning, three doors down from the entrance to Charing Cross Station at a cafe with the homely name of the Busy Bee. I have some good news.

Chapter 28

THE BUSY Bee was not busy. At eleven in the morning, maybe a half dozen customers, including Bill, at an isolated table in a corner, looking, as he usually did, stylish in a navy blue suit. Also now wearing a moustache, perfectly barbered and, yes, with a few flecks of grey.

Wes walked to the table and before sitting, pointed at his own upper lip.

'What do you think?' said Bill. 'Mere vanity?'

'Yes, vanity.'

Bill signalled the waitress, a young woman in a parti-coloured blouse with exceptionally long black hair, and ordered coffee for two, one with milk, one without.

'Is this good news for MI6, or good news for Beth?'

'For Beth.'

Bill looked left and right, in the classic manner of a spy, before continuing.

'As you will not know, Wesley, your government and the Soviet government are negotiating to resume diplomatic relations. The Soviets will, in some months' time, reopen their embassy in Canberra, and Australia may open an embassy, or at least a consulship in Moscow.'

The coffee was set down on the table by the waitress, who smiled at Bill.

'As I was saying, resumption of diplomatic relations, down the road a way. The Russians, as a goodwill gesture, intend to release your Elizabeth early.'

Wes involuntarily came to his feet.

'When?'

'Today, if you happened to be in Moscow, which you are not. Sit down.'

Wes sat, his heart banging in his chest like a bass drum.

'The Russians are prepared to fly Elizabeth and yourself—I nominated you as the family member who would accompany her—to London, and then to Sydney. Elizabeth and your good self will be required to sign agreements in Russian and English forbidding disclosure of any possible ill-treatment endured in prison. Of course, there is nothing to prevent you telling all back in Australia. They're trusting you. It's droll, the way the totally untrustworthy are prepared to exploit the trust of those of a far more reliable character. But Wesley, the real reason the reds want her out of prison is that they're afraid she will die. They don't want her to die in their keep. A lot of strife. The UN, Red Cross inspections. She's been badly abused, up until two months ago, when they became worried. Apparently she doesn't eat, or very little. MI6 have been handling the negotiations. We handle nearly all of your country's relations with the Soviets.'

Bill sipped his coffee then sat back and inhaled deeply.

'Wesley, Elizabeth in Moscow, it's largely my fault. What we did was completely illegal, and your government let it happen. At first I was flippant about it. A silly girl, no loss. But I've come to see that she is a finer human being than I have ever been. And you, Wesley. Cynicism is decayed passion. Most of my professional life has been given over to cynicism. But since I've known you, it's more shame than cynicism that inhabits my heart.'

He reached over the table and took Wes's hand. 'Forgive me, if you can.'

He reached down and produced a briefcase, black leather, well-worn; opened it and handed Wes a large envelope.

'Copies of the documents you'll need to sign. Your tickets from Moscow. Your passport and visa. The Moscow police have Elizabeth's passport. We've booked Elizabeth into a private hospital in Kensington. She and you will spend time there before flying to Sydney.'

He paused. 'And Wesley, my name is Wallace. Wallace Durham. Never Wal, or Wally. Wallace. My father's name was Wallace, too, always called Wally. I prefer to distance myself from him. He was a swindler. But then, perhaps there's not a vast distance between my father's swindling and my own. I hope with all my heart that Elizabeth survives and that the two of you enjoy a happy life together. That's my most sincere hope, Wesley.'

Chapter 29

WES FOUND Anna in the line of hopeful visitors. She had shared the news that he would be taking Beth home today, and when he hugged Anna and kissed her, there was the expected clapping and cheering. The weather was not nearly as cold as on his first visit and the actual shapes of the visitors were visible in light coats and dresses. The form of Moscow itself was more revealed, not so drab, many of the trees still in foliage.

Anna would act as interpreter, with Yevgeny's approval. He led Wes and Anna to the gates of the prison and the two guards on duty there, after some animated discussion, let them both through. Inside, they met the prison commandant, a tall man dressed in a splendid blue uniform with epaulets in four colours and gold braid on the lapels and peaked cap. He spoke in a low, confidential way to Anna before meeting up with a squad of ten policemen, not guards, all carrying rifles. Anna whispered to Wes, 'Might be trouble. Stay calm.'

They went past the turn-off to the cell in which Wes had met Beth, and after a number of changes of direction ended up in what would have to be assumed was the commandant's office, spacious and well-furnished as it was. The commandant left the door open, with the ten policemen grouped outside. He sat, and asked through Anna for the documents Wes was carrying in a large envelope. Each document was made up of two stapled pages, one in Russian, one in English. On each document, a space for the commandant's signature, for Wes's, for Beth's. The commandant, mumbling something, signed the three documents rapidly, then pushed them over his desk to Wes, who signed, six times, the Russian documents in English just as the commandant had signed the English copies in Russian.

There was some sort of commotion outside the door. The police parted and let Beth through, accompanied by a woman guard, this one young and slim. But nowhere near as slim as Beth who, in a black dress, had the appearance of a survivor at the gates of Auschwitz. She looked no worse than when he'd visited her seven months earlier, but it would have been impossible for her to look worse than that and still have a heartbeat and respiration. She kept her eyes downcast, and had to be supported in standing by the woman guard.

Wes made a move towards her, to embrace her, and called her name. The commandant barked something, and Anna translated: 'He says, no talking, no touching.' The guard helped her to the desk, to the documents. The commandant, who seemed edgy, told her in Russian to sign the six copies, but she couldn't hold the pen. Anna intervened and guided her hand, without any objection from the commandant. Then the commandant put the documents into a drawer of his desk, and locked it. He said something further in Russian and Anna said, 'He says to follow him.'

Beth required the support of both Anna and the guard to walk. The ten policemen followed. Progress was slow. Around one corner, they came upon a squad of soldiers with their rifles aimed at the commandant, at Beth, at Anna and the woman guard. The commandant was furious, and an argument broke out. Anna translated in a whisper to Wes. 'The commandant told them to get the fuck out of the way. The senior KGB officer told him he is not taking Elizabeth anywhere. The commandant says they will all be tried for treason. These KGB soldiers are from a renegade faction.'

Now the police joined in the argument and the other KGB soldiers shouted back. The corridor was full of shouting, and everyone, the police, the KGB soldiers had their rifles raised. Nobody's voice was louder than that of the commandant, who had drawn a pistol from the holster on his belt.

But then another voice, louder than that of the commandant. Striding down the corridor came a soldier who appeared to have more authority than anyone else, even the commandant. He was taller than the commandant, powerfully built and exceptionally handsome, in the broad-browed Slavic way, and he was smiling, even as he roared. The police parted to let him through. He walked straight up to the KGB soldier who was in command, took his pistol out and pointed the barrel at the soldier's right eye. He spoke some quiet instructions. Anna said softly to Wes, 'This is Igor Yurivich, a top KGB general. He's on Khrushchev's side. The people love him. He told the other fellow to make his men put their weapons on the floor, or he'd be dead in ten seconds.' The weapons were speedily set down on the floor and a way opened for the commandant and the police, Beth, the woman guard, Anna and Wes to get through.

No further crises. The commandant led the party not only to the door, but with the police surrounding him, all the way to the gate where an official government car was waiting. He handed Wes Beth's passport, then said something in an angry way to Anna.

Once Beth was in the car with Anna and Wes, she translated the commandant's message. 'He said, "And don't fucking come back."'

~

272

The doctor at the Kensington hospital, Ewan Thomas, spent two hours examining Beth and when he'd finished called Wes to follow him to his office. The hospital was obviously a destination for those with money. The walls of the corridors were decorated with etchings of medical instruments, and of the faces of people, men and women, recovering in beds, pillows plumped up behind their heads, and smiling. The furniture was plush. Ewan Thomas's office was designed to impress. In place of the utilitarian chairs doctors usually provided for their patients were two red velvet armchairs. On the walls hung facsimile reproductions of three Rembrandt self-portraits. Doctor Thomas spoke in the manner of a man who did not expect to be contradicted, or even interrupted.

'Miss Hardy is your fiancée, as I understand?'

'Yes.'

'And has come to us directly from a Russian prison?'

'Yes.'

'Mister Cunningham, I must tell you that Miss Hardy has been badly abused, physically, and judging by her silence, also mentally. She is severely traumatised, in every way. She will need to stay here for three weeks, and I cannot guarantee that she will live. She is dreadfully malnourished, and only one-half of the weight of a healthy woman of her age and build. Her ribs, which were taped when I examined her, and taped badly, are terribly bruised. I would conjecture that she has been kicked while lying on the floor. Her kidneys are also bruised, quite seriously. No broken bones, fortunately. The remnants of bad bruising to her face can also be detected. Punching, I would assume. I am not able to say whether she has been sexually abused. I have ordered her ribs to be retaped, and have put her on a protein drip. Mister Cunningham, can you stay for three weeks? As I say, she may die well before that. She doesn't answer my questions. Does she speak to you?'

'Not so far. But she held my wrist on the plane.'

'Then good. We'll do everything we can for her. If you want to stay at night, we'll make up a cot for you beside her bed.'

He asked her questions to which he received no answer. But she wanted him to sit on her bed and hold her hand. Above her bed hung a picture of W. G. Grace in his cap, resting on his bat before the wickets. The script on the frame confided that this picture was dedicated to a certain Lawrence Hungerford, who had died in the bed that Beth now occupied. Wes asked the nurse to take it away, and she did. In the blank space, she hung a picture of Monet's, a woman in a floating white dress in a field of flowers. Far more acceptable.

Most of the time, Beth didn't look at him, but she held his hand. Feeling the strength in her grip, he was sure she wouldn't die. On the fourth day, the drip feeding into her left arm, he asked her if she would like him to read to her. She shook her head, but then reached up and pulled his head to her lips and spoke the first words she'd uttered to him since Moscow. She whispered, 'Famous Five.'

The Enid Blyton books. 'Really?'

She shook her head.

'Nothing, then?'

She gave no response.

He stroked her short hair. He remembered when it was so much longer, and how it curled down her forehead but turned away from her eyes, as if she were being granted clear vision. He said, 'Beth, I'm here forever.' She reached behind her for his hand and put her lips to it.

She was given, each day, five medications: three for her bruised kidneys, a painkiller and an ointment that was rubbed into her ribs when the tape was removed. The ointment smelt like burning rubber. Wes and a nurse helped her to the bath in the late afternoon of each day. Beth indicated that she wanted Wes to stay while she was bathed, but the nurse told him that only a husband could remain in the bathroom. Wes waited outside to help support Beth back to her room. The nurse evidently thought that singing contributed to her patient's therapy and sang as she bathed Beth. Always the one song: 'How Much Is That Doggie in the Window'.

Early each day, Beth was administered a sedative that put her to sleep for three hours, and while she slept, Wes wandered the corridors, made friends with other patients, played chess with one aged woman who beat him every game. 'I'm not going to last terribly much longer,' she said, 'so it's good to get a few more wins under my belt. Wesley, I must tell you, don't lead with your knight every time. It makes your game so predictable.'

One midday, after her sedative had worn off, Beth turned onto her back and made a writing gesture.

'You want to write something?'

She nodded.

He had a notebook in his coat pocket, and a fountain pen.

She wrote with difficulty: *Dickens.*

The hospital kept a small library made up of books left behind by former patients. The only Dickens on the shelves was *Barnaby Rudge*. Wes brought it back and showed it to Beth. She shook her head. Then wrote on the notepad: *Oliver.*

'I'll get it for you.'

She then wrote: *Lenin, What Is to Be Done. The book.*

He went by tube to Foyles in Charing Cross Road— he knew how to get there after his earlier stay in London.

When he returned, Beth was asleep. He waited for her, and for her to be fed her lunch—she was now eating twice a day small servings of solid food. When she was done—how little she ate!—he held up *Oliver Twist* in his right hand, the Lenin in the left. She nodded at the Lenin. He pulled a chair closer to the bed.

'Skip the introduction?'

She nodded, and he launched into the opening. Ten pages in, she waved her hands and shook her head. She wrote on the pad: *No more. Oliver.*

For the next two hours, he read her the Dickens.

At the end of the Oliver reading, he asked her why she wouldn't speak, but she said nothing and wrote nothing.

She seemed to Wes and to the doctor to be improving. Ewan, the doctor, no longer thought there was any danger of her dying. 'But there is still blood in her urine. Always a concern. Ten more days.'

Four days were enough to finish *Oliver Twist*. Beth gazed at him steadily while he read. She wrote on the notepad: *More.*

'More Dickens?'

She wrote: 'You choose.'

Wes went to Foyles again and came back with an armful of books, including a Barbara Pym, an anthology of English poetry, *Martin Chuzzlewit* and a couple of Raymond Chandlers recommended to him by an assistant who claimed they far exceeded in quality any of the Agatha Christies.

He was reading her *The Big Sleep* in the afternoon of her eleventh day in the Kensington hospital, displaying a knack for rendering the various voices of the characters, particularly that of Marlowe, when one of the nurses showed in a small man in a cream-colored suit. Beth was on her back with pillows holding her almost in a sitting position. The man, smiling and deferential, begged the pardon of everyone—Beth and Wes—for interrupting. He was holding a large envelope. He said in heavily accented English, 'I regret to say that Miss Elizabeth must sign one of the documents again. One of the Russian documents which, most unfortunately, was signed below the line.'

Beth who had said nothing for two weeks, glared at the little man with implacable hatred.

'Get out!' she shrieked.

Wes seized the man by one arm and hauled him to the door, and out into the corridor to a nurses' station, where two nurses were chatting. He told them to make themselves scarce, and they did immediately. Wes threw the man against the wall and held him by the throat with his feet off the floor. 'If you ever come back here, I will strangle you. Do you understand?'

The man was not in a position to answer, either by nodding or by speaking. His face was a violent scarlet.

Wes let the man down to the floor. 'Do you understand?'

The little man coughed for a good two minutes. Then nodded and said, 'I understand.'

'Now get out.'

The man paused at the door, and turned back to

Wes. 'The bureaucrats,' he said. 'For me, I honour Miss Elizabeth for her bravery. I am sorry with my heart.'

Then he left, with his envelope which he'd retrieved from the floor.

The two nurses, who'd been eavesdropping a short distance away in the corridor, returned.

'Sorry,' said Wes. 'KGB.'

Beth was on her back holding a pillow over her face. Wes removed it gently. She kept her eyes closed.

'I told him I'd strangle him if he came back. I meant it. You've given up on the Soviet Union. I've given up non-violence.'

He'd known for some time that there was violence in him that could emerge now and again. 'In New Guinea,' he said, 'I was out with a mate, Lance Sherlock, Shirley. He was one of the few troops who would come with me looking for dead Japs to bury. I didn't carry a gun, you see; I was no use in a firefight. We came across a couple of Japs, probably doing the same thing as us. They fired at us, Shirley fired back. Then he gave me his pistol and told me to shoot. I did, and missed, and the Japs took off. But the thing was, Beth, I enjoyed it, firing a pistol at the enemy. I wanted to hit him. I loved the feeling of the pistol in my hand. At the same time, it made me sick.' A pause. 'I never fired a pistol again. But I wanted to. Will I read?'

Beth shook her head. She lay staring at the ceiling, hour after hour. Wes chatted about his family, and hers, how happy Franny was with her baby, Bella, how her dad's leg had mended and all his old vigour returned, how his mother was writing a novel full of Quaker characters also, full of goodness and virtue and pretty awful. Beth didn't want to hear any reading the next day either, but she wanted him nearby. She wrote him a note: 'Two apostates.' When she was sleeping, he wrote a telegram to his brother, Teddy. He'd only once sent a telegram before. He might have telephoned but the connection was iffy and crackly. But he'd read telegrams and knew it was the job of the writer to put 'stop' at the end of sentences. He wrote:

> i am good beth improving stop still two weeks here stop start work again on the channel stop get morty to do the dozing one yard and nine inches deep stop tell morty the banks have to be six inches deep on both sides stop width of the dozer blade stop blasting use only geoff brooks stop never bobby burton stop for felling use derek and harvey stop fill holes with rubble from the quarry mixed with mortar stop roll flat stop let max take charge of chinese town and the italians stop work sundays if you can but not on the channel stop respond care of me at kensington hospital of light stop loving brother wes stop

He took the message to the post office close to the Victoria and Albert. It cost four pounds.

At the beginning of Beth's final week in hospital, a story appeared on page four of the *News of the World* headed *Red Torture Victim in London Hospital*. It was illustrated with a photograph of Beth in bed, asleep.

An Australian woman of thirty is recovering in an exclusive London hospital after thirteen months of horrendous torture in a Red prison in Moscow. Her injuries are said to be the worst seen by the doctors treating her, meaning five broken ribs, head gashes, broken fingers, and shocking sexual abuse. A spokesman for Her Majesty's Secret Service offered no comment. A spokesman for the Australian High Commission confirmed to this reporter that the woman was an Australian citizen but would not provide a name. A Soviet Embassy spokesman said that the woman had been released from a Moscow prison on 'humanity grounds'. He said in his broken English that the woman had 'made a crime against the Soviet people'. He had no comment to offer about the alleged torture.

Neither Beth nor Wes had seen the story on the Sunday of its publication, but on the Monday, Doctor Thomas had. He sent a nurse to fetch Wes to his office, where he showed him the newspaper, opened at page four.

'How the reporter got hold of the story, we don't

know. And the picture. The information, inaccurate though it is, must have been obtained from a nurse, for a fee. As for the picture, some complicity between the informant and a *News of the World* photographer. Or maybe the informant, whoever it was, took the picture. The *News of the World* personnel are capable of anything. If they'd been around at the time, they would have interviewed Jesus on the cross. I've contacted MI6 and it has banned any further reporting of the story on national security grounds. That doesn't always work. Wesley, I'm dreadfully sorry. There will be an enquiry. You will want the story kept from Elizabeth?'

'No, I'll show her. If she found out, she'd be disappointed in me. And I'm disappointed in the hospital. It seems you can get into any room you choose, even if you're dressed as a vampire.'

He took the newspaper back to Beth and showed her. She was surprisingly sanguine about it.

Am I that ugly? she wrote.

'It's a rotten shot of you, darling. Your mouth's open. You're probably snoring.'

She wrote, *Keep reading the Chandler. His people are real people. There are no people in Agatha.*

Chapter 30

THE BRITISH Government sent a car to take them to Heathrow once Doctor Thomas decided Beth was fit enough to fly. He provided a detailed report of her treatment for whatever doctor saw her in Australia, and also a bottle of sedatives to administer every six hours of the flight.

At the terminal, a good seven or eight reporters were waiting for her and with the practised eyes of journalists, recognised her despite the distortions of the newspaper photograph. Wes held her close, but pictures were taken and a welter of questions were thrown at her: 'Elizabeth, did they pull your fingernails out? Miss Hardy, were you subjected to electrical torture? Miss Hardy, do you hate the Russians?' Policemen arrived and held the reporters back. Once through check-in, they were alone. Beth was trembling violently and it took Wes a half-hour in the departure lounge to calm her. How the reporters had come to know her name was a mystery.

She slept for most of the flight, even during the stop-overs. He put up the armrest and she lay with her head on his lap, acutely uncomfortable for Wes but he bore it. During one period of wakefulness, she wrote him a note: *I didn't betray anyone. I said nothing.* He ate his meals with difficulty. Beth was brought meals when she was awake. The cabin staff were aware of her story and situation and were kind to her. One of the stewardesses bent down and kissed her forehead while she slept. She said to Wes, 'So brave.'

At Sydney, they were met by Bob Hardy and Franny, in her old Jaguar. No reporters. Beside her frail sister, Franny looked like Rita Hayworth, gushing good health and voluptuous beauty. Franny and Bob shared the driving. Beth kept awake for hours at a stretch, but didn't speak a word. Wes had warned them, quietly, that she wouldn't speak. Every time Bob turned to look at her, being prone to tears, his eyes grew moist. They stopped at a motel in Albury and Wes and Beth shared a bed. She clung to him fiercely.

Another one hundred and fifty miles from Albury to Almond Tree. Her mother put her hands to her face and groaned. 'My darling, what have they done to you?' Franny bathed her and put her to bed in her old room.

Doctor Rowe from Canada Falls came to see her the next day. He was acknowledged as the best doctor in the shire. He read what Doctor Thomas had written and said, 'Bloody hell.' He examined her and came to the conclusion that she should be dead, and said so. 'She weighs about as much as a famished pup.' He told Lillian to feed her scrambled eggs and bacon for breakfast, rissoles for lunch and some sort of hearty casserole for dinner, followed by as much dessert as could be forced down her throat. 'I've heard of Ewan Thomas. He's held in high regard. He says here there's no more blood in her urine. That at least will keep her out of hospital.'

Wes had to work, but he came to see Beth for two hours each morning and two hours each evening. She still wouldn't speak. Patty was visiting from Hiroshima with Esther and Francis and she spent an hour at Beth's bedside telling her about Hiroshima, and her work there. Patty showed her Esther's hands and Beth put them to her lips and kissed them. She wrote a note for Patty: *I said nothing. I betrayed no one for thirteen months. Do you see?* Patty sat back and thought, and she believed she did see. 'And now you can't?' she said. 'Talk, I mean.' Beth nodded. Later in the morning, Patty explained it to Lillian. 'She had the living daylights beaten out of her for more than a year and kept her mouth shut. They must have wanted the names of her fellow conspirators, something like that. She told them nothing. And now she can't speak. It's locked up in her.'

'It's what? Is she mad, then?'

'No, no. I'm sure speech will come back to her. You have to be patient.'

Lillian couldn't make her daughter speak, but she made sure she ate, sitting her up in bed with a tea towel around her neck feeding her by spoon and fork, and talking.

'Your trouble is you're too brave for a woman. Men don't like to see so much courage in a woman. Men of a certain sort. There you are, putting up with punishment they couldn't bear themselves, and it irritates them. Too much bravery, honey. They want to see you break, and cry, beg for mercy, and I bet you didn't even shed a tear. I would of. Franny, Gus, Maud. It's not what we're made for. They would of killed you in the end.'

Franny took her for walks about the farm to build up her matchstick legs. Each walk, they stopped halfway and sat on the ancient red gum log by the dam. Since there was no conversation coming from Beth, Franny had to do all the talking. 'It was the baby that made all the difference to me. It was like heaven when I first held him. Ricky was there, but I didn't take any notice of him and wouldn't let him hold the baby. He's the ideal husband for me. Asks for nothing, expects nothing. I let him have sex with me, but I couldn't care less about it. Just a favour twice a week. You know, I might have been the same way with Wes. Just the baby. I'm pregnant again. I haven't even told Ricky yet. If he got sick of me and buzzed off, I doubt I'd care. It's not a real marriage. When men look at me, they see my figure and get crazy. But when Wes looked at you, he saw a real person. I envy you. Not because you have Wes, not anymore. I envy you, the person you are. I haven't got your make-up, your mind, your guts, all that means more to me now. But I have to work with what I've got, right?'

When Beth began to gain weight and strength, it was Wes who took her for walks. She brought her notebook with her and wrote him message after message. She told him about Anna and her son and what a superb poet she was, and what a wonderful painter her son was. She said she had to acknowledge that in Australia Andre would be considered a genius and Anna would be a celebrated poet. That by itself was enough for her to concede that Australian culture was to be preferred to Soviet culture. She wrote out one of Anna's poems for him. She tried to speak, but could only manage a stutter. She wrote: *Please darling don't give up on me. I couldn't bear it.*

It was a day of special beauty, the sky an unblemished blue from horizon to horizon and the myrtles on the hills shining. The Ayrshires in what was known as the Boston paddock, named by the American who first owned the land, were lolling as if they'd reached the highest possible level of cow contentment. Beth wrote: *I'm trying to be happy. I should be, shouldn't I? With the man I love on such a gorgeous day. No beatings to fear. A loving family all around me. But something is jammed in my heart, darling. I saw the most horrible things you can imagine and they haunt me.*

'Time,' said Wes.

Two weeks later, Beth was what could almost be called healthy. Colour had returned to her face, she had gained weight, her hair was at shoulder length. She told Wes she wanted to come to work with him.

'Ah, you see, the men don't like it, a woman on site. It makes them feel they have to watch their language.

Wes for God's sake, I've been in prisons on two continents. I've heard everything a thousand times.

'I'll ask them, darling.'

He did. They agreed with reluctance. More out of respect for Wes than for the sensibilities of Beth, they kept their language civil, a novel experience for most. Whenever one slipped up and called an uncooperative tool a cunt of a thing, he always turned to Wes to apologise, not to Beth, sitting with her book, unperturbed. Every so often she looked up to watch Wes, busy with a crosscut saw, a plane, a hammer and felt gladness rise in her heart. His competence, his physical strength, his concentration; it moved her.

She had sandwiches prepared by Lillian for both of them and they ate side by side. She wrote a question: *Is the workforce here unionised?*

'Everyone is. I insisted. But John Li owns the site. He's paying for everything, and he hates unions. He thinks they're all communists. He only puts up with it because I told him he had to. But up in the hills where he's clear-felling a thousand acres, he won't hire anyone in a union. He's got a hundred and fifty men living in tents. Earthmovers, dozers, lifters. No safety regulations. He's already had two men killed and five injured. You'd think the union would take an interest, but all the workers are migrants— the union ignores them, and no penniless migrant wants to pay six bob a month to the union anyway.' He shrugged. 'John's underpaying them by more than six bob a month, but they don't know that. He's got Marty Dunne and Dick Polly patrolling the camp, acting like armed guards. Marty and Dick, they're not about to shoot anyone. I went up there to look around and told them if they shot me or anyone else for venturing upon what remains Crown land, they'd hang for murder. They got out of my way.'

Beth wrote: *Wes, something has to be done.*

Wes laughed. 'Get your voice back and give a speech, my love.'

The channel had been excavated to within two yards of the Nazareth Lake shoreline. A further four yards down, a concrete wall had been built across the channel with a gate that rose and fell on a pulley device fashioned by Vinny Toole from Almond Tree. When the concrete wall and the gate were ready, the last of the shoreline earth was blasted away with gelignite so that the water rushed against the wall. The pulley device hadn't yet been tested with the weight of the Nazareth water against it, so on a Sunday, when work was usually suspended on the channel, Wes asked Beth if she'd like to come and watch himself and Vinny test the apparatus. She wrote: *Of course.*

Vinny was one of few men under Wes who didn't know that Beth was silent. He shook her hand and said, 'You must be the missus?'

Wes said, 'Not quite yet, Vin. And Vin, Beth has been through a terrible time in a Russian prison. She's not speaking for the time being.'

'Yeah? Bloody Russians. Yanks oughta bomb them.'

Wes showed Beth the channel, and the concrete wall with its gate. The wall was holding back the water from the channel. 'When the water's flowing, orchardists can tap off as much as they like. They pay a fee, but it's the same if they take ten thousand gallons or ten. Not much.' The water eventually made its way into Picnic Creek, miles away, and Picnic Creek in turn ran into the Goulburn River.

'So Vin, let's see if this works, or what.'

Vin attempted to spin the upper pulley to open the gate, but no result. The pulley was jammed.

'What in Christ's name?'

Vin jumped down into the channel to see if he could free the pulley.

'Vin, get out of there!'

But it was as if Nazareth were waiting for someone to commit the very episode of folly that Vinny Toole had just enacted. The iron gate burst from its fixings and the water of the lake rushed through in a torrent, carrying Vin with it. Wes and Beth ran for the ute, Beth assuming it was to follow Vin flailing in the rushing water, Wes knowing there was a net across the channel a hundred yards down. It was there to trap debris, tree boughs, bark, logs, animal carcasses from the lake, forming a dam. The shire workers were supposed to clear the net once a week. Vin would be caught there, but would probably be dead. It was obvious he couldn't swim.

Wes stopped the ute at the net, plunged into the channel boots and all and found Vin caught in the net with his head underwater. Wes grasped him under the arms and worked his way back to the bank, where Beth helped him drag Vin out and lay him on his back. He was dead, so far as Wes could see, but Beth pushed him aside and started mouth-to-mouth. She had saved distressed lambs this way—all the Hardy girls knew the method—while the ewe circled complaining loudly, and she had practised on humans in the first-aid course everyone in the union had to take, years back. She put Vin's head on one side, got his tongue out of the way, breathed into his mouth and pumped his chest. She kept it up for ten minutes, fifteen.

Wes, watching, considered the attempt hopeless. Vin was dead.

Then he convulsed and spewed water from his mouth and nose, convulsed again and began coughing. Beth maintained the pumping of his chest until water stopped running from his mouth. They stretched him out in the back of the ute for the trip to hospital and Beth took his head in her lap. Vin's eyes were open and he was breathing. They carried him into emergency and waited for Doc Halliday to come out and give them a report. 'Technically, he was dead, I would say. But he'll need to stay with us for a week. Sometimes revival with mouth-to-mouth can switch itself off after a bit.'

Two days later, on the way to visit Vin, Beth gestured for Wes to pull over on Gold Road. She gazed at him for a minute or more, then spoke. She said: 'Marry me.'

'Dear God, you can speak. What...how?'

Her voice was thin and whispery. 'Don't know.'

'Beth darling, it's wonderful. Kiss me.'

They kissed, at first tenderly, then more voluptuously.

'Marry me?' she said.

'Yes!'

'Soon?'

'As soon as ever.'

'A Quaker marriage?'

'Certainly. We have beautiful marriages.'

They continued on to visit Vinny; Beth allowed him to kiss her on the cheek. He said: 'They tell me you saved me.'

Beth said: 'Learn to swim.'

'Oi! You're talking.'

'Yes, I'm talking. Learn to swim.'

Not so complicated, arranging a Quaker wedding. No officiating clergy, and a lot of silence. Wes and Beth had informed Sylvie Farebrother of their desire to marry, and Sylvie, as clerk of the gathering, had passed the request to the oversight committee and the clearness committee (to make sure that neither of the two parties wishing to marry was already married, or a felon, and so on) and the clearness committee took only two minutes to authorise the marriage. The oversight committee made all the legal arrangements with the court and the shire. The wedding was set for March 10th 1960. Usually, cakes and sausage rolls were not offered at a Quaker wedding, but this wedding was a hybrid, and the Cunninghams, at whose home the gathering would meet for the wedding celebration, thought it a nice touch to send plates of food around after the service. The sausage rolls would have to be outsourced to Noleen Addison, an expert, since nobody in the Quaker congregation knew anything at all about their production.

Two weeks before the wedding, Wes took Beth to

a Quaker gathering at the Richardsons', and something happened that had never happened before. As soon as Beth walked in, the entire gathering stood and applauded, children as well. Beth blushed to her hairline. Two seats had been left vacant for the couple and, before sitting, Beth thanked everyone and even stretched her gratitude to God in heaven, without hypocrisy, since she had over the past year come to concede that something or someone with divine attributes was hovering over her. Possibly.

Silent prayer, then Wes sang. One of the Richardson dogs, a black Labrador, wandered in and sat at Wes's feet, and Wes took the opportunity to sing, 'The Dog Sat on the Tucker Box'. Not appreciated by the full gathering, but certainly by the kids.

Chapter 31

AS A QUAKER bride, you could be married in a cardie and the daggiest skirt in your wardrobe if you wished, but Lillian Hardy insisted on something more traditional: white silk tulle, full length, lacework at the hem, and a fully shaped bodice. She was a brilliant sempstress and put her whole heart into the gown. Fittings galore. Beth said: 'Mum, I'm not a beauty queen.' Franny, who was helping, told her to shut up. 'You're going to look regal, just put up with it. Can you imagine how gorgeous Wes will look in his new suit? Woman, you have to measure up.'

Wes and Beth entered the house together for the ceremony. Seventy people in attendance, half of them Quakers, half a mixture of other faiths, mostly Catholics, since the Hardy family were Catholics, of a very nonchalant sort, and the relatives they'd invited were also Catholics, also fairly nonchalant. A few foot-washing Baptists were scattered about, looking censorious. Chairs of all sorts had been provided and an aisle left for Beth and Wes to stroll down to their rather plain Quaker seats at the front. No flowers, and the living room was unadorned. Beth looked nothing like herself in her trailing wedding dress; but, yes, pretty.

The silent worship part of the service was abbreviated for the sake of the Catholics, who were not used to going for more than thirty seconds in their services without a voice or voices filling their ears. Without anyone officiating, it was left to Wes and Beth to stand and face each other and make their vows, which were brief, more or less a version of, 'Met you, married you, and I'm sticking around.' Beth had been tutored in what to say. Wes had also been asked to sing after the vows, and he sang his old favourite 'The Water Is Wide'.

> The water is wide, I can't cross o'er
> Nor do I have light wings to fly
> Build me a boat that can carry two
> And we will row, my love and I.

For the next two verses, a surprise, the Quakers in the gathering stood and joined in, while the non-Quakers looked about in bafflement. The signing of documents was quick, and that was it. Beth and Wes were husband

and wife. Sandwiches were passed around on genuine crockery by Bernice Richardson and her sister Eloise without any to-do, but when it came to the cakes, the Tudors, Quaker mother and four daughters, put them on plates as if they were hot coals being handled with bare fingers. In the Tudor household, cakes were regarded as the sort of food demons were weaned on. Beth helped in the distribution of the cakes and sandwiches, and Wes knew who to avoid in offering cakes, perhaps half the Quakers, but not the Farebrothers, who ignored tradition, and gobbled down eclairs with gluttonous enthusiasm.

Without alcohol, the feasting could not become as protracted as a reception among Catholics, or even Presbyterians, and the whole event was over in two hours. Beth and Wes waved goodbye, drove back in Wes's ute to their house, undressed rapidly, fell into bed and made love with inexhaustible appetite.

'We're not doing anything about birth control, darling.'

'Okay, after this you have to use condoms. That's all right?'

'Yep.'

'I'm hoping I can still have children. They used to punch me in the stomach and more than anything, I worried about my womb. But they didn't rape me, Wes. They weren't allowed to rape the foreign women. They didn't want them going home and telling stories of rape in a Russian prison. They raped the Russian women every time they came.'

'Ewan Thomas in London says he doesn't think there's been any damage to your womb.'

'I think of Patty's courage, having babies in Hiroshima. And baby Esther's poor little fingers. That's courage.'

'Patty has always had guts. At school one time she stood up at her desk and told off a teacher who had been humiliating a boy because of his awful handwriting. She called him a fat, ugly bully.'

'Good for her!'

'But she's also in Hiroshima because of God. Quakers believe that God gives each Quaker a task in life and once he or she understands the task, it's permanent. Patty believes that God wants her to help the people of Hiroshima. She can never escape that task.'

'What's your task from God? Me? Please say no. I don't want to be a task.'

'No, no, darling. I haven't discovered my task yet.'

The next day, Wes left for work late and said he wouldn't be home for lunch. 'You might like to do some shopping, Beth. You can take the old Ford in the garage. The keys are in the ignition.'

Once he was gone, Beth wandered the house, so beautifully made, trying to imagine what a housewife did. There was not a housewifely bone in her body.

What, cook and clean, wash clothes? She couldn't cook, she couldn't clean, and the only laundering she had any experience of was at a laundromat years ago. In Pentridge, your uniforms were washed and returned to you; all you had to do was rinse out your knickers and bras; same in Moscow, only less frequently. When she was in university and working for the union, she was living at Di's and being cooked for. She couldn't be a housewife.

Wes had the phone on. She called her mother.

'Mum, I don't know how to be a housewife!' she wailed.

'I'll come round tomorrow, sweetheart.'

Beth drove to the shops and asked Ruth at the butcher's what she should buy to make a meal for dinner. Ruth was Herb the butcher's wife, a burly woman who looked as if she could carry half the carcass of a pig over her shoulder with ease. She said, 'Sausages.'

Beth bought eight sausages, then four potatoes from the greengrocer, Lukey Phelps, and from the grocer, Ern Morrison, a high-tin loaf and a can of Monbulk strawberry jam. Also a large bottle of Rosella tomato sauce.

She could see that the sausages would have to be fried in a large pan, and found one in a cupboard. The stove was electric, so that was easy. She let them bake on the bare surface of the frying pan. The potatoes were more difficult. She found in a drawer what she assumed was a peeler, but couldn't make it work, so she boiled a pot of water and dropped the four large potatoes in unpeeled. She set the table with bowls, knives, forks and spoons, and placed the can of jam in the centre with a number of slices of bread, cut haphazardly to various thicknesses. The can would have to be opened by Wes. She had tried but couldn't get the can opener to work.

When Wes arrived home from work she served the sausages, which she'd forgotten to turn, charred side up, and the potatoes.

'I overcooked the sausages a bit. But maybe with some tomato sauce?'

They were inedible, and the potatoes were raw. She tried a sausage herself, and attempted a piece of potato, then whisked Wes's plate away and emptied both plates into the rubbish bin.

'We'll go down the shops and get some fish and chips from Alec Di Roma's.'

On the way, she fretted, 'I'll get better. Only I don't know anything about cooking. Mum's coming round tomorrow to help me.'

Lillian turned up in the middle of the next morning with bags and baskets of food and a big baking dish. 'Doesn't help you to cook, communism, does it? Anything in Marx about casseroles?'

She had a leg of mutton with her. 'Gonna make him

a roast. I hope Quakers enjoy a roast. Gave him one at our place one time and he gobbled it down.'

'Wes is not a very observant Quaker, Mum.'

'One thing's for sure, you don't see any fat Quakers. Must live on peas and turnips.'

She went on, after she'd unpacked everything: 'Now you serve your mutton baked. You know what baking is, sweetheart?'

'Mum, I'm not completely stupid. In the oven.'

'Good. In the oven. So we'll preheat the oven to 350 degrees. While the mutton's baking, you peel your taters, about five of them and cut them into quarters because you're going to bake your taters while you're baking your mutton, also your pumpkin, so you'll want to cut up your pumpkin into sections.'

'Only Mum, I don't know how to peel potatoes.'

'Oh Gawd, it's like teaching a little child. Here, give me a spud and the peeler.'

Lillian instructed her daughter in the mystery of peeling, and made her practise until, after fifteen minutes, she had succeeded in ridding one large potato of its peel. Then another.

'It's hard, Mum.'

'About as hard as pouring a glass of water. Now let me see you cutting up the pumpkin.'

This was a real challenge. Beth had to use the largest knife in the drawer to cut the big piece of pumpkin in half, then cut each half into three and scoop out the seeds.

'And next?' said Lillian.

'Cook it?'

'What about the peel? Do you want to eat pumpkin peel?'

Then came the leg of mutton, big. Lillian showed Beth how to coat the baking dish with dripping, then placed the mutton in the dish. 'Put it in the heated oven at about three in the afternoon and let it cook for an hour before adding the potatoes and pumpkin and let the whole thing bake for a further forty-five minutes. Fifteen minutes before you take the cooked mutton and vegies out, boil some beans and peas and cauli. Then put it all together and serve it. Oh, and the gravy. Add a little bit of flour to the juices left in the baking dish and stir it. Pour the gravy over the mutton, then your salt and pepper and away you go. Okay?'

'Okay,' said Beth, disguising her confusion.

'Have to go and get Dad's lunch. Call me if you get into any strife.'

Beth followed the instructions as best she could, and made a fair job of it, although blood oozed from the middle of the leg of mutton when she attempted to slice it.

On the way home from the shops the next day with two tomatoes and a can of peaches, she pulled over on Mason Street and said aloud, 'I can't do this.' She turned the Ford around and drove to the mouth of the channel, where

Wes was working, installing a new gate. She found him and embraced him and said that if he wanted a divorce she wouldn't make any trouble but she couldn't be a housewife. 'Wes, it goes on forever. It's impossible. I feel as if I'm suffocating. I don't know how other women do it, but I can't, I just can't.'

He took her aside from where the other men were at work. 'Dear heart, of course you can't be a housewife, any more than I could be a ballet dancer. I didn't fall in love with you because I wanted a housewife. I fell in love with you because of your convictions. What you want to do, you work it out. It's your task, not mine. You work it out. I have to get back to the channel gate.'

She worked it out. A couple of days later, she phoned Di Porter and asked her if she knew anyone at the Australian Forestry Union. She knew Audrey Hirst. Why? 'I'll tell you later.'

She phoned Audrey and asked if she could come down to the city and see her about the possibility of becoming an organiser for the AFU. 'I'll explain it all if I can see you.'

Audrey said: 'I know what this is about. John Li's hundred and fifty un-unionised workers?'

'Yes. We have a situation here.'

'I can't say no to someone with your experience. We thought you were dead, Beth.'

~

That night, after a meal of cold cuts and a tomato, she told Wes. He said, 'Darling, it's dangerous. He only allowed a unionised workforce at Chinese Town because I told him I wouldn't oversee the whole thing unless he did. If you end up going to the site, I have to go with you.'

Beth drove down to the city the next day in the old Ford and parked in Lygon Street. Audrey's office was on the second floor of the trade union building. She was a woman in her fifties who'd been working for the unions for thirty years. She said, 'God, Beth, I saw a picture from the *News of the World* of you in hospital. I thought, "Beth's a goner." Now look at you. You're lovely. Now, you want to become an organiser on John Li's operation. The concession is on Crown land. You can't exclude anyone from Crown land, concession or not. But we sent a man up there and he was chased away by two stooges with guns. We decided to leave it until the concession ran out.'

'What about the cops?'

'They don't want to get involved in union stuff.'

'So the workforce don't even know their rights?'

'John had them recruited in Italy and Greece and signed them up as soon as they got off the boat. They were at Station Pier one day, up in the bush the next. He put them in a camp with tents and told them anyone who joined a union would be sacked, the slimy bastard. It's illegal, but these poor buggers don't know that. He pays them twenty per cent below the union rate. And safety rules don't exist. You're not supposed to fell two trees at one time unless they're two hundred yards apart. He's got them felling trees side-by-side. That's how those two blokes were killed. The coroner sitting was Bobo Watkins, anti-union from way back, the arsehole. We can pay you ten quid a month at first. Is that okay?'

'Yep. But I want you to halve the monthly subscription for the men I get to join up. Three shillings for the first six months, and no joining fee. Also, I'll need a document to say I'm an official of the union.'

'We can do that, but Jesus Christ, Beth, I don't like your chances.'

Chapter 32

PATTY'S MOTHER-IN-LAW died in Hiroshima early in 1960, and her father-in-law one month later. Both had been ill for months and were very aged and there was no need for autopsies. Patty and the children went once again to the master to ask him to bless the spirits of the children's grandparents. But Patty found the master himself in very poor health, not yet bedridden but capable of only hobbling about with two walking sticks. He smiled to see her and the children. 'It would be better,' he said in English, 'if you came to bless me. I am two hundred and fifty years old, and my dear friend Hero has died. He was five hundred years old. Come, I will show you where Hero is buried.'

With difficulty, the master led Patty and the children

behind the stable to where a broad area was set aside for beans and capsicums and peas. An area, a big square, was the last resting place of Hero. A board with carving on it was set upright at one end of the square. The lettering, in classical Japanese read: *Hero, a horse, our beloved friend. He worked hard every day and never once complained.*

Patty and the children watched as the master wept.

'Now he is in heaven,' said Patty, mainly for the children's benefit.

'Is he? I thought he was in the ground,' the master said. 'No, Missus Patty. In the land where your body rests, that is heaven, if you wish to have a heaven. Hero's life came to an end. He is not running around in green fields in the sky. He is in the ground. He cannot think or see or feel anything, because his heart has stopped.'

'Is he not in the cosmos?'

'The cosmos?' The master chuckled. 'No, he is not in the cosmos. He is in the ground. I come here to mourn him because that is where he is. In the ground. Where the cosmos is, I wouldn't know.'

The master took his guests to the kitchen, where four novices were preparing lunch for the fifty-five monks. The novices quickly formed a line and bowed to the master when he entered. He chuckled again. 'Here, I am boss. In the world, nobody.'

The monks were preparing what appeared to Patty to be a salad of fruit and capsicums and beans.

'Will you eat with us?' the master asked, and Patty

thanked him and said yes, they would. The monks carried stacks of wooden bowls from the kitchen to an adjoining hall where long, beautifully carpentered wooden tables were arranged in lines of four. Patty and her children were given seats on benches side by side while the four novices who had prepared the food carried in large, deep terracotta bowls of the salad and served each monk. The meal was to be eaten not with chopsticks but with narrow, silver spoons with flat ends. Before they sat to eat, the monks bowed to their guests, and Patty and the children, familiar with the custom, stood and bowed in turn.

As the monks ate, they chattered loudly. Patty said to the master that she understood that Zen monks ate in silence.

'Not here. To talk while you are eating is good for the digestion. I have been chastised for allowing my monks to talk while eating. My answer is simply, "What is so good about silence?" My own master would sit in silence for ten hours at a time. Then one day, he said, "Enough." He had come to see that Zen is speech, not silence. And so it is. One person speaking to another, that is human. I want my monks to be human. They were born human, they should remain human.'

When they had finished eating—the salad was a wonderful creation—the master said: 'Now that your in-laws have died, you are thinking that you might go back to paradise. No. I have seen many, many of your patients who have come here to bless you for saving their children. You cannot stop. You are here forever. While a child can breathe, there is life. What you are doing is Zen. Giving breath. Zen is breath. You cannot leave. I am sorry, but you must stay.'

And that was it. She must stay. Patty had known what the master would say. There were now fifty hospitals in the Hiroshima region, and they would cope without her, if they had to. But she had become the guru of radiation sickness, she headed three committees, even the surgeons deferred to her opinions. She must stay. Except not all year. She wanted her two children to grow up in a Quaker community. It was important to her for Francis and Esther to be in touch with God, and the Quaker God was her preference. She had arranged to spend two months in every three back in Almond Tree, living with her parents, she and the children. The third month she would return to Hiroshima, without the children, and administer her hospital and oversee the administration of a number of others.

She explained this to the master, who nodded in agreement. The Japanese Government had agreed to fly her to Japan and back to Australia every third month, such was her value. The master said: 'Take me with you. I need a holiday.'

'Master, I doubt the government would fly you to Australia and back just because you need a holiday.'

'No? Then what is the use of a government? When

you return each three months, come and see me. If I am in the ground next to Hero, say a Quaker prayer for both of us.'

'I will. But stay above the ground, please.'

Chapter 33

EVERY WORKER in the state of Victoria has the right to join a union. It is illegal for an employer to prevent workers from joining a union, or to punish workers in any way because they have joined a union. If you are a union member, your rate of pay is guarded by the union, and your safety is also guarded. I am here to offer you membership of the Australian Forestry Union. If you join up, the union will make sure you are paid a fair rate for the work you do. At the moment, you are being paid twenty per cent less than the union rate, and there are no safety regulations to protect you. The two workers who were killed on this site four months ago died because of safety regulations being ignored. I urge you to recognise that many workers in the past, going back more than a hundred years, fought hard for the right of workers to form unions—not only fought, but died, many of them, some of them murdered. Membership of the union will only cost you three shillings a month for the first six months, and the union will not be asking for a joining fee. I will be handing out application forms for union membership, and I encourage you to give serious thought to joining.

Professor Tomas Kruipers of Melbourne University, well known to Beth, agreed to write translations of what she'd written on a Gestetner blank in Italian and Greek (he spoke sixteen languages) and sent it back to her in a large envelope, which she provided, stamped. His accompanying note read: *This will get you into strife, Beth my dear.* She persuaded Mary Anne at the library to run off two hundred copies on the Gestetner machine for two pounds. She already had two hundred union application forms from Audrey. She kept the application forms and the printed version of her address to the workers in separate small cartons and the two cartons sat on the back seat of the Ford when Wes drove her up to the timber camp on the concession at five in the afternoon.

The road was wet and full of potholes, slippery from

recent rain. Wes expected they'd be met by a couple of ratbags with guns at the gate, and they were. Different ratbags than on his first visit, but they put down their guns just as meekly when he told them to. It was now five-thirty and the men had all returned to camp and were sitting around smoking and drinking tea, campfires burning. Wes called out: 'I need you all to gather around Beth here, who is a union organiser. She has something to tell you.'

The men, whether Greek or Italian, all wore the same dubious expression, as if they were about to be conned into buying a lame horse. But they were courteous to Wes, whom most had seen before and knew his reputation. It was Wes who handed out the sheets of paper on which Beth's message was written in three languages. Beth found a tree stump she could stand on while she waited for Wes.

She wore her union uniform of daggy skirt and frumpy cardigan, but she wore lippy, pink, unusual for her, as if she wanted to concede something to the men's expectation of a woman. She had seen men, not so different from the men before her, treat women brutally, horribly, but she wasn't afraid of the men here. She was in a position of authority. It made all the difference. In Moscow, she had no power at all, nothing. Here, her authority, as she knew, came from Wes, the men respected him. But when she spoke to them, they would respect her, too.

When Wes had done, he climbed up onto the stump with his wife and told the men to listen. 'This woman has been through hell in a Moscow prison for the sake of justice. She lived through that to offer justice to you. You listen to her. Understand. Put your hand up if you understand.'

Hands went up, all of them finally. Most of the men had a grasp on English, up to a point.

Wes jumped down as Beth read her message from the stump. She had a carrying voice with a low timbre and the men could follow her easily with the help of the handouts.

'Any questions?'

Hands went up.

'He sack us. How I eat?'

Beth said: 'He can't sack you for joining the union. It's against the law.'

'But he will.'

'We will take him to court. It will cost him thousands of pounds.'

'Three shillings, I can't pay.'

'Is justice worth three shillings?'

After the questions, some of them difficult, and maybe a certain amount of disingenuousness here and there in Beth's replies, Wes handed out the union applications. Beth had also thought to bring biros, and she left a dozen of them on the stump.

Beth said: 'I will come back tomorrow, same time.'

For the visit the next day, Beth changed five pounds into shillings and florins. Wes took his chainsaw, and he needed it because a tree had been felled across the track to prevent him driving any further. He cut the tree into lengths and hauled the lengths aside. Then drove on. Waiting for them at the gate this time were six men with rifles. Billy Hunter from Almond Tree was foremost. Wes hopped out of the Ford and strolled up to him.

'Good afternoon, Billy. Give me the gun.'

Billy, after a few moments of embarrassment, handed the gun over.

Wes said, 'Now the rest of you, open the breech of your rifles and eject the shell.'

The men did as they were told. By this time, Beth had joined her husband. 'This is Crown land,' she said. 'Anyone can enter it. If you shoot us, it's murder. The sentence for murder in this state is hanging. I have seen men hanged and it's not a pretty sight. So if you want to hang at Pentridge, go ahead and shoot us.'

Then she opened the gate and entered the camp, where the workers were waiting, and climbed up onto the stump. Wes stood to one side.

'I should have asked you yesterday if any of you wanted to speak. Take the chance now.'

For a couple of minutes, nothing. Then a worker stood and came forward.

He said to Beth, 'I speak in Italian, okay?'

He spoke for five minutes. Many of the workers, evidently Italians, applauded him, not loudly. Then he said to Beth: 'I tell to them, join the union. I come from Napoli. Many of us coming from Napoli. In Napoli, the unions are belong to Camorra, what you call mafia here in Australia. No justice in Napoli. If your union is honest, we want it. Okay?'

'We are honest, we work only for our members.'

'Good. We all join, all the Napolitani.'

Then another man came forward. He said to Beth, 'I Greek. I speak to us in Greek language.'

He also spoke for five minutes, to applause.

He said to Beth, 'We go to your union.'

Beth and Wes read and corrected the application forms of seventy-three of the men. Each paid three shillings. It was dark when they finished.

Beth said, 'I'll come back tomorrow.'

Wes told Billy Hunter to show some courage and stand up for workers.

'I oughta, oughtn't I?'

'Jesus, Billy, you're a working man. What did John Li tell you? That we would run away?'

'Yeah.'

On the way home, Beth sang 'The Ballad of Joe Hill' at the top of her voice. Wes had never seen her so happy, except in bed. 'You have seventy-three, my darling. But that still leaves seventy-seven.'

'We'll get them. Oh Wes, isn't this a good thing, isn't this a good, good thing?'

'Better than cooking, is it?'

'Sure is!'

'But Beth, John's going to retaliate. You realise that, don't you?'

'Let him.'

After dinner that night—an omelette with cheese and bacon, prepared by Wes—Beth told him she wanted to go to the site by herself tomorrow. Wes settled back in his armchair and exhaled deeply.

'Beth, are you insane? There're all those men up there. You're probably the only woman they've seen in six months. No, no, no. I have to be there.'

'Wes, I want to go by myself. The men won't touch me. I'm the union official, not you. It's my job and I want to do it myself.'

'They won't touch you if I'm there. But if I'm not, Beth, think about it.'

Beth reached forward and patted her husband on his knee. 'It's my job, Wes. I took it on. You have to let me do what I want.'

'I'll drive you and stay in the Ford. In any case, you can't get along that track. It's a truck track. You couldn't do it.'

'Yes I can. I'm a good driver, Wes.'

Wes raised one objection after another. What if she broke an axle? What if the men ignored her?

'Wes, trust me. I believe in this. I have to win back my life. Do you see?'

'What time do you want to leave?'

'Say, ten. I'll be doing a safety inspection. I'm also the safety official.'

'Come back to Chinese Town. If you're not back by two, I'll come after you.'

No men with guns at the gates of the site the next day, but John Li was. He was puzzled not to see Wes.

'Where is Wesley?'

'He's building your stupid town, or your town with a stupid name, at least.'

John Li folded his arms and planted his feet wide. 'You can't come in.'

There was a pedestrian pass beside the gate, and it was this pass that John was blocking.

'Yes I can,' said Beth, and pushed past him with her tin box of coins and her application forms.

'I will call the police!' John shouted after her.

'Yes, why don't you do that, John? I can tell them that you attempted to keep a union official from a worksite.'

Only one man in the camp at 11.20 in the morning; a short, stocky man with a bandaged hand.

'What is your name, if you don't mind me asking?'

'My name? Lorenzo. Italy.'

'How did you hurt your hand, Lorenzo?' She pointed to his bandaged hand.

'My finger broken.'

'Have you been to the doctor?'

'Doctor? No.'

Beth took out her notebook and wrote in it.

John came up beside her. 'What are you doing?'

'This man was injured on the worksite but has not seen a doctor. I'm conducting a safety inspection.'

'His finger is broken. It is nothing. Next you'll be wanting a man to see a doctor if he gets bitten by an ant.'

'And where are the toilet facilities?'

'Toilets? This is the bush! You take a spade and dig a hole.'

'So no toilet facilities.' Beth made a note. 'And where do the men bathe?'

'Bathe? In the creek.'

'So no hygiene facilities?'

'The creek!'

'I assume that's where the fresh water comes from, too? The creek?'

'Of course. What a stupid question.'

She asked Lorenzo: 'How many days do you work, Lorenzo?'

'How many days?' He reflected. 'Six days and one half.'

'And do you get paid while you are injured?'

Lorenzo held up his bandaged hand. 'This? Pay? No.'

'It's what they agreed to!' said John.

Beth said she wanted to see the felling site. John, in a rage, said she wanted to ruin him.

'No, I don't want to ruin you. I want to see that your workers are treated fairly. Is that too much to ask?'

He muttered under his breath, 'Communist.'

'Maybe. But I have suffered at the hands of the Soviets more than you can possibly imagine. So don't say that, John. Open the gate so that I can go to the felling site.'

'I have to come.'

'If you like.'

There was only one track to follow. As Beth drove, John kept up a constant muttering in Chinese. She parked two hundred yards from the felling site, and even from the Ford she could pick out a dozen or more problems with the safety regulations. She stepped out of the car and approached closer.

Men were everywhere among the mountain ash, felling with chainsaws; often no more than ten yards from each other. When they noticed her, they waved and smiled. Trees came crashing down, one after another, the men striding nimbly to get themselves out of the way. They called warnings to each other in Greek and Italian. When the logs were trimmed, they were loaded on the truck with mechanical devices attached to the tray while two men stood on the load of logs and handled them into position. One slip and the men risked having their feet and legs crushed.

'Don't you see how dangerous that is?' said Beth, shouting above the racket of the machinery.

John shrugged. 'They have experience.'

She made one note after another before driving John back to the camp. She had collected nine more union applications from the men.

'I'll come and see you tomorrow at your office.'

'What time?'

'Ten.'

That night, she went through the list in her notebook with Wes.

'Isn't it appalling? He's exactly the sort of bastard who would have sent children down coalmines in the nineteenth century.'

'He'll ignore what you've written, Beth.'

'Then we'll strike. We have eighty-two in the union now.'

Beth typed out the entire list of objections and their various remedies on Wes's old Smith Corona. It took three hours. Wes came up behind her each half-hour and rubbed her shoulders, and also fed her mouthfuls of steak and veg.

She said: 'Wes, you do realise I'm still a communist?'

'I do. Of course.'

'But the Soviet Union—that's what communism looks like when it's corrupted. But don't think I've given up on communism, will you?'

'No I won't think that. Something good will come of it one fine day.'

'Do you think?'

'Yes, I do, Beth, I do.'

John Li kept an office at the back of Robert Harding Real Estate in Almond Tree. There was no such person as Robert Harding. John Li had inherited the agency from his father, Hoong Li, who had believed that an Anglo name would attract more clients than a Chinese name. The walls were ornamented with framed colour photographs of John Li's favoured football team, Footscray, red, white and blue, and a large picture of the team's great champion, Teddy Whitten, signed.

When Beth called in, she was greeted cheerfully by Marge Miller, John's receptionist.

'Poor baby, what you copped from those reds, but it's all good now, I hope.'

'I'm fine, Marge.'

John was at his desk, waiting for her, and he was not smiling.

'Let me go through the list of safety violations, John.'

John didn't reply.

Nor did he reply to any of the items on Beth's list.

She then went on to the matter of wages. He would have to raise the wages of his workers by twenty per cent, effective immediately.

'You want to make me a pauper?' he said. 'You want me to give all my money to communists?'

'They are not communists, John. They are ordinary

working men. They deserve a fair wage for their hard work.'

John sat back in his chair and raised his chin. 'No.'

'No?'

'No to twenty per cent. No to safety. This is theft.'

Beth nodded. 'John, your concession expires in two months. Do you know who the Forestry Minister is? Lindsay Thompson. He will not grant you extra time because he didn't want that old-growth forest cut down to begin with. He was under pressure from other interests. If you do not address all the items on my list—all of them—we will go on strike and you will never exhaust your concession with less than half your workforce in two months.'

'I will hire more men.'

'Scabs? Not in time, you won't. Think about it. I'm going up to the site in two days.'

And so she did. Waiting at the gate were twelve or so men with rifles in a long line. One raised his rifle and pointed it at her. He was a boy of about sixteen, seventeen. Beth walked up to him and allowed his rifle barrel to press against her chest.

'Are you going to shoot me, junior?'

The boy shook his head, and gulped.

'No, I didn't think so.'

She waited at the camp for the workers to return from the felling site. The men with rifles waited with her.

As the men returned in couples and mobs, they appeared appalled at the men with rifles. One stepped forward, a tall man with long hair and a bandana, and told them in English to get the hell out of here. He waved his hands as if chasing chickens away, and she watched the armed men slowly retreat.

Beth stepped up onto her stump and called to the workers to gather around. She had gained recognition as a serious political figure, someone the men were willing to listen to. She told the men that John Li had refused to attend to their safety concerns, and had refused to increase their pay to the union standard. 'We have to strike.' The men whose English was up to it translated for those who couldn't quite understand. 'It should take two weeks. John Li won't allow you to stay in the camp while you're on strike. We will find you places to stay in the towns around here. And we will feed you. You have plenty of well-wishers in the towns, particularly in Almond Tree. This is a fight we can win.' She had already won approval and offers to help from forty families, and would apply for money from the union to pay for food.

A letter came in the mail, addressed to Beth. She opened it and read two words written in red pencil on the single sheet of paper: 'comunist cunt'. Responding more to the bad spelling than to the epithet, she showed it to Wes and asked him if he thought John Li had sent it. 'No, not John. He wouldn't use language like that.'

On her next visit to John's office, she told him that ninety-two of his employees would go on strike beginning on Monday. 'To avoid it, you know what to do.'

He rose up from his desk in a rage, fists clenched. 'My father's mother and father in Guangdong were murdered by communists. By Mao Tse-tung, murdered. By his soldiers. I do not feel sorry for communists. They were only in Guangdong for a visit. They had no politics. Murdered. You want me to give money from my pocket to communist murderers? No! Go on strike. You will get nothing from it.'

Wes organised a convoy of trucks, utes, Land Rovers and cars to pick up the strikers from the camp and take them to the many places where they would be accommodated. Wes also had to borrow tents from all his mates and fellow workers on the channel and on the rebuilding of Chinese Town. The workers slept on floors, on sofas, in sleeping bags on back verandas, in tents in backyards. Often the workers cooked for themselves with ingredients purchased and distributed by Beth, but just as often their hosts cooked for them, cheerfully. Beth's incompetence as a shopper was evident to everyone. One family was expected to make a meal for eleven men out of Brussels sprouts and lettuce. After three days of Beth's shopping, she was told, politely, to simply hand over the money and leave the shopping to the hosts.

A good forty of the workers were put up by Quaker

families with borrowed blankets and sleeping bags. It was a squeeze, but at least the houses all had two bathrooms and two toilets, one downstairs and one upstairs to serve the two guest rooms. The Quakers of Almond Tree had a native sympathy for unions, being themselves, in a certain way, a union, but even more sympathy for Beth and Wes's cause. The twenty-seven workers at Beth's place had more liberty than at any other Quaker household, it would be fair to say. They were all Italians and must have come from a region of Naples where singing was as common as conversation because they sang all day, Italian folk songs, opera, even an Italian version of Elvis's 'Heartbreak Hotel'. Wes was asked for a song, and he sang the only two he knew in Italian, 'Ave Maria' and 'O Solo Mio'. The workers sitting around the living room were spellbound. After 'Ave Maria', tears flowed. One by one, the Italians came up to him and embraced him. And again after 'O Solo Mio'.

'Better than Caruso.'

'My friend, I love you with my heart.'

Beth went with three carloads of workers each day to picket the entrance to the site. The scabs came in dribs and drabs from New South Wales, driven down by a friend of John's in Sydney. But the friend didn't want any scuffles, and turned around with shouts of 'Scabs!' in an Italian accent following him. He'd return the next day with the same men, and sometimes a second truck behind him. The workers surrounded the trucks and threatened the scabs on board with everything from a broken neck to murder. The scabs in the trucks looked daunted. They clearly hadn't been told much. After a certain amount of shouting and abuse, Beth would raise her arms, asking for quiet. Then she would explain to the daunted men in the trucks that this was a union worksite and the workers were simply protecting their jobs, were being paid twenty per cent below the union rate and that all safety regulations were being ignored. Then the shouting and abuse began again and the truck drivers, fearing as much as anything damage to their vehicles, would back into the turntable and head down the road. The workers responded as if they'd enjoyed a mighty victory and embraced Beth, kissed her cheeks.

She went to see John each day.

'I give you nothing.'

'You're going to lose a lot of money, John. More than the twenty per cent you owe these men.'

The offensive letters came each day, always with 'communist' misspelt. She screwed them up and tossed them into the rubbish bin. Letters came, too, for Wes from Anna in Moscow, sent and addressed by a neighbour because all Anna's letters had to be approved by the police and the police did not approve any of them. The letters had been more frequent in the past, brief and full of Moscow chit-chat. One revealed the news that the East Germans intended to build a wall across Berlin months before it became public.

But the latest letter, which came in the midst of the strike, began with the news that her son had died of pneumonia in the prison hospital.

> They didn't give him any antibiotics, nothing, no achromycin, no penicillin, they just let him die. They didn't let me see him until he was dead. They told me he was sick and in the hospital, and I begged them to give him medication. They said they had no medicine to spare for anti-Soviet prisoners. Wes, the grief was horrible, and it still is. I had his body sent to Israel for burial, to some family members. I couldn't bear the thought of his body buried in the soil of this country that treats its people like vermin. As soon as I can arrange it, I am going to Israel to live.

One night after dinner, the men danced to folk tunes played on a fiddle by Franco, who regarded his fiddle as his most precious possession. Beth joined in, although her dancing was awful—like a baby giraffe learning to run. And then, just when the merriment was at its peak, three shots were fired from outside and shattered the upper panes of two windows that faced the street. Most of the men knew what gunfire was from the war, and flattened themselves on the carpet as Wes and Leonardo raced for the door and ran outside.

A red Holden ute was speeding away, but the driver misjudged a bend and smashed into the granite wall Wes had built along the front of the property. Leonardo reached the ute first and hauled the driver out. He pushed him along with a hand around his neck until he reached Wes.

'James? What the hell?'

It was James Li, John's son—widely regarded in Almond Tree as a fool of a boy, indulged by his father—home from Scotch College. He drove around town in the red ute his father had bought him, too young to have a licence, and he drove badly. He was a skinny kid with hair that grew down over his eyes. At the moment he looked terrified, with twenty men threatening to knock his teeth out. Wes called Ernie Connell. Not at the police station, where he never was after three in the afternoon, but at home, where he always was after three in the afternoon.

'James Li? What's he done now? This is union stuff is it? Please don't tell me you rung me at nine at night because James pissed on your front door.'

'He fired three shots through our front windows, Ernie. Then crashed his car. We have him here.'

'Jesus Holy Christ! What, he's gone from being an idiot to mass murderer. Anyone hit?'

'No. But you need to get yourself over here to my

place, Ernie. I'm going to ring John Li and get him here, too.'

Beth retrieved the most recent of the vile notes from the rubbish bin, flattened it out and showed it to James. 'What do you know about this?'

James averted his eyes.

'Did it come from you? All of them? They did, didn't they?'

James nodded.

Ernie, in all his corpulence, arrived first, being closer to the house. But John wasn't far behind. Wes showed Ernie the shattered windows, then the crashed car. Ernie picked up the rifle from the car by the barrel tip to preserve the fingerprints and brought it inside. John appeared profoundly ashamed.

'Is this his rifle?' Ernie asked.

John nodded. As soon as he got close enough to his son through the men hemming him in, he slapped him again and again, until Ernie restrained him.

'Here, here. If there's any rough stuff to be administered, it'll be from me.' And to demonstrate, he whacked the boy across the chops, just a single blow, but expertly dealt. The boy was howling now.

'Sorry, I made a mistake. Sorry.'

'So what have we got here,' said Ernie, scratching the back of his neck. 'Driving without a licence, driving underage, and attempted murder. Mate, you're up shit

330

creek. Come on, we're going down to the station. That's me and the master criminal here, and you Wes, and Beth, you might want to come, too. And John.'

Ernie had to unlock the station and turn on the lights. He found chairs here and there and sat everyone in a circle, himself presiding.

'Okay, idiot, what's the story?'

James, sniffling, murmured that he was trying to help his father against the communists.

John jumped up and gave his son another whack across the face. 'Did I tell you to shoot them, fool?'

James had to agree that his father had not sanctioned murder. 'Sorry, a bad mistake, sorry.' Then: 'I wanted to scare them, that's all.'

Ernie said: 'Two ways this can go. If Wes and Beth press charges, John, your fool of a son is on trial in the juvenile court for attempted murder. If they don't, we put him in front of a magistrate in Shepparton for reckless use of a firearm. Attempted murder, he'd be in juvenile detention and then Pentridge for five years. Reckless use of a firearm, maybe a fine, a big one. I'm going to put the kid in the clink out the back and leave you to discuss it. Might make an arrangement, who knows? You might have something to offer, John. What do you think?'

Ernie took the sniffling boy out the back door. Alone with Wes and Beth, John said, tears in his eyes, 'Don't put my boy in prison, I beg you.' He got down on his knees to further dramatise his plea. 'I beg you with my whole heart.'

Beth said: 'There were more than twenty people in that room. James could have easily killed one of them, two of them.'

'Forgive him, please. He is a stupid, stupid boy. But his mother loves him so, so much. It would kill her if he went to prison.'

Beth looked at Wes. It was a questioning look. Wes grasped the question, and after a minute, conceded.

Beth said: 'An immediate twenty per cent raise for all the workers, even those not in the union. Every safety issue on my list addressed, once again, immediately.'

Without a moment's hesitation, John said, 'Yes, I agree. I will do it.'

They told Ernie that they would not press charges if John signed a document that Beth would write up.

'Any objections if I let the kid go home with John? He's going to wet his pants in there.'

'No objections.'

In the car on the way home, Wes said, 'It's a bit like blackmail, Beth. Not all that comfortable.'

'It's not blackmail. John wanted something we had, we had something he wanted. It was a swap.'

'Still, maybe we should have let justice run its course.'

'You wanted to see that wretched boy in prison?'

'No, only...'

'Wes, justice can't always be pretty.'

'Okay. It leaves me a bit uneasy, is all.'

'Not me.'

Beth the next day typed up an agreement on behalf of the union. It took hours of negotiating all the contingencies in legalese. She took it to John's office late in the afternoon. She had made a carbon copy, and John, deeply unhappy, followed one copy while Beth read the whole document aloud. John grunted after each clause. When Beth was finished, John belted himself on the head with his hand.

'Okay! That foolish, foolish boy. I should let him go to prison. Now you.'

He pushed a document across his desk for Beth to read. It was brief. It was an undertaking never to prefer charges against James Li, neither she nor Wes, nor any of the men in the room when James fired his rifle through the windows. Beth had sent Wes to let all the men know of the deal she was about to make, and none had complained. She felt confident in signing both agreements. Marge witnessed them.

Chapter 34

IN FEBRUARY, 1962, Patty made plans to come home to Almond Tree for what was to be the last time. She had been feeling unwell for months, and two doctors at her hospital diagnosed heart disease of a sort common among those who had survived the bomb. It was nearly always fatal. She was thought to have no more than three months to live.

Before she left to fly back to Australia, she made a journey to see the master, just in case he had better news for her. But the master had died and was buried beside the beloved horse, Hero, as he had wished. It was unusual for a Buddhist to be buried rather than cremated, but the master had been an unusual man. A second wooden monument had been erected beside Hero's. The master had carved it himself. It read: *With my friend.* Patty kissed the monument, then sat weeping for an hour. A monk brought her tea.

Before she left, she sold the hospital to the Japanese government for a hefty sum that reflected the great reputation of the place. And a ceremony was held in the reception area, attended by the Minister for Health and Welfare who presented her with a medal to be worn around the neck on a red ribbon. On one side of the medal was inscribed, in English, *Beloved of the Japanese People*, and the same inscription in Japanese on the other.

Patty had sent a letter ahead asking Wes (as the single most competent member of the family) to arrange a special gathering of Quakers for the evening following her midday arrival. It was so arranged, and held at the Cunningham house. Patty revealed nothing before the meeting, but unwelcome news was anticipated. The only previous special gathering had concerned a member who was threatening to hang himself after blowing up the Farebrother house. He was placated, but had to be placed in a mental hospital, where he still resided.

At the meeting, Patty stood before the gathering and told those assembled of her illness. She was home to die, she said, among Quakers and family. Her message was followed by five minutes of total silence, respectful silence. The Friends formed a queue and each in turn shook Patty's hand. The family members hugged her. Beth was holding Esther, and Patty took her from Beth's arms and held her while the hand-shaking and hugging continued. All the other children in the gathering kissed Patty's hand. No words were spoken, and all the members of the gathering left.

She met with her family in the Cunningham living room after the honouring. Patty's mother and father had been caring for Francis and Esther during Patty's regular month away, but it was evident that they were too old, too frail to keep it up. She asked Beth and Wes whether she and the children could live with them for these final three months. Beth said, 'Yes, of course.'

'Also,' said Patty, 'I want you to care for the kids after I'm gone.'

Beth said, 'Yes, we will, gladly.'

It was do-able. Wes had persuaded his mother to allow Francis to attend Almond Tree Primary for the sake of giving the boy more kids around him. Also, Wes's mother's teaching hadn't altered in sixty years: simply too much of God's goodness and too little of the way the world really went about its business. Esther, meanwhile, went to Nanny Hall's kinder with ten other children of three and four. Nanny Hall's kinder wasn't registered, but she did such a good job that no one bothered. It was all singing and dancing and crayons and plasticine and building blocks, God left out in the backyard alone. Of course, you had to accept that Nanny smoked like

336

a chimney, Capstans, but the children were loved and cared for.

Patty, Esther and Francis moved into the two spare rooms on the second floor. The children came to her bed each morning and said, 'Don't die, Mum.'

Quakers don't place any emphasis on an afterlife. Patty might have said, 'I will be with God,' but it would have been false. She didn't believe she would be with God. She didn't believe anyone could be with God. She was candid about death. She told the children she had to die. 'But you will be with Uncle Wes and Aunty Beth. They love you.'

Still, the kids said each day, 'Don't die, Mum.' That death was involuntary, when it came to their mother, was impossible to grasp.

Wes had finished work on Chinese Town, or Feenix, and the channel was long past completion, but he had another project to occupy him—the sealing of the many open mine shafts off the spur road, one of which had recently claimed the life of a bushwalker. And Beth was busy each weekday, too. She was now regional secretary of the union and had ten sites to visit each month. It was Franny who took on the task of caring for Patty each day. She came with her two children (Ricky's two kids from his previous marriage were at school) and was endlessly cheerful and attentive. While she chatted with Patty—Patty was propped up on three pillows—the children played with toys and colouring books.

She asked Patty to tell her about Hiroshima. Patty said that when she first saw Hiroshima, there was no Hiroshima to see, just a huge black and orange scar with a few badly damaged buildings tottering on their foundations. 'But some grass had begun to grow, or weeds. If you picked one of them and put it to your nose, it smelt like chemicals.' She said that the survivors of the atomic bombs, known as *hibakusha*, were reluctant to get themselves to the hospitals outside Hiroshima for treatment. 'Something had come out of the sky and scorched the life out of thousands and thousands. The survivors were traumatised. Many lived with terrible burns for months before going to one of the remaining hospitals. When they did finally come, we saved hundreds and lost thousands. Hiroshima was America's Auschwitz.'

One Saturday, with Beth at her bedside, Patty said she felt much improved. The sun flowed into her room with a creamy gentleness, as if the goodwill of the heavens had come to visit.

'I think I'm getting better.'

'Really?

'The pain has gone. Beth darling, can you drive me around Almond Tree? I want to see the trees in fruit.'

With the kids in the back seat of Beth's new Falcon sedan, since the old Ford had given up the ghost, they drove up and down the rows of apple trees at Ma Parkinson's orchard (with Ma's permission), the Johnnies flushed red, then to Cooper's pear orchard, with permission once again. Finally to Harper's raspberry spread. Leo Harper told the kids they could pick and eat as many as they liked, and they took him at his word. Patty and Beth sat on the grass, watching.

'This must be the most beautiful place on earth, Almond Tree,' Patty said.

'Just about.'

'I knew a Zen monk in Hiroshima. A master. I told him that Almond Tree was paradise and I was thinking of going back. He said I had to stay in Hiroshima and care for the victims of the bomb and the radiation. He said my god expected it of me. My god, not his. He had no god. He said paradise is nothing. So I stayed. Francis suffered because I stayed, and poor little Esther, and now me. But we did save a great many people, lots and lots of kids. He was right, the master. God expected it of me.'

'Well I don't know what God expects of me. Signing blokes up to the union, probably. Your god, Patty, is he a unionist?'

'Oh, sure. You get to heaven, you pay your dues at the Pearly Gates to Saint Peter. Actually, Beth, we Quakers don't put much store in heaven. Heaven is here, such as it is.'

~

Feeling better didn't last long. Beth had to drive Patty and the kids home after Harper's. She made simple sandwiches of cheese and tomato for lunch—working within her limitations—then asked Patty if she'd like to be read to. 'The New Testament, maybe?'

'Oh God, no. I've had all the wisdom I can bear. No more wisdom. You know what I'd like to hear? Do you think you could go and get my Just William books from my old bedroom at the house? Loved them even though I was fifteen when I read them. That's what I want to hear.'

Beth took the kids with her and fetched the Just William books, then returned and read the first in the series aloud to Patty over a period of days with kids nestled on the side of the bed.

Later, Wes took the kids for a picnic, then he showed them Chinese Town—Feenix—completed, and pointed out how the brick houses were closer to the forest than the wooden houses, and explained why. Back at the house, Esther wouldn't get out of the car but sat picking at her cardigan. She had seemed a bit bleak all day. Wes got in beside her and pushed his hand though her long, chestnut hair.

'What's the trouble, sweetheart?'

'Mum shouldn't die.'

'She shouldn't, sweetheart. She shouldn't. None of us should. It's a rotten system.'

'She shouldn't of let herself be sick.'

340

Wes picked her up and carried her inside, and upstairs to her mother.

'She's upset about...well, you know,' he told her.

Patty took her and cuddled her and crooned endearments. She revived and agreed to go down to the kitchen, where Beth would give her a glass of orange Tarax. But now it was Patty who was in tears.

'Wes, it's so difficult to die.'

'I told her it was a rotten system, and so it is. A rotten system.'

'The Zen monk I knew in Hiroshima, he told me that the ground you are buried in is the only heaven we can know. I want to be buried, Wes. My piece of heaven. And the children can come to my grave and kiss my headstone. The Zen master died and I went to his grave and kissed his plaque, it was made of wood. And Wes, I knew he was right.'

On the Monday, with her kids in school, Gus took a turn caring for Patty. When she came by, Patty was up and about and saying once more that she felt so much better. She didn't look better. She walked in the garden with Gus, then said she'd like to be by herself for a few minutes. Gus let her go and Patty walked around the corner of the house, but after ten minutes, hadn't returned. Gus went, and came upon Patty on hands and knees with blood bubbling from her mouth and nose. Gus helped her to her feet and got her inside and stretched her out on the sofa.

She found a tea towel and wiped her mouth and nose and begged her to please hold on. She called the hospital and asked for an ambulance, but the ambulance was miles away on another call. She was told a doctor would be sent. Gus next called the Cunninghams and told Patty's mum to get to Wes and Beth's place straight away. Then her own parents and gave them the same message. Beth and Wes were at work and a long way out of contact.

The Cunninghams and the Hardys arrived at the same time. Patty was breathing, small bubbles of blood escaping from her mouth. All sat by her side where she lay on the sofa. They expected her to die, and so she did, her eyes open and still glittering.

The Cunninghams sat in silence. The Hardys sobbed and wrung their hands. When the doctor arrived, a locum, he introduced himself as Cyrus Fate, no recognition of the irony. He looked about sixteen and just out of high school. He examined Patty, felt for a pulse, put his stethoscope to her chest, and announced that she was indeed dead. Patty's mother rose from her chair, and closed her daughter's eyes and crossed her hands on her chest.

Beth arrived home in the middle of the afternoon from a forestry concession fifty miles away, saw the cars gathered, and knew what had happened. She walked into the living room where Patty's body still lay, nodded to the Cunninghams and to her own mother and father, then went straight back outside to weep. When Wes drove up, half an hour after Beth, he saw her still weeping on the front porch and he, too, knew instantly who the tears were for, and why. He parked and walked over to her.

'Patty?'

Beth nodded. 'I have to pick the kids up.' She left him to farewell his sister.

Francis and Esther could see that something was wrong with Beth, but didn't ask. She waited until she was back with the kids, still in the car, before turning in her seat to face them.

'Mum has died. While you were at school and at Nanny's.'

Francis nodded. 'That's what I thought,' he said, and he climbed out of the car and hurried inside. Esther stayed where she was. 'Come inside, lovely,' said Beth.

'I don't want to see.'

'I know. But you have to. You have to say goodbye to Mum.'

Esther opened the door and in a flash was running down the driveway toward the road. Beth chased after her but stumbled and fell headlong and by the time she was on her feet again, Esther was standing on the side of the road while a car approached, Frank Dyson's big black Humber. Esther waited until it was close then stood in its path.

Beth screamed at Esther but it was only Frank's acute swerve at the last second that saved the girl. It put him in the ditch under the cypresses, the engine still ticking over. He called to Beth from the Humber, 'Beth, Jesus, what the fuck?'

Beth had grabbed Esther and was holding her close. 'Some strife, Frank. I'll get Wes to haul you out.'

She carried the child back to the house. Those inside had heard her scream and were waiting outside.

'Leave her to me,' she said. 'Wes, go down with the ute and haul Frank out of the ditch. If there's any damage to the car, tell him we'll pay for it.'

It was possible to get to the stairs inside without passing through the living room, and Beth took Esther that way, up to her room. She sat her on the bed and closed the door. Then sat beside her, holding both her hands. Esther was howling.

'There now, sweetheart, *shush, shush.*'

It was *shush, shush* for fifteen minutes. Only clichés came to mind, best avoided. Patty was dead. It couldn't be diminished in its finality by something like, 'Mummy would be sad if she knew you were crying for her.'

Patty had told her a month before: 'Esther will be inconsolable, I'm afraid. Let her cry.'

The child's distress gradually ebbed, until she was no longer howling but sobbing softly.

'Do you want to kiss Mummy goodbye now?'
Esther nodded.

Beth led her down to the living room and space was made so that the child could kiss her dead mother's forehead. Then Esther went to the furthest corner of the room to sit with her legs drawn up and her face buried in her dress. Francis, meanwhile, sat with his head on his mother's lap.

The ceremony was simple in the Quaker tradition, held at the Cunningham house. George Farebrother spoke first, and was brief: Patty had done service to God, which God surely recognised, and had honoured the example of Jesus. Those among the gathering of seventy who felt moved to speak were encouraged to do so, and a number did. The Japanese Government had, at very short notice, sent a representative, a man of sixty or so who had known Patty in Hiroshima when he was employed as an administrator in the Ministry of Health and Welfare. He said of Patty: 'Mrs Patty brought justice to Hiroshima. Hundreds of people are alive today because of her.'

Usually, Quakers choose cremation, but Patty had made her wishes plain. A second short service was held at the grave side in the cemetery. Wes spoke. He said, 'My beloved sister, farewell, and since we are where we are, forever farewell.' Francis and Esther stood silently until the end of the service, then Francis said in Japanese a very few words. He translated for the gathering. 'I said, "This is a sad day for me and for Esther."'

Chapter 35

IT TOOK six months for them to become a family. But Esther still had to be taken to the cemetery each day to kiss her mother's headstone and tell her about the household, and about Nanny. 'Wes is blowing up holes in the ground so people don't fall down them. It's a bit dangerous for him. Beth is having arguments out in the bush. I went with her one day and heard her shouting at a man in a sawmill. She's very angry at work but she's never angry at home. I did this at Nanny's.' She displayed a drawing in coloured pencils of a sheep.

Francis was more philosophical. He didn't need to go to the cemetery more than once a week. He did a lot of reading and was enjoying the William books that Beth had been reading to Patty. When Esther spoke of her mother, he had only the one comment: 'Everyone dies.'

It was true that Beth spent a lot of time shouting in the bush. She had discovered an appetite for thumping the desks of mill managers and leaning forward with her teeth bared. Her nickname among the senior executives of forestry companies and among mill managers was 'the dingo'. She had taken union membership in the ten concessions she oversaw to a hundred per cent. The members trusted her; they knew she would fight tooth and nail for their rights.

But among the union members there were some who were capable of making secret deals with management, cutting corners here and there for a bonus. Whenever she found out—and she usually did—she was furious. She sat two of the workers she'd uncovered working in cahoots with a mill owner on a log and walked up and down ranting like a maniacal school principal who'd caught two students drawing dirty pictures on the toilet walls. 'Isn't it enough that you have the highest rates of pay in the industry? Isn't it enough that you have a safe workplace? You have to go under the counter with that pig in the office? I'm ashamed of you, yes that's right, ashamed.'

It had occurred to her that her fierce advocacy of the men's rights was related to what she'd endured in Moscow—that the justice she had to do without in prison now filled her to bursting with the need to see that what was right was recognised. It was possible she was a bit mad. She still considered herself a communist, but the gentle, charitable communist she'd been as a teenager, as a young woman, that was gone. In prison, she had seen a woman twice her age hung by her hair for an hour when she was caught reciting the Lord's Prayer. The image was in her mind forever. It was there when she thumped the table in the offices of mill managers: anger and a type of distress. At home with Wes and the kids, she never raised her voice and her devotion to Francis and Esther could not have been more tender.

And yes, the work Wes was doing for the shire was dangerous. The abandoned shafts had to be blown up with gelignite, collapsing them, then the remaining depression filled with gravel. Wes had hired a long conveyor belt that ran from the truck loaded with gravel up to thirty yards to the collapsed shafts. The spur road had been built way back in the day by gold miners searching for veins of quartz, and they'd extended the track as they moved along. All the shafts were within thirty yards of what was no longer a track but an unsealed road—all the shafts Wes was going to bother with, at least. The miners had tried east and west of the track, never going too far up or down.

It took Wes and his crew two days to close a shaft completely. The downhill shafts were easier—the men could stand above the shaft when the gelignite exploded and the rubble would all roll away further from where they stood. The uphill shafts were dangerous. The explosion would loosen rocks well above them and they would need to keep wide of the shaft to avoid the inevitable avalanche. Wes would hook up the conveyor belt to the engine and steady it at the other end with metal pegs driven into the hillside with sledgehammers. Wes was usually the last to get clear of the avalanche, making sure all the men were safe.

It was boring work. You found a hole in the ground and filled it in. Wes was used to seeing something more substantial as a reward for labour—a construction. And really, only two bushwalkers had ever fallen down the shafts; one died, the other suffered cuts and bruises. You'd have to be half-asleep to fall into one of the shafts, with their square-yard opening.

It was probably his lack of enthusiasm for the work that led to the accident that almost killed him.

On the day of work on the last shaft, the avalanche came so quickly that he was caught by the rocks and rubble and buried. He was the only one struck by the rocks. The other men worked with furious haste to dig him out, and found him still breathing but unconscious with a huge gash on his head.

No way of calling for an ambulance, so they lifted him as gently as they could up the slope and laid him out on the back seat of Charlie Camp's big old rusty Chev parked on the side of the road. Then Charlie drove down through Chinese Town like a bat out of hell and along Gold Road to the highway, and so to the Almond Tree hospital. With Charlie on one end of a stretcher and Doctor Fate on the other, they carried him in and Doc Fate checked him over. 'No broken limbs.'

Wes was now conscious. 'What the hell?' he said. Doc Fate, much more competent than his boyish looks suggested, examined the gash on Wes's head and declared no fracture to the skull. Charlie and the doc stripped Wes naked and found him covered in bruises all over. 'Could of been worse,' said Charlie. Doc Fate had a nurse shave around the head wound, then sutured it, fourteen stitches.

It was four in the afternoon before Beth arrived. Wes was now in a ward. His bruising had been treated with an ointment and his body, still naked except for his underpants, glistened.

Beth burst into tears the instant she saw him. 'Oh, you idiot. You utter idiot.'

His head was bandaged. She kissed his lips, which had been left intact. 'You look like me in Moscow. No more of these jobs with explosives. I mean it. No more.'

'It was a freakish thing, darling.'

'I don't care. You have to keep alive. I'm pregnant.'

'What?'

'You're going to be a father, you oaf. I'm not doing it all by myself.'

Chapter 36

THE CUBAN Missile Crisis of October 1962 scared the daylights out of everyone in Almond Tree, except for Beth. She told Wes, 'The Russians won't go to war to get a few missiles into Cuba. They know perfectly well that the Americans would win a war.' It was no surprise to her when the Soviets backed down. She understood the Soviets, and what they were bluffing about and what was vital to them, as she hadn't in the days when she worshipped them. She always needed to believe with all her heart in something, and in those days it was communism and the Soviets. Now it was justice for working men and women. And communism. And her husband. And the baby.

She kept on working for the first seven months of

her pregnancy and as soon as she began to show, was treated to the hearty best wishes of the senior managers of the timber companies and mill owners, who couldn't wait to be rid of her. The work she was doing was going to be taken over by Herby Crenshaw, who was crooked as a dog's hind leg and could be relied on to endorse all sorts of under-the-table arrangements. As soon as Beth found out it was to be Herby who would be her stand-in, she reduced her time off to two months after the birth. She would take the baby with her.

She enjoyed being pregnant. Despite the discomfort, she liked the idea of it: out of the wreckage of Moscow, her body had made a baby. Also, her sex drive soared, for some reason. She couldn't keep her hands off Wes and was forever leaving the children with colouring books and little chores while she bustled him into the bedroom.

Lillian told her, 'I won't lie to you, childbirth is bloody painful. You were the worst, and they say if your birth was especially painful for your mum, when you give birth it will be awful for you. But the thing is, two minutes after the birth, you can't remember the pain.'

Franny said, 'Piece of cake, Beth. Don't worry about it.'

In the event, Franny was right. The baby was born after a single hour of labour. A fair bit of pain but nothing compared to being kicked in the stomach in Moscow.

When Wes was shown in, the baby was on Beth's breast.

'Madeleine,' she said. That was the agreed name for a girl.

Beth looked lovely, her face shining. 'Wes darling, a baby girl. It's a miracle. That's how it feels. Like a miracle. Are you going to cry?'

He wasn't. But his happiness was making his features wobble about as if he were about to bawl.

'This is what I wanted.' He was stroking the back of the baby's neck as she suckled.

'You are going to cry, aren't you, you sook? God, wait till Dad gets here. He'll be bawling for hours.'

When Madeleine was two months old, Beth took her along to the Hoskins mill up north to accept the handover of the forest concessions and the mills from Herby Crenshaw. Herby was tall and skinny and wore his hair in the Beatles' fashion. Also pointy-toed Beatle shoes. He was forty-four. Beth met him in the mill manager's office, which the manager had vacated to give them privacy. She was cradling the baby.

'So which one are you, Herb? John, Paul, George or Ringo?'

'It's not a crime to like the Beatles, is it?'

'No, but other things are. And Herb, every rotten deal you've made, I'll find them and squash them, believe me. Every single one.'

'You going to carry that baby with you to every site? And that big bag of stuff? What's in it? Nappies?'

'Yep.'

'You're breastfeeding, right? That's why you have to bring the kid. The blokes, they don't want to watch you breastfeeding. You know that?'

'I'll cope. And so will the men.'

Herb shrugged.

'You're the boss.'

She breastfed the baby at first, because it was easier than fooling around with bottles and formula. She shielded her breast from the men when she was feeding Madeleine. Not to save herself from embarrassment, but the workers. They became used to Beth turning up with the baby. A few asked to hold Maddy. They cleared spaces on the forest floor for her to lay out the blanket and change the baby; heated water for her to wash Madeleine while changing her. That she could keep it up for long, they doubted, but she persevered, until finally she had to admit she couldn't bring the baby any longer.

She reduced her work to three days a week, and had to leave Madeleine and a container of expressed breast milk with Franny for five hours once a week; with Teddy's wife Julia another day, and with Gus another day. Madeleine didn't like the sound of the thirty-inch circular saws at the mills or the chainsaws at the felling sites. Apart from Madeleine's distress, it was dangerous.

It was a vast relief for Beth, and for the baby, when she was left behind.

Wes said: 'Beth, do what you must to keep that union doing what it's supposed to do.'

Yes, but every time she left Madeleine behind to be cared for by Gus or Julia or Franny, sometimes Maud, she felt sick with remorse. No thought of resigning; but still.

'Wes,' she said, 'all this chopping and changing of Maddy from one woman to another, it can't be doing her any good. I want to leave her with one woman for five days a week, six hours a day.'

Wes was clearing away plates from the dinner table. He said nothing for two or more minutes, as the sound came through the window of Francis and Esther outside in the waning daylight, catching crickets.

At last Beth said, 'Let's ask Nanny Hall.'

'Nanny Hall. Dear God. Beth, she's sixty-three.'

'So what? She was terrific with Esther before Esther went to bubs. Wes, it was a wonder we even had Maddy. I should have been dead after Moscow. I hate to say this, but the union won't work as it should without me. My heart aches when I plonk Maddy into the lap of a stand-in mum. But Nanny Hall is different. She's—she's nonchalant. And I think Maddy likes nonchalance.'

'She likes nonchalance?'

'She does, yes.'

'You're not going to regret it when you're pining for her?'

'Of course I will. But if I'm all that stands between all that bullshit and an honest union, then I have to stick at it. Do you see?'

'I do see. But Nanny Hall. Nonchalant Nanny Hall. Have you thought this through?'

'I'm not going to do the job forever, am I? But for now, yes.'

Wes sat down across the table from Beth. She took his hand.

'Wes, Maddy will have us all her life. We give these three kids a good home, don't we? They don't miss out on anything. Maddy needs to be fed and changed and given love and affection. We don't have a sacred obligation to her. Just love and affection and decent care.'

Esther came running into the kitchen with her hands clasped. 'We caught one!' she said. She opened her hands with their distorted fingers and let first Wes then Beth peep in at the cricket.

Francis wandered in. 'She caught it herself,' he said.

The baby in her cot began to make the demanding noises she'd mastered when she wanted a feed.

'Yes, yes, coming!' Beth called.

Chapter 37

BETH WAS on the back veranda with Madeleine and a book. A Saturday, one of the two days of the week on which she was with Maddy the whole twenty-four hours. Wes in town doing the shopping. The baby, on a blanket, wriggling her hands and feet in the air, gurgling contentedly, and when the fit took her, attempting to roll over on her belly. Eleven months old now. Francis on the banana lounge, reading his way through a stack of his own books, including *The Last of the Mohicans*, somehow. And a dictionary in which he conscientiously looked up words unfamiliar to him. Esther was playing with two lambs from the Hardy flock, rejected by their mothers and being raised in the backyard on bottled milk. The lambs chased Esther about, attempting to nuzzle against her. As far as the lambs were concerned, Esther was their mother. They never approached Francis, who had not the slightest interest in them.

Reading from Patty's selected Auden, Beth came to her dead sister-in-law's favourite, 'September 1, 1939'.

We must love one another or die, she read, and she realised that she'd heard it quoted before, without paying much attention. Her immediate thought this time was, 'It's not true.' Auden was saying either universal fraternity, or we wipe ourselves out? She had once loved all the people of the Soviet Union, the entire mass of them, or so she'd thought, and it had all been a lie in her soul. We could love those we could—in her case, maybe twenty people in the world. The rest of the members of the human race had her goodwill. Most of them.

Let people everywhere find some justice. Goodwill and justice. That should do it.

The screen door opened and Wes appeared, back from shopping. 'Scrambled eggs with fried tomatoes for lunch,' he said, bending to crouch beside Beth.

'Wes, I was reading Patty's selected Auden. I remembered at the cemetery this morning that she had a favourite poem she said I should read. "September 1, 1939". It was written on the eve of the war. He calls the 1930s, "a low, dishonest decade", as if there's any other sort. There's a famous line in it, "we must love one another or die". Do you think that's true?'

'Of course.'

'Really? Is that what Quakers believe?'

'Yes, we do.'

'But Wes, look at these three kids. Francis and Esther, Hiroshima almost destroyed them. And me, I was almost too dead to become a mother. They're loved, that's how come they're here. Patty's love and yours and mine, it left these kids alive. But it didn't stop the Americans dropping those bombs, it didn't stop those bastards in Moscow from almost kicking me to death. Do you really think we must love one another or die?'

'I do, Beth. And another thing we Quakers say is don't get into arguments about what you believe.'

Beth dribbled the last of the milk from the bottle onto Esther's fingers; the lambs sucked madly.

Francis called to Wes and Beth, 'The Mohicans, were they a real tribe?'

Wes said, 'Yep, they were a real tribe. And some survived.'

Francis said, 'They're not in my dictionary.'

'Maybe you need a bigger dictionary.'

'Love one another or die, hmm?' said Beth. 'I'll think about it.'

She put the baby aside and kissed Wes.

'Are you going to make lunch, Quaker man?'

Acknowledgments

I would like to acknowledge the invaluable editing of Mandy Brett, which made this a better book than it would otherwise have been.